Affliction

by

Marilee Brothers

The Soul Seekers Series

Affliction

Contact Information: info@thewildrosepress.com

Cover Art by *RJ Morris*

The Wild Rose Press, Inc.
PO Box 708
Adams Basin, NY 14410-0708
Visit us at www.thewildrosepress.com

Publishing History
First Fantasy Rose Edition, 2016
Print ISBN 978-1-5092-0620-9
Digital ISBN 978-1-5092-0621-6

The Soul Seekers Series
Published in the United States of America

His cheek scrapes across mine,
his mouth just inches from my lips. "Look at me, Minnie," he whispers. "Tell me what you see."

I lift my gaze and stare into his eyes, fully expecting to see my own face, possibly streaked with bits of sticky syrup and framed with flattened helmet hair. Nothing scary. Just something I'd rather not experience right now. But someone changed the channel.

My breath hitches in my chest. "Fire," I say. "I see a smoldering fire."

Billy's mouth grazes my cheek. "Smoldering, huh? Let's make it burn hotter."

His lips touch mine, tentative at first, until I wrap my arms around his neck and try to climb inside his skin. He deepens the kiss, his silky tongue slipping into my mouth. I'm transported to another place. My world consists of all things tactile. The sound of our breathing. The smell of his leather jacket. The warmth of his body against mine. The softness of his lips. The heat spiraling through my body like wildfire. More. I want more.

I'm brought back to earth by the sound of a honking horn and a raucous shout, "Hey, you two, get a room!"

Embarrassed, I push away from Billy and stare at the ground, trying to get my breathing under control. Billy grabs my hand and kisses the back of it like an errant knight wooing a fair maiden. This strikes me as hilarious and I snort laugh. Also embarrassing.

Billy releases my hand and tilts my chin back. "I'm not leaving until you look at me one more time. I promise you, it's safe."

Kudos for Marilee Brothers

Winner of First Place
in the Booksellers Best Contest in 2012

Dedication

To all my wonderful friends and readers
who have encouraged me,
supported me, and lifted me up
when my writing journey hit some bumps in the road.
I appreciate you more than I can say.

Chapter One

April 2010

Slightly buzzed, I stagger out the door into the warm spring air, redolent with the odor of orange blossoms, a sweet relief from the musky smell of weed permeating the party house. I'm a cheap date. At one hundred and five pounds, getting buzzed requires only a single beer. It's not like I had a date. No way. But it is the reason I'm a few minutes late following my best friend, Dani, to her car.

Dani is my ride home. But, I'd hesitated when she was ready to go. I thought I had a chance with a cute guy I remembered from school. Long story short, I didn't. A willowy blonde chick named Heather beat me to the punch. I'm not a good loser. Disgusted by the fickleness of the male species, I decide to split.

Pausing for a moment outside the door, I notice a black BMW with tinted windows parked next to the curb, engine running. I try to clear the fog from my brain. Where the hell did we park the car? I'd just stepped off the porch when I hear muffled cursing and a yip of pain. Female pain.

"Get your hands off me, asshole!"

Dani's voice. High pitched with fear and rage.

Two figures emerge from the shadows. The smaller one jerks free and runs for the street. Her much bigger pursuer covers the ground in three strides and grabs her as she reaches the sidewalk. He wraps both arms around her and lifts her off her feet.

"Dani!" I yell, racing after them. "What's going on?"

At the sound of my voice, the guy holding Dani turns to face me. I recognize him from the party. He and his friend were sharing a joint and looking around the room with bored expressions. I'd glanced into his eyes, didn't like what I saw and steered clear of him. Should have warned Dani.

He looks at me and sneers, "Get the fuck outta here. We're having a little disagreement. Nothing major."

"Bullshit!" Dani cries, struggling to free herself.

"Let her go." I reach for my cell phone. "I'm calling 911 right now."

"Go ahead." He tips his head toward the BMW. "We'll be gone when they get here. We're going for a ride, aren't we, sweetheart?"

He gives Dani a little shake and starts toward the car. "You're going to learn not to be such a prick tease."

No time for 911. I jump in front of him. "Let her go. Now."

The guy grins down at me, his teeth flashing white in the darkness. "Who's gonna stop me, pipsqueak? You? I don't think so."

Nobody calls me pipsqueak. I double up my fist and swing from the heels for his perfectly shaped, aristocratic nose. Because of the disparity in our heights, I miss. Instead of his nose, my fist plows into his throat. Gagging, he drops Dani, clutches his throat with both hands and stumbles backward. His knees buckle and he crumples. The back of his head bounces off the curb. Wide-eyed, Dani and I watch in horror, willing him to move. He doesn't.

The door of the BMW swings open and his friend pops out.

"Call 911. Your friend's hurt," I yell.

I grab Dani's hand and we run like hell.

*****

May 2014

The baby's soul is spotless. Unlike her mother's. I have to save her. If I don't, her soul will soon be stained with fear and pain like her three older siblings. I have a plan. Yes, it's half-assed, but a half-assed plan is better than nothing…right?

I'm at the end of my shift as a nurse's aide. Visiting hours are over. I check the nursery window for proud daddies and grandparents. Nobody. Still in my scrubs, I slip into the nursery and call to the overworked nurse on duty, "This one is needed in the lab."

She nods. I tuck the tiny baby girl in my right arm and hold her close to my body, similar to a running back clutching a football. Head down, I step out into the hall and walk to the door leading to the stairs.

"Hey, you!" Male voice.

My heart leaps in my chest. I stop and turn. Stan, from the janitorial staff, pushes his mop down the hall in pursuit of a cute, young LPN who gives him a coy finger wave. I take a shaky breath and slip through the door.

I gallop down the stairs and stop on the second floor landing. Breathing hard, I use a fingernail clipper to remove the baby's ID bracelet. She opens her eyes and, I swear, she smiles at me. It's not a gas smile. I know the difference.

"Okay, baby girl, let's do it," I murmur, trotting down the remaining stairs.

The lobby is milling with people. Good or bad? Too soon to tell. I straighten my shoulders and try to behave like I'm acting in an official capacity. That's the thing about hospitals. There's a bajillion employees going hither and yon. If you look like you know what you're doing, nobody bothers you.

I can see the front entrance. It's so close. I pray Lydia will be parked at the curb, an important part of the plan. My friend, Lydia, can't get pregnant and really wants a baby. She has a pretty good soul. A little spotty from past indiscretions, but whose isn't? Plus, it's *waaay* spiffier than the soul of the kid's lazy, abusive mother. Lydia has a good job and a steady boyfriend who will be a good father. Win-win situation.

Such was my thinking at the time. My mother often says, "Honor Melanie Sullivan, things are not always black and white." To which I always respond, "They are to me."

A scant five steps from the door, I hear, "You with the baby. Stop!"

I look over my shoulder. Mary Lou Schwinn, Director of Nursing, is closing in fast. Damn nurse shoes. Never heard her coming. I send a silent apology to Lydia and hand over the kid.

*****

My mother, Sandra Sullivan Morales, and I sit side by side in hardback chairs across the cluttered desk of my probation officer, Stan Abbot. Despite the warm weather, a cardigan sweater is draped across Sandra's knees. The sweater's purpose has nothing to do with style or warmth.

Abbot's office chair creaks in protest as he leans back, studying my file with a puzzled frown. A bit of his plump, hairy belly protrudes from a gap in his buttoned dress shirt. I avert my eyes but know I can't *unsee* the image. It's burned into my retinas.

He glances up at me. "Honor Sullivan," he intones.

"Stan Abbot," I reply, earning a reproachful look from my mother.

I wonder what his frown indicates. Is he trying to connect my face to my name? Or, does the frown mean something more ominous. Like maybe he found out what happened at the hospital. Doubtful, since the hospital bigwigs decided not to press charges. Technically, I was still inside the hospital when Schwinn stopped me and, upon questioning, I told her I had no intention of leaving with the baby. More importantly, the hospital doesn't want folks to know how easy it is to snag a kid from the nursery. They settled for my resignation and promise to never darken their door again.

Abbot clears his throat and places my file on his desk. "So, Honor, this is our exit interview. After today, you'll be off probation."

Okay, he doesn't know about the incident. I nod.

"Just a few questions and you'll be free to go."

I nod again, fixing my gaze on the file folder.

"I see you're still not making eye contact. Are you taking your meds for Aspergers?"

"Yes," I lie.

My mother squirms in her chair. Technically, I

don't have Aspergers. My so-called affliction is something entirely different. From age six, I could look into people's eyes and read their souls. Most of the time, I don't like what I see. Consequently, I stare at the ground a lot.

"Clonidine for impulsivity…right?" Abbot says.

"Me? Impulsive?" I joke, risking a quick glance at Abbot's face. I really don't want to know what is in his soul. He holds my future in his hands. What if I see something truly awful? Then, I'll have to leap from my chair and karate chop him across his thick neck. Okay, it's possible I may have a touch of Aspergers.

"It's in your psych report."

Is this the first time he's read my psych report? I decide to test him. "What else does it say?"

Obviously unprepared for the question, he compresses his lips and scans the paper.

"It says you had a language delay and received special services in the first and second grade."

Sandra speaks sharply. "Does it say why? You do know she'd just witnessed the death of her twin sister?"

A buzzing sound fills my head. Not a good sign. Sandra's hand creeps under the sweater and grips my leg, grounding me.

Abbot continues, "It says she and her sister communicated in their own language, and Hope was struck by an automobile when the twins were six."

He lifts his gaze from the report. "Hope and Honor, huh?"

I cover my mother's hand with my own and take a deep breath. Let it out. "Hope is dead. So is Honor. I go by Melanie now. Mel, for short."

Sandra says, "I believe my daughter has met all the

6

conditions of her probation. Do you have further questions?"

Abbot ignores her, opens my file folder and extracts a sheet of paper. "It's been four years since Adam Boyle's untimely death, Mel, which makes you now twenty two years old. Since you were eighteen when this occurred, may I remind you how lucky you are not to be sitting in a prison cell?"

My mother bristles, slowly morphing into Mama Grizzly.

I fix my gaze on Abbot's wobbly double chin. "May I remind you he was assaulting my friend? Yeah, I punched him, but when he fell, his head hit the curb. That's what killed him." *Adam Boyle was a damn bully. So I punched him a little harder than I meant to. Karma.*

My mother adds, "If Adam hadn't been Senator Boyle's son, the incident would have been a non issue."

Abbot peers over his half glasses at my mother as if assessing the danger. Finally, he sighs. "Frankly, Mrs. Morales, if not for the psych report and diagnosis of Aspergers, your daughter would have been incarcerated. You should count your blessings."

"Count my blessings," she repeats, her eyes flashing with anger.

My turn to remain calm, I squeeze her hand and murmur, "Let it go."

She snatches her hand away and gives Abbot the stink eye. "Are we done?"

"Almost," Abbot says. He shuffles through the papers again. Extracts a single sheet, peruses it. "So, Honor, er, Mel, how's your job going? You've been at the hospital two years now?"

"Fine," I say. "It's going fine." *Operative word: Going. As in going, going, gone.*

My mother pinches her lips together.

After a single knock, the door flies open and the secretary who guards Abbot's door appears. "You're way behind schedule, Stan, and you've got a lunch meeting in five minutes."

Abbot mumbles, "Got it."

He closes my file folder and stands.

Are we done?

Abbot says, "Your job evaluations have been excellent. So, as long as you are gainfully employed and stay on your meds, you're good to go."

I glance over at Sandra and rise from my chair. "Okay."

Strike one. No meds. Strike two. No job. One more strike and you're out, Honor Melanie Sullivan.

Chapter Two

The sky is black as pitch at five a.m. Sandra reaches up into the cab of the massive eighteen-wheeler and hands me a cooler packed with enough food for five hungry truckers, even though there are only two of us. Jimmy, the driver, and yours truly. Jimmy drives for my stepfather, Abel Morales, owner of Able Trucking for which my mother is a dispatcher. I've chosen to ride with Jimmy because his soul reinforces my notion he's a good guy who won't try to feel me up on our 600-mile journey north to Redding. I will disembark there and hitch a ride with Brett for the second leg of the trip, Redding to 3 Peaks, Oregon. I've chosen stud muffin Brett for the exact opposite reason of the first.

What can I say? For the last few years, Sandra has kept a tight rein on my carnal desires. And, frankly, my previous sexual experiences are nothing to brag about. In other words, I'm still looking for the big O.

Sandra's brow is crinkled with worry lines. "I wish you didn't have to go, but you know it's for the best."

I drop a kiss on the top of her head. "Yep. New start. Time to get the hell out of San Berdoo." I use the slang term for my hometown, San Bernardino, California, birthplace of the Hells Angels and considered by some to be "the armpit of California."

"You're sure Dani knows you're on your way?"

"Yeah, I emailed her."

The fact I hadn't heard back from Dani, now living in 3 Peaks, would remain my little secret.

"Give the baby a kiss for me."

"I will."

"And don't try to steal her."

I check Sandra's expression and determine she's kidding, so I grin. "I'll abort my kidnap plan."

"You have your résumés?"

I pat my backpack. "All four of 'em."

My mother has a shady side. She created a set of impressive résumés to assist me in my job search once I arrive in Oregon. She now has a designated cell phone to receive calls from prospective employers. I expect rave reviews.

"Gotta hit the road, kid," Jimmy says.

My mother climbs into the cab and wraps me up in her arms. I feel the warmth of her tears against my cheek. A wave of sadness sweeps over me. It may sound strange, but the two of us have never lived apart. I was more than ready to move out at eighteen. Then, Adam Boyle happened. Good old Stan Abbot decided it would be best if I remained at home under Sandra's watchful eye.

Reluctantly, I pull away and swipe at my eyes. "I'll be fine. Don't worry."

She grips my hand, leans close and whispers, "Just think before you act, Mel. Is that too much to ask? I know it's hard when you see things the rest of us can't. But, it's not your job to save people."

Even though I totally disagree, I nod and kiss her cheek. "I'll call when I get to 3 Peaks."

She jumps down, shuts the door and lifts a hand in farewell. I press mine against the window.

The big engine rumbles as Jimmy works the gears and pulls away from the curb.

"You okay, kid?"

"Yeah," I say, even though my heart feels ripped from its moorings. I curl up on the seat, my head resting on my backpack and close my eyes, willing myself to escape into a deep, dreamless sleep.

I awake to the heavenly aroma of greasy food and coffee. I sit up, stretch and try to get my bearings. We're in a super market parking lot across from familiar golden arches.

Jimmy is slurping coffee and grinning at me. "Got your favorite food. Fries and coffee...right?"

I smile back at him. "Yum."

Jimmy and I share the same taste in food. Grease and salt. Nothing green. Despite Sandra's efforts to train me up right, nutrition-wise, I've resisted. I know I'll regret it someday. Every now and then, I lay awake at night and imagine I hear the sound of my arteries hardening.

"Where are we?" I peer through the window for a clue.

"Halfway to Redding." He cranks up the engine and pulls out onto the street. "Rest stop a few miles up the road if you need to pee."

Jimmy's a good guy. He understands the female bladder.

We meet up with the studly Brett at a truck stop south of Redding. I wish I could say my plans for seduction were successful, but the idea of screwing the boss's stepdaughter puts Brett in a bad place. I do everything but strip down to panties and bra.

With both hands clasped firmly on the steering

wheel, Brett shoots me a heated glance and a smile of regret. "It's not that I don't want to, Mel. I think you're real cute. But, I'm sure you know Abel has a nightstick under his seat, and then there's your mom. She'd help Abel beat the crap outta me. Plus, we're already behind schedule and I really need this job."

"No problem," I mutter, my cheeks burning with embarrassment. *Thanks, Mom.*

It's twilight when we roll into 3 Peaks. I punch Dani's address into the GPS. 3315 Pine Drop Drive. I thank Brett for the lift, grab my backpack and climb out of the truck.

Brett calls, "I'll wait if you want. Make sure somebody's home."

"It's okay. I see lights on inside."

I definitely don't want Brett hanging around. If it doesn't work out at Dani's house, he'll feel compelled to report to Abel, who will immediately call Sandra. Before I have time to blink, I'll be on the flip-flop, back to San Berdoo.

When Brett pulls away, I stand on the curb and check out the house. As if living up to its address, a humongous pine tree dominates the front yard. Littered with desiccated pinecones, the grass looks like it's holding on for dear life. Patchy, brown and sparse, the whole front yard has the look of neglect with one exception. A shiny black Toyota Tundra is parked in the weed-choked driveway.

I'm having a hard time placing Dani in this setting. Dani, who insists on perfection? Yes, I know. It's a conundrum. Why did she choose someone like me—so far from perfect—for a friend?

I rationalize, thinking maybe the yard is her

husband Eddie's responsibility. I hate to be a know-it-all, but I told her not to marry him. His soul is speckled with mud. Eddie is not good husband material. But, Dani was in *luv* and paid me no mind.

As I walk up the crumbling sidewalk to the front porch, I bite my tongue. When Dani answers the door, I won't say, "Look at your front yard. You should have listened to me."

I press the doorbell and listen. Nothing. Must be broken. Another strike against slacker Eddie. I double up my fist and pound on the door.

The drapery in the front window twitches and a face appears. Definitely not Dani's face. I begin to get a sick feeling in the pit of my stomach. Something's wrong.

The door flies open and Eddie appears, glowering down at me, a cigarette hanging from his lips. Clad in baggy jeans and a black AC-DC T-shirt, he looks bigger and meaner than I remember.

"Um, hi Eddie," I stammer. "Is Dani here? I emailed her I was coming."

"Dani's not here."

He gives the door a shove. I catch it with my foot. "Hey, remember me? Mel Sullivan? I was in your wedding. Where is she?"

It's painful to watch Eddie trying to collate the information. I imagine cogs and gears grinding slowly inside his thick skull as he formulates an answer. Finally, he gives me a big, cheesy grin. "Oh, yeah. Mel. Guess you didn't hear. Dani's in the hospital. She had a fall."

"What?"

He reaches under his shirt and scratches his belly.

"Yeah, it's real sad. She was painting the bathroom and fell off the ladder. Hit her head on the tub. She's in a coma at St. Charles."

The air gushes out of my lungs and I see stars dancing in a field of black. I lean over, place my hands on my knees and gulp in air. I have low blood pressure and sometimes a sudden shock puts me over the edge.

"You gonna pass out or somethin'?" Eddie asks.

I straighten up. "I'm fine. Can I see the baby?"

Eddie's gaze shifts upward and back. "She's not here right now. She's with, um, some friends of mine."

Something tells me not to ask, but I do anyway. "Who are they? I'd like to see her."

"Not a good idea," Eddie says, attempting to arrange his face into that of a concerned parent. "You know, she misses her mother and all. I don't want her any more upset."

"Well," I say. "I don't plan to upset her. I just want to see her."

Eddie looks like a cornered wolverine. Come out fighting. Never say die. "I'm gonna have to say no."

"Okay, no problem. Have you called Dani's dad?"

Dani's mom took off when Dani was eight. Shortly after, Dani's dad re-married and had three kids with the new wife. He cared about Dani but was rarely home, having to work hard to support his family.

Eddie heaves a sigh and rolls his eyes. "Yeah, of course I called her dad. "

"Sorry," I mutter. "Thought I'd let him know if you didn't."

He folds his arms and stares down at me. "Anything else?"

I shake my head, shoulder my backpack and head

for the street.

Now what, Mel?

Chapter Three

As I trudge toward the commercial loop of Highway 97 in the gathering darkness, I call Sandra and describe the warm welcome I received from Dani, Eddie and their beautiful baby girl, Destiny. No need to make my mother worry. I'll figure something out. During my teen years, I spent a lot of time skipping school and hanging out with ne'er-do-wells, as my mother called them. It was probably the best education I ever received. Long story short, I can take care of myself.

First order of business: Locate St Charles Hospital. Check on Dani. I hail down a city bus. Thirty minutes later, I stand in the lobby of the hospital, trying to pry information out of a woman with characteristics not unlike my mother. Fortunately, I've had a lifetime to hone my skills. And, I know my way around hospitals.

"Immediate family only." She glances at her watch. "And, it's after eight. No visitors after eight."

"But, I'm her sister. I had to hitchhike to get here. Please let me see her. What if she dies tonight? It would be on you."

The last bit gets to her. Doubt clouds her sharp, gray eyes. "Third floor. Room 312. Don't stay long. Your brother's there. Guess you'll be glad to see him."

My brother? I stare at the floor to disguise my look of surprise. "Haven't seen him for a while." *Or ever,*

16

since I don't have a brother.

The third floor is quiet. The nurse behind the counter is pecking away on her keyboard, pausing occasionally to peer at the screen with a puzzled frown. Quickly, I make my way to 312. The door is closed. I open it a crack and peer into the darkened room. Bed number one. Older lady, mouth agape, hooked up to multiple wires. Not Dani.

I peek around the drawn curtain. Illuminated by dim light filtering through the open window blinds, Dani lies on her back, her hands resting on her belly, her long blond hair splayed across the pillow. A purple bruise covers her left cheek. An IV tube sprouts from the back of one hand. Electrodes dot her chest and a blood pressure monitor hisses as it squeezes and releases her left arm. Tears well up in my eyes.

"Another long-lost family member, huh?''

I turn toward the deep voice. A man is sprawled in a chair tucked into a shadowed corner. He rises, unfolding his lanky body in segments. Legs. Hips. Shoulders and head. He's a big guy, standing at least six feet tall. Hard for me to judge, though, since I'm vertically challenged.

I step around the curtain and let my backpack slide to the floor. "I heard my *brother* was here. Who the hell are you?"

He walks toward me into the light. "Since I know Dani doesn't have a *sister your age*," he says, "Who the hell are *you*?"

"You go first."

He scrapes his fingers through his reddish-brown brush cut, grins down at me and extends a big hand. "William Henry McCarty. You can call me Billy."

I give his hand a little squeeze and scoot away from him. "I'm Mel."

"Mel's a guy's name."

"Also a nickname for Melanie."

This guy is beyond irritating. Why does he care about my name? "Why are you here?" I slide between the curtain and Dani's bed. I pick up her right hand, the one without the IV, and press it to my lips. Her fingernails are bitten down to the nail bed. So unlike the Dani I know, who always has perfectly manicured nails.

"You tell me. Then I'll tell you."

"Because she's my best friend and I think Eddie's a lying sack of shit."

Billy steps to the other side of Dani's bed and studies her battered face. "Me too. Not the best friend part. The lying sack of shit part."

"So, Eddie's not your friend?"

"No way," he says. "My sister, Kendra, and Dani are tight. Kendra and Dani had plans to pick out paint for the bathroom. Then Kendra was going to help out with the kid while Dani painted. She doesn't buy the falling off the ladder story. Says there's no way that could have happened."

Should I believe this guy? I frown at him. "Then why isn't Kendra here?"

"Kendra's got two little rug rats. No time to play detective. Since I was a military cop, she twisted my arm."

The black seeds of suspicion, sown earlier by Eddie's remarks, sprout into noxious weeds. I squeeze Dani's hand, willing her to wake up. "Did Eddie tell your sister who was taking care of Destiny?"

"When Dani ended up in the ER, Kendra offered to

take the baby. Eddie turned her down, said she was with some friend of his." Billy's jaw tightens and he shakes his head. "We're talking about the same day Dani had her so-called accident. And the baby's already gone?"

"He told me the same thing."

Billy grips the side rails of the bed. I glance at his face. The friendly-Billy face is gone. He's morphed into a different man. Eyes focused and intense. Lips compressed in a tight line. All hard angles and edges. "Son of a bitch," he mutters. "What'd he do with the kid?"

Fear roils deep in my belly. "Do you think he'd do something to her? Hurt her?" *Or worse? Don't go there, Mel.*

"If he's lying about Dani's accident, it's possible."

I still have my doubts about William Henry McCarty. Is this guy for real? He's a complete stranger to me. Maybe he's lying about not being Eddie's friend. Maybe he's here in Dani's hospital room to make sure she doesn't wake up.

One way to find out. Although every fiber of my being screams, "No!" I force myself to look into his eyes, to read the contents of his soul. Unblinking, I stare into his clear, hazel eyes and gasp with surprise when I see my own face. It's like seeing one's reflection in a plate glass window. Is he blocking me? Is it possible he's a fellow soul reader?

His gaze narrows to a squint. "Something wrong?"

Gathering my wits, I shake my head, reach for my backpack and then pause. No way will I leave Dani with Billy standing over her. "How long do you plan to stay here?"

"Heading out right now." His gaze sweeps over my

faded jeans, black tank top covered with an unbuttoned flannel shirt and comes to rest on my backpack. "Why? Need a lift home."

"No, I'm good." What I *needed* was to get away from this guy with the piercing eyes and crystal clear soul. As well as time to figure out if I can trust him. The fact I'm currently without a home is none of Billy's business.

"Do you live here in 3 Peaks?" he asks.

"Sort of." I drop a kiss on Dani's forehead.

"How do you sort of live somewhere?"

I shrug and make my way into the hall. I have a plan and it doesn't include Billy, so I stop outside the room and re-tie my shoes, waiting until he walks past me to the elevator. I head for the stairs when the doors slide open and he steps inside.

Once in the lobby, I spot Billy leaning against the information desk, schmoozing with its sober-faced guardian of hospital information. She's giggling like a thirteen-year-old with her first crush. I roll my eyes; check the signage and head back to the stairs.

Second Floor. Surgery. From my checkered past, I know the surgical floor will have several areas for families to wait while their loved ones go under the knife. Big areas with TVs and magazines. Little areas tucked away in a corner for those who want privacy. I hit the jackpot at the end of the hall. A darkened room with an overstuffed chair, comfy couch and small coffee table. Nice big window overlooking the city of 3 Peaks. I stow my backpack next to the wall and curl up on the couch. Anyone checking will think I'm waiting while a family member has emergency surgery. I have my story ready in case some hospital employee on a

power trip challenges me.
     But then, he shows up.
     Billy.

Chapter Four

I'd just dozed off when the lights flip on and a familiar deep voice jolts me from dreamland.

"Thought I'd find you here."

I open one eye. "Go to hell."

He stands in the doorway, a smug smile lifting the corners of his mouth. "You don't have any place to stay, do you?"

I struggle to a sitting position and glare at him. "Wow, you must be a detective."

He moseys into the room and drops into a chair. "What's your story, Minnie Mouse? Runaway? How old are you anyway? Sixteen?"

Because I'm undersized, I've been called Squirt, Pipsqueak and/or Short Stuff my entire life. Normally, it ticks me off. Big time. Tonight, I'm too tired to get mad. I sigh, reach for my backpack and began pawing through it for my wallet. Apparently, it migrated to the bottom. Frustrated, I pull out my battered laptop and set it on the floor. Then, I grab pajamas, bras, panties, tampons, prescription bottles, toothpaste, cell phone and flip-flops. Pile 'em all on the coffee table. I retrieve my wallet. I flip it open to my ID, stand and shove it into Billy's hands.

"Here you go, Ace,"

Billy's gaze flicks back and forth between my picture ID and my face. He gives it back to me. "Honor

Melanie Sullivan, age twenty-two, fully grown woman, I humbly apologize for my remarks."

"Alrighty then." I begin re-packing my things.

The way my life is going, I could have predicted what happens next. The card containing my punch-out birth control pills slips from of my hand, hits the floor and lands at Billy's feet.

He picks it up, reads the label and hands it to me with a wink. "Like I said, fully-grown woman. Safe sex is a good thing."

I ignore him and sink back into the couch. "Turn out the light when you leave."

Some people can't take a hint. He refuses to budge. "Honor's a nice name. Why don't you use it?"

"Long story and I'm tired."

"So, you're from San Bernardino. When did you get to 3 Peaks?"

"A few hours ago," I mutter.

"No family here?"

"I planned to stay with Dani, but it didn't work out."

He stands and stares down at me. "My sister has a big house."

I wave him away. "I'm okay. It's late. I'll figure out something tomorrow."

"What happens tomorrow?"

"I'll check on Dani and look for a job."

After a long moment, the light goes off. I sense he is leaning over me and open my eyes. He presses a warm hand against my cheek. "Take care, Minnie. See you around."

He tiptoes from the room and closes the door. The touch of his hand lingers on my skin. In its wake, a tingle of pure unadulterated lust spirals through my body, setting fire to every nerve ending. Thanks to William Henry McCarty, I am now wide-awake.

Later, when sleep finally comes, it is fitful and filled with dreams of Dani. The dreams take me back in time to my six-year-old self.

I hate first grade. I hate recess. All the other kids have friends. Not me. Not anymore. I curl up in a ball next to the fence and try not to think about Hope. I clap my hands over my eyes so I don't see her running out into the street. I know it's my fault. I threw the ball too high and it went over her head. "Stop, Hope!" I screamed. "A car's coming." But she didn't stop. No matter how hard I rub my eyes or plug my ears I still hear the sickening thud as she collides with the car. I see her flying through the air, landing on the sidewalk, her face covered in blood. I can't unsee it because it's inside my head. I bury my face in my arms.

I sense a presence before I lift my head and open my eyes. The girl is crouching next to me, her blond hair tumbling around her face. Her blue eyes are filled with tears. She reaches out a hand and touches my arm. "I don't want you to be sad. Will you be my friend?"

I can't find the words so I just nod. She takes my hand and pulls me up. "Let's go swing...okay?"

When I free myself from the dream, my face is wet with tears. Dani. If not for her, I'd have been a first grade dropout. We were best buds during our school years. In fact, we were so tight, the other kids called us *Danimel*. It soon morphed into *Danimal*, as in, "Hey, Danimal, you two coming to my party tonight?" Instead of fighting it, we embraced the nickname, signing yearbooks with a paw print.

Other than Sandra, Dani is the only person who knows of my ability to read souls. Instead of believing it's a curse, Dani thinks it's cool. One time, though, she didn't listen to me. It was when I told her not to marry Eddie and it caused a rift between us. After Destiny was born, we re-connected and she began urging me to come to 3 Peaks. Did she want me here because she needed help? I try to remember our phone conversations. Mostly, she talked about the baby, how much she loved being a mom. She rarely talked about Eddie. Maybe I should have paid more attention.

Is the dream a cry for help? My first impulse is to run to Dani's room. *Think before you act, Melanie*. My mother's voice. It's three a.m. Popping up at Dani's bedside in the middle of the night is probably not a good plan. If somebody calls security and I'm ejected from the hospital, I'll have a hard time getting back in. Better stay put until morning. My mother would be proud. Instead of acting, I thought it through. Exhausted by the unaccustomed cerebral workout, I close my eyes.

Seven a.m. I waken to a sudden increase in the noise level. A shift change is underway. I grab my backpack and find a restroom. After taking care of my bursting bladder, I splash cold water on my face, peek in the mirror and gasp in surprise. Prior to leaving home, I'd hacked off my long, unruly hair. New life. New hair. Each time I catch a glimpse of myself, it's like looking at a stranger. A stranger with spiky black hair, a permanent tan, bright blue eyes and a tiny mole next to a mouth turned up at the corners despite my pessimistic personality. The blue eyes and permanent tan are compliments of my sperm donor father, or as Sandra refers to him, *that damn Spaniard who knocked me up and split.* I finger-comb my new do, pinch my cheeks to add some color and head up the stairs to Dani's room.

An LPN is attending to the older lady in Dani's room. She looks up when I enter. "It's a little early for visitors."

"I'm Dani's sister. Just got here last night. I'll brush her hair and wash her face."

The LPN shrugs. "Be my guest. I've got a bunch of others to take care of." She hands me a plastic basin, a fresh towel and washcloth. "You might try talking to her. I told her husband too, but he hasn't been around much. Sometimes people in a coma can hear you."

Dani had shifted during the night. The bedcovers are tangled and twisted as if she was thrashing around. Seems like a good sign. I tidy her bed and fill the plastic basin with warm water. I wring out the washcloth and gently pat her forehead and cheeks. The bruising on her face is more apparent in the harsh daylight.

"Hey, girlfriend, it's Mel. I'm so glad to see you. I can't wait to tell you what's up with me." I lower my voice to a whisper in case the LPN is eavesdropping. "I'm off probation. I'm now a free woman."

I jabber like a jaybird while I give Dani a sponge bath. After ten minutes, the water is cold and I'm running out of words. I rub moisturizer on her dry lips and drop a kiss on her cheek. "Can't wait to see the baby."

Her eyelids flutter. Whoa, should have mentioned the baby earlier. "Love the picture you sent me of Destiny. She looks just like you."

I blather on, trying to recall every baby description

26

I can come up with. Cute as a button. God's little angels, etc. I run out of steam after, "I bet she even burps on command."

In the silence that follows, Dani moans and rolls her head from side to side.

I take hold of her hands, lean close and whisper, "What is it, Dani? Look at me so I can help. You don't have to say a word. I'll know. Okay?"

Her eyes fly open. I stare into her clear blue eyes, unchanged since the first day we met. Her eyes are unchanged, but sadly, her soul is not. Dani's soul has always been bright yellow, filled with sunshine. I've always loved Dani's soul. Looking at her soul made me happy. Now, it makes me want to cry. Dani is suffering and not only from physical pain. The light in her soul has been extinguished and her shiny soul is now a putrid brownish-yellow, streaked with flaring hotspots of anguish.

I put my mouth next to her ear. "What's happened to you?"

Her eyes fill with tears. She squeezes my hands and struggles to form words. "Baby. Want baby."

"Where is the baby? Where's Destiny?"

Dani sighs and the light leaves her eyes. Her grip on my hands goes slack. I charge out of the room and run to the nurse's station. "Room 312. She's waking up. Call the doctor."

Chapter Five

I huddle in the hall and watch as official-looking medical folk trot in and out of Dani's room. At first, I tried to remain in the room, tucking myself into a corner. A sharp-eyed nurse looked me over and barked, "*You. Out.*"

Thirty minutes later, I spot Eddie emerging from the elevator. Unshaven and rumpled, he wears jeans and a flannel shirt not unlike my own. When he sees me he stops. "You're here?"

"Where else would I be? Dani's my friend."

"Huh," he says, as if puzzled by my strange priority. "Is she awake?"

"She woke up for a few minutes. It's the reason they called you."

He shifts from one foot to the other. "She talk to you?"

I shrug. "Not much." I can think of no good reason to tell the big jerk anything.

He reaches for the door.

"Let me know what's happening."

"They kick you out?"

I nod.

He pushes the door open. Before it closes, I listen for the sound of Dani's voice, but hear nothing but the low murmur of her medical team and the hissing of machines. A few minutes later, Eddie emerges, flanked by the nurse who'd ousted me and a man dressed in slacks, dress shirt and tie. Her doctor?

Eddie points at me. "She lied to you. She's not Dani's sister."

I bristle. "I'm the closest thing she has to a sister. She needs me. When I talked to her, she opened her eyes."

The nurse turns to Eddie. "You're the husband, Mr. Morgan. It's your decision. Can this person see your wife, or not?"

His expression hardens. "Not."

The man speaks up. "I'm afraid you'll have to leave, Miss."

My face grows hot with anger and frustration. I know it will do no good to argue, but poor judgment has never stopped me before. "Apparently you don't want her to get better. Did she wake up when Eddie talked to her? Or, did he bother to talk to her?"

The man and woman exchange a glance but keep silent.

I glare at Eddie and pick up my backpack "Yeah, that's what I thought. She responded to me. She was coming out of her coma. And now she's not."

The man holds up a cautionary hand. "I'm Dani's doctor and I can tell you these things take time. If she's really waking up, it will happen whether you're here or not."

"Yeah," Eddie sneers, happily reinforced by his wife's physician.

"Fine." I'm aware I sound like a pissed off teenager. I start down the hall and call over my shoulder. "But, I'll be checking. And, she better damn well get better or it will be on you, Eddie."

Still burning, I gallop down the stairs. I know the last statement I hurled at Eddie was incredibly impulsive and stupid. My hostility toward Dani's husband will make it nearly impossible for me to help her stay alive. "Damn you, Mel," I mutter. "Do you have to blurt out whatever passes through your birdbrain?"

I continue my self-scolding until I hit the main floor. I need coffee and food so I can start my job search. I follow the sign to the cafeteria, pick up a tray, and zero in on a big, gooey cinnamon roll, the last one left on the plate. Apparently I'm not the only unhealthy eater in the hospital.

After I pay for my roll and coffee, I have exactly eighty-two dollars and forty-nine cents left in my pocket. I need to find a job. Stat.

True, Sandra will wire money if I ask. No way will I ask.

I pick up a copy of today's newspaper and make my way to a tiny corner table. After a slurp of coffee and a big bite of roll, I turn to the help wanted section. Four glowing résumés burn holes in my backpack. All I have to do is find the right match. I will not be seeking employment in a hospital or work as a nanny. My mother is scared to death I'll snatch another baby even though I've assured her I won't.

I searched the want ads for jobs fitting my résumés. Dog walker/pooper-scooper. Zip. Gardener. Nada. House painter. Nothing. Waitress. Score! A café called Nick's Place needs an experienced waitress. According to my résumé, I am over-qualified, having worked for several years at an establishment called Sandy's Pub and Eatery. True, the restaurant is my mother's kitchen.

But, how hard can it be to take orders and deliver food?

I finish my breakfast and head for the restroom. Job interviews require I don't look like I've just hitched a ride on an eighteen-wheeler. After changing into my job-hunting clothes, I check out my image in the mirror A disheveled pixie clad in black jeans and a wrinkled scoop-necked T-shirt glowers back at me. I hope body heat will smooth out the wrinkles. I remind myself to look pleasant.

The bus drops me off in front of a shabby-looking establishment. The sign across the top of the building assures me this is Nick's Sports Bar and Motel. Motel? Sure enough, I spy an L-shaped line of cinder block motel rooms behind the main building.

A *closed* sign hangs in the front door window. I peer around the sign, detect movement inside and rattle the door handle.

The door opens a crack. "We're closed until 4." A man's voice.

"I'm here about the waitress job. Have you filled it yet?"

The door flies open. A muscular thirty-something guy looks at me with an appraising brown-eyed gaze. "How old are you, honey? We serve adult beverages here."

I pinch my lips together for a brief moment. *Now is not the time, Mel, even if he did call you honey.*

I try to keep my expression neutral and stare at the bridge of his nose "I'm twenty-two. Would you like to see my qualifications?"

"Sure, come on in." He steps away from the door so I can enter. He leads me through a dimly lit dining area consisting of booths and tables. The back of the dining room features a long bar topped with polished dark wood. An open window to the kitchen is visible behind the bar. Despite the gloomy interior, the place smells of soap and furniture polish overlaid with the aroma of French Fries. Damn, it smells good!

"I'm Nick Holloway," the guy says, as we step into a long hallway. The restrooms are labeled Jocks and Jockettes. Action photos of athletes, both male and female, line the walls. Holloway takes a right turn into a sparsely furnished office.

He waves me into a chair. "And you are…?"

Oh, yeah, job interviews require social interaction. Remember, Mel?

"Melanie." I hand over the document lovingly crafted by my over-zealous mother. "Melanie Sullivan."

He scans my résumé, places it on the desk and folds his arms across his chest. I risk a glance into his eyes, just long enough to search for the telltale signs of an evil nature. Fortunately, his soul looks fairly bland.

After a brief silence, he says, "Your qualifications are fine, Melanie. Here's my problem. Things can get rough in here. I keep the ruckus down to a minimum, but I can't be on your tail, protecting you every minute. If some guy grabs your ass, tell me and I'll toss him out, but, bottom line, so to speak, you have to be able to take care of yourself. You're pretty small, so I'm afraid you might get pushed around."

I narrow my eyes and stand, pointing at the résumé. "Did you read the bottom section, the part about my hobbies?" Nestled between the lies, there is a shining beacon of truth.

He picks up the paper and reads aloud. "Knitting scarves. Gardening. Brazilian Jiu Jitsu. Black belt.

What the hell is Brazilian Jiu Jitsu?"

His office is pretty small, but there's plenty of room for what I have in mind. I drop to a crouch. "Come out from behind the desk and I'll show you."

He laughs. "You're kidding. Right?"

"No."

His brows shoot up in surprise. "Are you going to hurt me?"

"Not if you submit."

He pushes his chair back and stands. "And if I don't?"

"Then, I hurt you."

Looking wary, he steps to the side of his desk. "Now what?"

I move closer to him. "Try to grab me."

He lunges at me like I knew he would. Sidestepping quickly, I grab his wrist with both hands and whip my left leg around his body, striking the back of his knee. Caught off balance he crashes to the floor, face down. I land hard on his upper arm with both my knees and use the strength of my body to force his hand back in a wristlock. Inside my head, I hear the voice of my instructor. "Apply enough pressure and the pain will drive all rational thought from your opponent."

"Ouch, goddammit!" he yelps.

"Do you submit? Say it."

"Hell, yeah. I submit."

Grinning, I help him up. He rubs his wrist and collapses into his chair. "Jesus, girl, how did you learn to do that?"

"Brazilian Jiu Jitsu teaches smaller, weaker people how to use ground fighting and leverage. Plus the joint locks cause severe pain. My mom wanted me to be able to protect myself, so she started me in BJJ when I was twelve."

I don't tell him the main reason behind Sandra's decision. My bad attitude and social awkwardness attracted bullies like iron filings to a magnet. Nick Holloway doesn't need to know that.

I stand in front of his desk and look down at him. "So, are you going to hire me?"

Nick grins and raises his hands in the universal sign of surrender. "I submit. You're hired."

Chapter Six

After we hammer out the details, I can barely contain my glee. I'm now gainfully employed. Plus, I have a roof over my head and two meals a day. The roof over my head is in exchange for my services as a motel maid when one of Nick's regulars doesn't show up. Apparently, this happens frequently. How hard can it be to change bed sheets?

Since Nick's Place is mainly a sports' bar, the doors don't open until late in the afternoon which will give me time to sneak back into the hospital and check on Dani.

My room is nothing to brag about, but it's scrupulously clean. Along with the requisite bed and bath, it has heat and air conditioning *and* a microwave oven *and* a small fridge. I'm feeling pretty proud of myself. In less than twenty-four hours, I have a job and a home.

It's a little short on personal touches, so I root around in my backpack and pull out the only picture I brought from home. Hope and Honor, age five. First day of kindergarten. Fighting back a wave of sadness, I trace the outline of our faces. Hope is dead. In my mind, so is Honor.

Nick asked me to come in at two-thirty so he can fill me in on my duties. Along with the key to my room, he'd tossed me a handful of V-necked pink T-shirts with *Nick's Place* emblazoned in big, black letters across the boob line. "Wear one of these. Your jeans are fine."

Clad in my waitressing outfit, I walk through the courtyard to the back of the restaurant. A sign next to the curb says, "Employee parking only." Four spaces. Two are filled. One with a battered blue pick-up truck. The other with a beige, older model Chevy Impala. I wonder which one belongs to Nick.

I step into the immaculate kitchen and see the back of a burly, muscular guy in jeans and a white T-shirt standing over the industrial sized stove. He's applying a whisk to a pot bubbling with something that smells yummy. I try not to drool as I breathe in the kitchen's glorious mingled odors of bacon, cheese and French Fries.

The guy glances over his shoulder. "So you're the new waitress?"

"Yeah, I'm Mel."

"Myron," he grunts and turns back to the stove.

Guess he's not in a conversational mood. Fine with me. I shrug and step through the swinging doors. I find Nick behind the bar, wiping down its already gleaming surface. When he spots me, he turns his head and calls through the open window, "Hey, Myron. The new kid is here and she looks hungry."

Is it that obvious? Maybe I am drooling. The big gooey cinnamon roll I'd scarfed down for breakfast was long gone.

Nick points at a bar stool. "Have a seat."

Myron appears. He's carrying a plateful of grilled cheese sandwich wedges and fries. It smells like heaven. He sets it down in front of me.

Nick says, "Meet Myron. He's one of my fry cooks. He and another guy, Sammy, each take a half shift so they can work their other jobs.

"Actually, we just met," I say.

Myron extends a hand the size of a catcher's mitt. I give it a shake and glance into his flat gray eyes. A second glance tells me more. I see three vertical iron bars bisecting his spotty beige soul. If I'm not mistaken, Myron has served time in the gray bar motel. His bulging, tattooed biceps are a testament to the heavy duty power lifting, a favorite activity in prison.

Not my business. Not when my tummy's growling like a jet engine warming up.

"Nice to meet you again, Myron. Thanks for the food."

Without further ado, I dig into my food while Myron and Nick shoot the breeze. When I come up for air, Nick says, "I'll show you around. Helen will be here soon. She's my other waitress."

He switches on the overhead lights and opens a low gate leading to an area adjoining the dining room, an area I'd missed on my first trip through the restaurant. Stools line the walls, but the room is dominated by two pool tables.

"We call this the Corral," Nick says. "It can get a little rowdy in here, so watch yourself. I'll try to keep an eye out, so give me a high sign if you need help."

Next, he leads me down the hall to a small storage room. He points at a bucket and mop. "Cleaning supplies here in case there's spillage. There's almost always spillage."

On the way back to the dining room, I glance at the photos of local athletes lining the hall and spot a familiar face. Clad in a football uniform, a helmet hanging from his right hand, William Henry McCarty stares into the camera with a surly gaze.

Nick turns and finds me studying the picture. "The Kid's one of our regulars. You know him?"

"We've met. Why do you call him the Kid?"

"You've heard of outlaw Billy the Kid…right?"

I nod.

"Our Billy was the best fullback to come out of 3 Peaks High School. A sports writer from the Oregonian found out William Henry McCarty was also outlaw Billy the Kid's real name and compared the two in an article. He said, 'The Kid flat mows 'em down like his famous predecessor.' I guess the name sort of stuck."

"Huh." I say it like I don't give a rat's ass.

By the time Helen bustles in, my head is swimming with confusion. Nick had tossed out a bajillion terms, thinking I would know what he's talking about. I don't, of course. Not wanting to admit my ignorance, I nod and pray I can figure it out later. Sum total of what I know? Each table needs a "setup." Silverware, napkins, salt, pepper, condiments. Since Nick's system isn't computerized, we take orders the old-fashioned way, written down on a pad. Each waitress is allowed to keep her tips, but breakage comes out of my salary. Also, if my customers "dine and dash," I'm stuck with the bill. Good to know.

Helen is a big-busted redhead with long, skinny bird legs and muscular freckled arms. She looks me over and hollers at Nick. "Better let me take the Corral. Those guys will eat her alive."

"She's tougher than she looks," Nick hollers back.

More confusion. Am I supposed to wait on

customers in the Corral or not? Instead of asking, I decide to wait and see how it plays out.

At exactly three fifty-nine, Nick unlocks the front door and two old couples shuffle in.

"They come in every day for the early bird special," Helen tells me. "Go ahead. It will be good practice for you."

I soon discover this isn't an act of generosity. After downing their meatloaf specials, each of the elderly couples gives me a one-dollar tip.

When happy hour starts at four-thirty, the place gets crazy. Drinks and appetizers, half price until six. Helen and I are busting our buns, trying to deliver food and keep pitchers of beer refilled. Nick's behind the bar, deftly mixing drinks while keeping a watchful eye on the crowd.

A shrill whistle splits the air, followed by, "Hey, Sweet Cheeks! Get your butt over here."

The summons comes from a table crowded with blue-collar guys. One of the men holds up an empty beer pitcher.

Helen brushes by me. "I believe he's talking to you, Sweet Cheeks."

Nick gives the guy a look, but says nothing. Is this a test to see if I can handle the situation? Even though I'm pissed off, I approach the men.

"Another refill?" I reach for the empty pitcher.

The jerk pulls it away, forcing me to move closer to him. He tilts his chair back, balancing it on the two back legs. His legs are spread like he's giving me an up-close, personal view of his manly junk. I feel the heat of his gaze crawling over my body. His buddies watch the action with anticipatory grins. Even though it's the last thing I want to do, I move in until my legs are touching his. We lock gazes and I look into his soiled mustard-yellow soul.

"You might want to be careful, sir," I say. "Looks like that chair's about to tip over."

My hand closes around the empty pitcher. *Just a teensy little bump, Mel, and over he goes*. I really want to do it, but then I remember Adam Boyle. Instead, I refuse to blink and move closer. Uncertainty clouds his eyes and he lowers the front legs of the chair to the floor.

Still staring into his eyes, I pull the pitcher from his grip. "Same as before? MGD?"

The corners of his mouth turn down. "Yeah, that'll work. And make it snappy."

I give him a sweet smile, knowing he's trying to save face with his buddies. "Right away, sir."

As I turn to leave, my peripheral vision catches sight of a hand moving toward my ass. I switch my hips the opposite direction and call over my shoulder. "Bad boy! No grabbing the help."

Thankfully, everybody at the table busts out laughing. As I approach the bar, Nick gives me a big thumbs up. "Way to go, Mel. Think you can handle the Corral?"

"Sure. No problem." At least, I thought I could at the time.

I deliver a platter of Buffalo wings to the boys in the Corral and hurry back for their drinks. I pick up the tray of eight frosty mugs filled with draught beer. Making sure the mugs are balanced on the tray, I take a tentative step. At precisely the same moment, a guy at the bar whirls around and flings out an arm to greet his buddy across the room. His arm whacks me in the back of my head and I lurch forward. The tray shoots from my hands. Beer mugs fly. A foam-capped tsunami of beer cascades across the floor. I stagger forward, trying to catch my balance but instead, *splat* face-first in the beer spill.

I struggle to my feet and without benefit of thought, scream, "Fuck."

After a brief moment of silence, the crowd begins to cheer, clap and yell comments.

"Way to go, new girl."

"Anybody got a straw?"

Dripping with beer, I clap a hand over my mouth, afraid to look at Nick. He has two good reasons to let me go. If the beer crash doesn't do the trick, the F bomb surely will.

A big warm hand grips the back of my neck. "Need some help?"

I turn. My forehead brushes against the stubbly chin of the man standing behind me. Billy the Kid is in the building.

Chapter Seven

My face is hot with embarrassment and I'm unable to string together a complete sentence. Instead, I stammer, "Um, well, uh…"

From the corner of my eye, I see Nick approaching. Fortunately, the guy who caused the accident slides across the beer-slickened floor to apologize. "Don't you worry, little girl. I'll tell Nick it was my fault." He slip-slides away and intercepts Nick who, I'm sure, is on his way to fire me.

My feet feel glued to the floor. Billy puts his hands on my shoulders. "Let's go get the mop. I'll help you clean up."

His kindness puts me over the edge. I bite my lower lip and blink back tears. *Do not cry, dumb shit. Especially not in front of this guy.*

I swallow the lump in my throat and croak, "Yeah, good idea."

I begin to pick my way through the mess.

"Hey, Mel." Nick's voice.

I stop in my tracks. I'm about to get the axe. I know it. Nick's expression is unreadable. I lift my hands and say, "Sorry about all this, especially the language." I dig around in my pocket and hold out the key to my room. "You want me to go?"

Nick's brows draw together. "Go? Why would I want you to go?"

To my amazement, he turns to Billy and gives him a big bear hug. "Back from sand land, huh Kid? Heard you landed a job with 3 Peaks P.D. When do you start?"

Billy delivers a friendly punch to Nick's midsection. "One of their detectives is due to retire. Have to wait until he decides to pull the plug."

Hmm, so Billy the Kid will soon be Detective Billy the Kid.

Helen bustles over and pats my arm. "Tough break, Mel. Shit happens. Then you die."

Still shaky, I make my way to the storage room, Billy trailing behind me. Armed with bucket, mop and a handful of old towels, we tackle the beer spill together. Out of the eight mugs, only two broke, so it's possible I may still be on the plus side, salary-wise. At least that's what I think until Billy says, "Me and the guy who caused the accident took care of the beer."

I stop mopping and give him a blank look. "Beer?"

He quirks a half-grin and points at the floor. "That beer."

Oops. My face heats up as I factor in the cost of the eight mugs, each holding sixteen ounces of beer. I stare at the floor and mumble, "I'll pay you back when I get my check."

Billy tosses a chunk of broken glass into the trash. "No you won't."

I lean the mop against a stool, put my hands on my hips and glare up at him. "Yes, I will."

Hands on hips, Billy mimics my pose. "We'll see about that."

Clearly, this guy has to have the last word. I shake my head in mock disgust.

We're almost done cleaning when Nick strolls over. "I'll finish up. Take five, Mel, and go change your clothes." He pauses and grins, "Not that the boys aren't enjoying the wet T-shirt."

I'm so rattled by the accident, I don't realize I'm a friggin' mess. My pink tee is soaked and clinging to my body. My nipples stand out like headlights on high beam. Suddenly self-conscious, I glance at the guys sitting at a nearby table. A young guy with a ponytail gives me a wink. His buddy says, "Nice tits, honey."

Face flaming, I hand the mop to Nick and head for the door.

The rest of my shift passes in a blur of activity. The noise level rises in direct proportion to the amount of alcohol consumed. While carrying heavily laden trays, my head swivels back and forth as I dodge the crowd clustered at the bar, always on high alert for the unexpected lurching drunk. When the place closes at two a.m., my ass is dragging, but I'm stoked about the tip money crammed in my pocket. First thing in the morning, I'll head to the thrift store up the street and pick up some jeans. After the beer spill, I'm down to my last ratty pair until I get a chance to do my laundry. Then, I'll check on Dani.

I'm learning things don't always go according to plan. I'm in a deep, dreamless sleep when a heavy fist pounds on the door and jolts me awake. Still groggy with exhaustion, I open one eye and check the bedside clock. Eight forty-two in the a.m.

A heavily accented voice accompanies the pounding. "Hey, you. Rosa no show up. You come help me clean rooms. Now"

I groan, drag myself out of bed and open the door a

crack, clad only in panties and bra. I'd been too tired to paw through the contents of my backpack in search of pajamas.

A short, plump Hispanic woman peers through the crack. "You Mel?" she screeches.

"Yeah," I croak.

"I'm Consuela. You call me Connie. Nick say you come help me clean rooms. Rosa not here. Put clothes on. Come with me."

I splash water on my face, throw on my clothes and stagger through the door where Connie waits with a cart loaded with fresh towels, sheets and cleaning supplies. She points at the cart and then to a room with its door ajar. "You start there."

She whirls and stomps away before I have time to form a reply. Muttering under my breath, I use my butt to push open the door to Room 8 and pull the cart across the raised threshold. Despite the fresh mountain air pouring through the open door, the smell of sex and stale bourbon overlaid with a sickly-sweet vanilla scent permeates the room. I hold my breath and flip on the lights.

"Oh, hell no." I back out of the room. Connie peers out of Room 6, a sly look on her face. "Gloves! I'm not touching anything in that room without rubber gloves."

Connie gives a snort of disgust. "You big baby. Gloves in cart. Go look."

I glare back at her, knowing she's already checked out Room 8 and decided it would be a good starter room for the newbie.

Since there are no surgical masks on the cart, I pull a hand towel across my face and tie it behind my head to block the odor making my stomach do backflips.

Rubber gloves firmly in place, I dump the wastebasket. Two spent spray cans of fake whipped cream and an empty bottle of bourbon tumble out.

I start by cleaning the mirror, obliterating the words, "WE HAD FUN" written in scarlet lipstick. The toilet is next. Whoever the guy was, his aim was damn poor. Before I tackle the sticky bed sheets, I step outside to breathe some fresh air.

"Morning, Sunshine," Nick calls as he saunters across the inner courtyard, a container of coffee in each hand. He hands me one of the cups and studies my towel-draped face. The corners of his mouth twitch like he's trying to hold back a smile. "Any serious damage in Room 8? I've got the guy's credit card information."

"You mean like a broken bed?" I ask. The words come out muffled through the towel.

Nick looks puzzled. "Bacon? There's bacon in the bed? Man, I've seen some kinky stuff but, what the hell...bacon?"

He brushes by me and steps into the room.

I pull the towel down and call, "*Broken*, not *bacon*."

When I go inside, I see Nick has stripped the bed. He holds a pair of pink thong panties between his thumb and index finger. "Found 'em under the pillow. No serious damage as far as I can see."

Silently, I hold out the wastebasket and he drops the panties in. He grins at me. "Looks like they had a real good time."

"According to the message on the mirror, they did." I shake my head in disbelief and blurt, "What kind of a place is this anyway? Do you rent by the hour?"

Nick's face darkens. "Hey, little girl, don't judge

me. I run a decent establishment. What people choose to do here is their business as long as they don't wreck the place."

I stare at the floor, wishing I could take my words back and mumble, "Sorry."

After a long moment, he cuffs me lightly on the shoulder. "Yeah, whatever. Put your burka back on and get to work."

"Thanks for the coffee."

He nods and strides away.

It takes another hour, but when I close the door to Room 8, I feel a sense of accomplishment. It is scrubbed, sterilized and spiffy, ready to rent to the next horny couple. Hold the Jell-O. Please.

Three more rooms. At eleven, my tummy recovers from the malodorous Room 8 and demands food. I find a vending machine and feed it four quarters for a bag of chips. They get stuck and refuse to drop down to the opening at the bottom. Tired and hungry, I curse and kick the side of the machine, which does the trick. I sit on the curb and eat my chips.

I'm about to tackle my final room when I hear the unmistakable sound of a Harley Davidson motorcycle, its subdued rumble bouncing off the cinder block line of motels.

Billy the Kid pulls up next to the curb. He dismounts and removes his helmet. His *aw shucks* grin is missing. I stand and search his face for a clue. When I look into his soul, I see my own face again and it is wet with tears.

I draw a shaky breath. "What's wrong?"

He places his hands on my shoulders. "Dani died last night. I'm so sorry."

47

Chapter Eight

I'm aware of an agonized cry escaping my lips and then, I see a darkening sky streaked with shooting stars. My stomach seizes up. I gasp for breath. My knees buckle. Before I hit the unforgiving pavement, I'm swept up and cradled against a warm presence. My ear is pressed against a muscular chest. I hear the strong heartbeat of the man who holds me and know I am safe. Then, blackness engulfs me.

When I open my eyes, I'm sprawled on a bed in one of the motel rooms. A clean bed. Recently re-made with fresh sheets. Possibly by me.

I lie still and listen while Billy reams out Nick Holloway. I open one eye and see they're standing toe to toe in the middle of the room.

"Jesus Christ, Nick! She works 'til two in the morning and then she has to crawl out of bed and clean up other people's shit? Did she eat breakfast? Hell, did she even get a dinner break last night? What is this, a slave labor camp?"

Nick's voice sounds conciliatory. "Listen, Kid. She has a room to stay in and two meals a day. She knew the deal when she took the job. If she doesn't eat, it's not my fault. And, besides, she's a tough little cookie. She knows Brazilian Jiu Jitsu. She put a move on me and had me begging for mercy."

"I don't give a damn about any judo crap," Billy

says. "All I know is she passed out when she found out her best friend died. What does that tell you? If I hadn't caught her, she'd have conked her head on the pavement. She needs somebody looking out for her." He stops his tirade and stabs a thumb into his chest. "Me."

"Yeah, I get it, Kid. She's all yours."

What? I swing my legs over the bed and sit up. "Quit talking about me like I'm a stray cat who needs to be rescued. I can take care of myself, thank you very much. And, just for the record, I don't belong to anybody."

I struggle to a standing position, a little too fast. I'm still woozy, so I brace my hands on my knees and take a couple of deep breaths. Both men turn and stare at me like I've just arrived from a far-off planet. The weight of Dani's death hits me like a punch and I bite my lower lip to keep the tears from flowing.

I stand as tall as possible and make eye contact with both men. "I have low blood pressure. The shock made me black out. The news about Dani." My voice trails off and I stifle a sob.

Total silence in the room. Obviously, these dudes are clueless when it comes to women's emotions. Damn, I don't like looking weak, so I take a shuddering breath and say, "Okay, I'm going back to work now."

"Like hell," Billy says. "You're going with me to get something to eat."

"I'm okay."

Nick lifts a hand. "No, he's right, Mel. You're no good to me if you're passing out from hunger and... whatever. Be back by three thirty."

"Come with me, Minnie." Billy takes my hand and

leads me from the motel room. He pulls a second helmet from his saddlebag and places it on my head, carefully fastening the strap beneath my chin.

I'm too tired, too hungry and too heartsick to argue. I climb on the bike behind Billy. Sitting erect, I maintain a few decorous inches of distance between his body and mine, hands clamped on the bars next to the seat. But then, he says, "Hang on," and punches it. With a little yip of surprise, I wrap myself around Billy like a baby orangutan clinging to its mother. The brisk wind in my face, the blur of asphalt beneath us and the sensation of flight creates a sensory overload that lifts my heavy heart.

The feeling of euphoria doesn't last. Billy gives me space, remaining quiet while I inhale syrup-laden pancakes, two strips of bacon and coffee. When I finish, all I want to do is go back to my room and sob into a pillow. But, what really scares me is the fact I have to call my mother and tell her the news. She'll contact Dani's father and, shortly after, figure out I've been lying to her since I arrived in 3 Peaks.

Finally, Billy breaks the silence. "So, do you plan to stay in 3 Peaks?"

Good question. I mull over the alternative. San Bernardino. Sandra micromanaging my life. No job. No future. And, what about Stan Abbot? By now, he might have heard about my little escapade at the hospital. Would he then place me on further probation? I feel safer with nine hundred miles between us.

I glance briefly into Billy's piercing gaze. I have no desire to see my own tear-streaked face again. "I'm staying here."

"Working at Nick's? Kind of a rough crowd."

"What do you care?" I huff. "I can handle it. Besides, I want to find out what happened to Dani."

He leans across the table and studies my face. "And what, exactly, do you plan to do about it?"

I scroll through my brain for an intelligent answer and come up blank. "Well, for starters, I want to talk to her asshole husband, Eddie. Yesterday, Dani woke up. She tried to talk to me. And now she's dead? It makes no sense."

"Yeah, I bet Eddie will be real glad to chat you up." He winks to take the sting out of his words.

Billy's right. I'd be as welcome as a case of virulent clap in Eddie's world. I think about my options and blurt, "I need to see Dani. Tell her goodbye."

"You'll have to wait until tomorrow. The body will be taken to the funeral home today."

The pancakes curdle in my belly. Dani, my dearest friend, is now *the body.* Suddenly, I'm so angry I want to howl and scream, make everybody in the restaurant share in my agony. I pinch my lips together and grip the edge of the table until my knuckles turn white.

The waitress drops off the bill and says, "Thanks, you two."

I reach for it but Billy snags it in a lightning fast move. "My idea. I pay."

I come down from my rage-fueled high and take a shaky breath. "Thanks. I owe you one. Actually, I owe you two after last night's beer spill."

"No way," he says.

"Way."

He shakes his head in disgust. "God damn it, woman. Why are you so stubborn?"

"I don't like to owe people."

He rises. "Consider the debt paid. Let's go."

No way was the debt paid, but rather than carrying on the verbal sparring match, I file it away under: *Things to deal with later.*

Two blocks away from Nick's, I tap Billy on the shoulder. "You can drop me here. I have to pick up a couple of things at the store."

He pulls into the super market parking lot and stops the bike. "I'll wait."

"Not necessary. I really need to be alone right now."

"You sure?"

The thrift shop across the street is my main objective, but I don't need Billy hanging around while I shop for second hand clothes.

I climb off the bike and hand him the helmet. "Yeah, I'm sure. Thanks for breakfast. Guess I'll see you around."

I start to turn away when I hear, "Wait."

Billy gets off the bike, removes his helmet and puts his hands on my shoulders. He leans close, his breath warm on my face. "Minnie Mouse. Why are you afraid to look in my eyes?"

I squirm under his touch and fix my gaze on his lips, which, by the way, are extremely sexy.

"Not afraid," I mumble and go for a diversion. I blurt out the first thing that comes to mind. "Shut up and kiss me."

His lips curve into a smile. "No problem."

He moves his hands to my waist and pulls me tight against his body. I gasp with pleasure at the sensation of his muscular body pressed against mine. He lifts a hand and slides it across my cheek, threading his fingers through my hair until his palm rests against the back of my head. He tilts my head back. I feel his lips brush against my ear and shiver with anticipation.

His cheek scrapes across mine, his mouth just inches from my lips. "Look at me, Minnie," he whispers. "Tell me what you see."

I lift my gaze and stare into his eyes, fully expecting to see my own face, possibly streaked with bits of sticky syrup and framed with flattened helmet hair. Nothing scary. Just something I'd rather not experience right now. But someone changed the channel.

My breath hitches in my chest. "Fire," I say. "I see a smoldering fire."

Billy's mouth grazes my cheek. "Smoldering, huh? Let's make it burn hotter."

His lips touch mine, tentative at first, until I wrap my arms around his neck and try to climb inside his skin. He deepens the kiss, his silky tongue slipping into my mouth. I'm transported to another place. My world consists of all things tactile. The sound of our breathing. The smell of his leather jacket. The warmth of his body against mine. The softness of his lips. The heat spiraling through my body like wildfire. More. I want more.

I'm brought back to earth by the sound of a honking horn and a raucous shout, "Hey, you two, get a room!"

Embarrassed, I push away from Billy and stare at the ground, trying to get my breathing under control. Billy grabs my hand and kisses the back of it like an errant knight wooing a fair maiden. This strikes me as hilarious and I snort laugh. Also embarrassing.

Billy releases my hand and tilts my chin back. "I'm not leaving until you look at me one more time. I promise you, it's safe."

I look and see my own flushed face, the ghost of a smile touching my lips.

He bumps my forehead with his. "See you later. Walk safe."

He climbs on the bike and tools away. I will my legs to stop trembling as I walk to the thrift store.

Chapter Nine

I'm standing in line at the checkout station, feeling righteous about the bounty in my shopping cart. Because I'm an unusual size (munchkin) I'm able to score some cool cast-off clothes. Two pair of designer jeans, plus a silk blouse and fitted blazer suitable for attending a funeral service, even though it hurts my heart to think about it. According to my calculations, the four garments will cost me less than fifty dollars.

The young woman in line ahead of me clutches a pair of stretchy pants and an oversized T-shirt. As she turns to place them on the conveyor belt, I see she is pregnant. Her belly pokes out in the space between her too-small shirt and jeans that gap at the waistband to accommodate the bulge. Her white-blond hair is pulled back in a ponytail fastened with a brown elastic band. A silver charm bracelet jingles as she fumbles for her money. She gives me a quick glance and a tentative smile.

I'm almost rendered speechless by the woman's natural beauty. Her particular shade of blond hair does not come in a bottle. Her eyes are deep aquamarine. In the fleeting look we share, I'm not able to peer deeply into her soul. But I don't need to see into her soul to tell she's anxious and afraid. Her shoulders are hunched, her breathing rapid. Her gaze darts to and fro as if she's looking for an escape route. I wonder what her story is.

What circumstances bring her to a thrift store to find cheap clothes for her expanding body? Maybe she's like me. Not the pregnant part; the broke part.

The cashier rings up woman's clothes. Six dollars and seventy-five cents. She clutches a five-dollar bill in her hand and offers it to the cashier who mutters, "Not enough."

The woman looks panicky. Her fingers grip the clothes as if the devil himself is trying to take them from her. In heavily accented English, she says, "It is all I have."

I step forward and thrust two one-dollar bills at the cashier.

The cashier grunts and digs in the cash drawer for change. The blond woman places a hand on my arm. Her brilliant eyes sparkle with tears. "You so very kind. Thank you."

My emotions are still shaky due to the news about Dani. I swallow a golf ball sized lump in my throat before I answer. "No problem."

"I am called Aida," the woman says.

"I'm Mel. When is your baby due?"

She flushes. Her gaze flicks away and back. "Soon," she says and moves from the check stand.

Impulsively, I call, "Aida, wait. I'll walk out with you."

She casts a nervous glance toward the parking lot. "You hurry. I must go."

I pay for my new duds (forty-eight dollars and twenty-two cents) and join her. Something about this woman who, after a closer look, is likely a teenager, gets to me. I know not why. I scribble my cell phone number on the back of the receipt and hand it to her. "If you need somebody to talk to, call me."

Her hand is shaking as it closes around the paper. "Thank you, girl called Mel."

I grin at her. "You're welcome, girl called Aida."

I follow her out of the store and watch her half-trot to a silver Toyota Land Cruiser and climb in the back seat. I peer through the tinted windows. Is there a baby car seat next to Aida? As the giant SUV pulls by, I see the driver is an angry-looking, sharp-nosed brunette, who is glancing over her shoulder and yelling at Aida. What the hell?

Aida is on my mind as I walk back to Nick's. She's obviously foreign. Obviously broke. The accent sounded Russian. Maybe a live-in nanny? If the woman driving the Land Cruiser is her boss, Aida has my utmost sympathy. If you drive a $70,000 SUV, surely you can afford to treat the help a little better.

Connie, Captain of the Motel Maids, is waiting for me when I return to Number Twelve, my home away from home. She pops out of the room next to mine. "One more for you," she says with an evil grin. "*Numero Dos.*"

"Yeah, okay," I mutter, wondering which of the nine shades of hell I'll be experiencing in *numero dos*.

I put my new used clothes in the closet, grab the cleaning cart and head for Room Two. The door is locked and Connie is the sole proprietor of the master key. I hear movement inside. The drapes part and a bristly face topped with wildly frizzy gray hair peers out at me. Now what?

"Check-out time is over," Connie screeches. "You tell him, get out!"

Thanks a lot, Connie. I tap on the door. "Maid

service, sir. Do you plan to stay another night?"

The door flies open and the space is filled by a large, hairy man wearing no clothes. He places his hands on flabby hips, and snarls, "You woke me up."

The shock has turned me to stone. I desperately want to close my eyes, turn away, do something, anything to block out the naked, disturbing image standing before me. All I can do is stare and stammer, "Um, sir, uh, I…"

"Jesus Christ, Harvey, put some clothes on and get the hell out of here." Nick yells, striding across the courtyard. "You want to stay another night, show me the money."

Harvey, looking sullen, steps behind the door—thank you, God—and mutters, "Bernice kicked me out again. I might be back tonight."

Nick gives me a friendly pat on the fanny. "Quite a sight, huh?"

I'm too stunned to respond.

"Harvey's one of my regulars," Nick says. "He and his wife have a contentious relationship so, more often than not, one of them shows up here for the night. Sometimes they stay here together for what they call 'honeymoon night.'"

I rub my eyes to clear the image. "Clothing optional?"

Nick laughs and turns to leave. "Such is the life of a motel maid. See you later. Be sure to take a dinner break. Don't want you passing out on me."

Turns out Harvey's room is a piece of cake. Once I haul out the empties (Pabst Blue Ribbon), all that remains is a moderately messy bathroom and hairy bed sheets. He leaves me a $10 tip and note of apology for the doorway flashing. Take that, Captain Connie.

When I finish up, I have time to do my own laundry and take a nap. When I wake, I'll call home and risk the Wrath of Sandra.

****

"Let me get this straight." Sandra's voice is ominously calm. "Not only is Dani *dead*, but she's been in the hospital since you arrived in 3 Peaks. In other words, everything you told me earlier was a lie."

Before I placed the call, I decided the best policy was to do the right thing. Spill my guts. Come clean. Walk the straight and narrow path of righteousness.

"I didn't want you to worry." *And nag me about coming home.*

A huge, put-upon sigh bounces off the cell towers and hisses into my ear. "I'll tell you what worries me," Sandra says, "The fact you don't trust your mother enough to tell the truth."

"Sorry." It's all I can think of to say.

A long silence follows while Sandra decides whether to stay mad or pump me for details. If I had to put money on it, I'd go for the second option. I stretch out on the bed and wait her out.

"Damn it, Mel, this sucks. I'm real sorry about Dani, but first, I need to know if you're okay. Where are you staying? Please tell me it's not a homeless shelter. Those places have bedbugs. Are you out of money? Shall I wire some to you?"

Option two.

I don't realize I'm holding my breath until it whooshes from my lungs in a gust of relief. I tell her about my job and living arrangements, possibly exaggerating a teensy bit. She's totally baffled I landed a job as a waitress.

"How can that be? You've never waited tables. Nobody called me for a reference. And, you're living in a motel? Is it safe?"

"Yep, got a dead bolt on the door. Besides, you know I can take care of myself."

Sandra says, "Maybe you should come home."

I'd been waiting for that comment and had my answer all prepped. No way I'm leaving 3 Peaks. But now is not the time to butt heads with my mother. "Maybe," I agree and count to ten. "Might stick around here for a while, though. See how it goes."

"I can be up there tomorrow if you need me."

I bite back a shriek of horror and convince her to stay put, ending with, "Trust me, I'm fine."

Our conversation winds down. I ask her to call Dani's dad and finish with, "I love you, bye." My finger is hovering over the *end* button when I hear, "Wait."

I lift the phone to my ear.

"Almost forgot," she says. "A letter came for you yesterday. From Dani. Want me to open it?"

The hair stands up on my arms and I'm slammed by waves of dizziness. I feel a strong sense of Dani's presence. Even though I feel ridiculous, I sit up and look around the room. My gaze is drawn to a shaft of sunlight streaming through the window and then I see it. Caught in the prism of light, Dani's soul shimmers like a butterfly beating its fragile wings against a windowpane, searching for escape. I gasp in surprise. Is Dani reaching out to me? A passing cloud blots out the sun and the image vanishes.

"Mel? Are you there?"

Though I'm desperate to know what's in the letter, I can't bear to hear it second hand. I find my voice and say, "Just forward it to me."

"I'll do better," Sandra says. "Cutie Pie Brett has a run up there tomorrow. I'll send it with him."

I thank her even though I know C.P. Brett will be in spy mode. His orders will be to check out the following: Mel's physical appearance. Does she look tired? Hungry? What about her living arrangements? Bedbugs? Is her workplace safe? Any new dings or bruises? Oral report due upon return to San Berdoo.

Can't win 'em all.

Chapter Ten

The next morning, the missing in action motel maid, Rosa, shows up, which gives me a much-needed break. My second night on the job is as challenging as the first, minus major beer spillage. At half past seven, Helen bumps me with a hip. "Darrell's back. He's asking for you."

"Darrell?"

"You know Darrell, the guy whose balls you wanted to kick through the top of his head."

"Oh, *him.*" I mutter a few choice words under my breath. Helen says, "Right on," and sashays away.

I turn in a food order and look for Darrell, determined to be pleasant. He's not with his buddies from the night before, but sitting in a booth across from another man whose back is to me. I approach cautiously, stopping well outside Darrell's reach.

He stares at me through hooded eyes and speaks to the guy across from him like I can't hear him. "Here she is. The chick I was telling you about. Cute but clumsy. Spilled about ten gallons of beer last night."

Forgetting my vow of pleasantness, I bristle and glare at his chin. I have no desire to look in his eyes because I already know Darrell's a damn bully. There's only one way to deal with a damn bully. Offense, not defense.

"What's your point? Do you want to order or not?"

Darrell winks at his friend. "Told ya she was sassy."

The guy turns his head to check me out. It's Eddie. His eyes widen with surprise. "You work here?"

"Yes." I take a deep breath to calm myself. "I needed a job."

Darrell is clearly confused. His gaze darts back and forth between Eddie and me. "You two know each other?"

"His wife is…" My throat closes and chokes off the words. I gulp back tears. "I mean she *was* my best friend."

"Then I guess you know Dani died," Clueless Darrell informs me.

I nod.

He reaches across the table and punches Eddie in the shoulder. "That's why I brought this guy here tonight. To cheer him up, ya know?"

I nod again. *What better way to mourn your wife's death than to drink yourself into a stupor?*

I take a step closer to Eddie. "I'd like to see Dani. Tell her goodbye. Maybe tomorrow morning?"

Eddie won't look at me. "The graveside service is the day after tomorrow. You can come if you want."

I persist. "Where is she? Which funeral home?"

"Oh, man, this is awkward," Darrell says, rolling his eyes.

"Why is it awkward?"

"You tell her, Eddie."

Eddie stares at the tabletop. "She was cremated this afternoon."

Shock waves radiate through my body like an electrical current. There are so many things I want to say. *Why so fast? What about her father? Couldn't you wait until after he gets here? What about me? I wanted—no—I needed to see her.*

I think about her beautiful soul dancing in the sunlight and, once again, wonder if she was reaching out to me.

I stiffen my spine and arrange my face into a neutral expression. I say none of the things I'm thinking. Instead, I pull the order pad from my pocket and clear my throat. "What can I get for you two?"

Billy comes in later, greeted with delighted cries of "Kid!"

He's with a woman. I experience an unaccustomed surge of jealousy and have to talk myself down. *You don't really know this man. He might have a dozen girlfriends. He might even have a couple of wives. So chill!*

Trailed by the woman, he follows me into the Corral. I act like I don't know he's behind me.

"Hey, Minnie, I want you to meet someone."

Can't very well pretend to be deaf as well as blind, so I turn to face him. I check out the woman. Tall and lean. Reddish brown hair. Her eyes are hazel, but swollen and red like she's been crying. *God, you're such a fool, Mel.*

I smile at her. "You must be Kendra. Ignore what your brother told you. My name is Mel, not Minnie."

She rolls her eyes. "Could be worse. He calls me Bugs."

Billy grins. "She likes carrots."

His gaze travels over my body, leaving a tingle in its wake. Somehow, it doesn't feel invasive like it does with some guys. He leans close. "Have you taken your dinner break?"

"I've been busy."

"I'll talk to Nick."

He spins on his heel, ready to ride to my rescue on his white charger. Before he takes off, I grab his arm and hiss, "I'll handle it. Go find a table. I'll take care of Nick."

Kendra shoots him an amused glance. "Guess she told you, big brother."

I join them fifteen minutes later. Billy is sipping a beer. An untouched Coke sets on the table in front of Kendra.

I hesitate before I dig into my mac and cheese. "You're not eating?"

Kendra says, "We already ate. We're here to talk about Dani."

I wave a fork in the direction of Darrell's table. "Eddie's here."

Kendra's eyes flash in anger. "Asshole had Dani cremated this afternoon."

"So he told me. Where's Destiny?"

"Good question," she says. "'With friends,' he tells me. When I ask *who*, he says, 'You don't know them.' He's a lying piece of crap."

Her voice breaks and the tears begin to flow. It's all I can do not to join in. Billy pats her shoulder and picks up the story line. "Kendra didn't believe him from the start. And now, with the cremation thing…why so fast?"

"Not to mention the brand new truck," I add.

"Exactly." Kendra says, blowing her nose on a napkin. "Dani said they were always strapped for money."

"Maybe they have good credit," Billy says.

Kendra shakes her head. "I doubt it. Dani was looking for a job to help out."

She turns her head and glares in Eddie's direction. "I'd like to go over there right now and rip him a new one."

"Me too," I say. "But then I'd lose my job."

"Probably a better way to handle it," Billy says. "Let me do some poking around. See how he paid for the truck."

"Will Dani's dad be at the service?" Kendra asks.

"I hope so," I say. "I asked my mom to call him."

"Maybe he'll want the baby."

I shrug. "Maybe, but he and Dani aren't close. After Dani's mother took off, he got re-married and had a bunch of kids with his second wife. I doubt he'll want to start over with a grandkid."

Billy adds, "Not his choice. Eddie's the father."

"Asshole." Kendra repeats, ripping the paper off her straw. She plunks it into the soda and slurps noisily.

I know how she feels. I want to join her and smash a wrecking ball into the person who more than likely knows the exact cause of Dani's death. But I'd defended her once before and got into big trouble. There had to be a better way.

Kendra pushes her drink away and reaches for my hand. "She loved you, you know. She talked about you all the time."

Now it's my turn to tear up. "I know. I loved her too. I'm not going anywhere until I figure out what happened."

Kendra glances over at Billy and then back at me. "I know someone who'll be happy to hear that."

Billy gives her a playful cuff on the side of her head. "Shut the hell up, little sister."

I don't mention the letter from Dani. Not sure why. Maybe because it feels like a betrayal to our friendship. Dani and I always trusted each other with our secrets. Maybe she and Kendra did too. But, this is different. Dani's gone. The letter will be her final words to me and I'm unwilling to share until I've read them.

Billy and Kendra leave when my dinner break is over. Billy's parting words are, "See you tomorrow."

My raging hormones scream, "Tomorrow? What about tonight, big boy?"

Fortunately, my hormones don't have vocal cords.

Chapter Eleven

Brett shows up around seven the next night while I'm at work. Instead of handing over the letter, he looks apologetic and says, "Your mom says I have to check out your living space before I give this to you."

I narrow my eyes at him. "You do realize you could lie about it, don't you? Or, are you wearing a wire? Trust me, my living arrangements are just fine."

Brett flushes. "Sorry, Mel. I'm not a very good liar and your mom, um, well she scares me. She can sniff out a lie in a New York minute. Like I told you before, I need this job."

Okay, now I know why Sandra sent Dani's letter via Cutie Pie Brett.

I hold up a finger. "Give me a sec."

I seek out Nick, explain the situation and ask for fifteen minutes.

"Mama Bear checking on her cub, huh?"

I pinch my lips together in disgust and nod.

Nick cuts his eyes at Brett who gives him a friendly salute. "Hurry back."

I unlock Number Twelve, step back and wave Brett through the door, which I leave open for decorum's sake. Then I realize my action is a bit silly. Hadn't I done everything but rip my panties off in order to seduce this guy just a few days ago? Talk about mixed messages. Hopefully Brett is too simple minded to put it all together. Turns out he isn't.

He gives the room a brief scan before checking out the bathroom.

"Satisfied?" I ask. "Since you now know I'm not in a crack house or brothel?"

"Not quite." He steps up close to me, puts his hands on my shoulders and gives them a little squeeze. "Guess what I brought?"

I frown at him. "Hopefully the letter my mother gave you."

"Yeah, I've got it."

He pauses and gives me a significant look.

I decide to play dumb. "Then I've got no clue."

He leans close and presses his lower body against mine. It soon becomes obvious he's glad to see me. He nuzzles my ear. "A rubber. I've been thinking about you a lot. Is your offer still on the table?"

I step away from him. "Uh, not really. I have to get back to work."

He clamps his hands around my waist and pulls me tight against his body. His lips graze my cheek. "Don't worry. I'll hurry."

Aggravated, I push against his chest. "As difficult as it is to turn down your offer of *speed,* I really do have to go. Remember the part about needing a job? You mentioned it earlier. I need this job."

But Brett, who appears to be in a lust-induced coma, has apparently lost his ability to process language. His hands roam up and down my body like he can somehow knead my flesh into willingness. Still locked in his grip, I'm aware he's walking me back toward the bed.

I'd just drawn a breath and was about to yell,

"Stop!" when I hear a deep voice drawl, "Excuse me, folks. The door was open. Didn't know you needed privacy."

Brett stiffens in surprise, releases me and pivots toward the door, now filled by Billy the Kid. He's wearing his scary face.

My cheeks burn with embarrassment as I struggle to explain. "Brett drives truck for my step dad. He dropped by with something my mom wanted him to deliver."

"Yeah," says the eloquent Brett.

"Oh, is that right?" Billy steps into the room and shuts the door. With two large men eyeing each other like mongrel male dogs, my room seems to shrink in size. I start to worry. Should I open the door? Try for a better explanation?

"Let me get this straight." Billy gives Brett an appraising look. His hands curl into fists. "Your mom sent this guy to do what? Grope you? Take you to bed?"

Now, he's making me mad. "Don't be an ass. Of course not. Dani wrote me a letter. It arrived after I left. Brett brought it to me. That's it."

"So what I just saw…?"

Brett finally finds his voice. "Total screw-up on my part, man. I thought I had a chance with her. Looks like I was wrong."

He pulls a small manila envelope from his coat pocket and thrusts it into my hands. "See ya, Mel. Good luck."

He makes a wide circle around Billy and bails through the door.

An uncomfortable silence follows. I stare at the

envelope in my hands like I've never seen such an amazing object in my entire life. I feel Billy's gaze on me. My emotions fluctuate between embarrassment, shame and anger. I know my previous encounter with Brett has set in motion his actions of tonight. He had every reason to believe I'd be willing. And then there's Billy. What right does he have to act like he owns me? I guess some women delight in the idea of two men wanting them. I'm not one of those women.

Finally Billy growls, "Aren't you going to open Dani's letter?"

As much as I'm dying to know what's in the letter, I stuff it in my apron pocket. "Later. I have to get back to work."

I try to duck around him, but he takes hold of my arm. "Want to talk about the other guy?"

The anger kicks in and I jerk free. "I told you, there is no other guy." I glance up at him. "What's it to you, anyway?"

Amusement dances in his eyes. "Tough little chick, aren't you, Minnie? Gonna try some of those special moves on me?"

"Don't think I haven't considered it. No time right now."

He reaches out and touches the tiny mole next to my mouth and then traces the outline of my cheek. I can't help it. I shiver.

His voice softens. "Maybe after work. Will you have time then?"

"You're in an awful big hurry to get hurt." My voice sounds rusty. Like it hasn't been used in a while.

He gives me a half grin. "I've got a few moves of my own."

I brush by him. "Yeah, I bet you do. Shut the door when you leave."

He follows me out of the room. "Later?"

"Possibly," I say.

Who the hell are you kidding, Mel?

****

At half past midnight, the place begins to clear out. A few hard-core drinkers remain, but the kitchen's closed so I'm able to take a quick break. I find a quiet corner and open the envelope from Dani. Several pictures tumble out along with a hand-written letter. I study the pictures first. Eddie's pick-up truck. A wide-angle shot of a sprawling palatial home. A commercial building with the words Medical Clinic printed on the door.

I unfold the letter, dated a few days before I arrived in 3 Peaks.

Mel,

I'm scared to death and not sure what to do. Eddie's up to something and it's not another woman. It started a couple months ago. After dinner, he'd take off and be gone for a couple of hours. At first, I thought he was out drinking, but then he told me he was helping his buddy re-build an engine. I soon figured out he was lying but didn't let on. I started following him. Check out the pictures I sent you. The big house. The medical clinic. That's where he was going. Totally weird. Shortly after, Eddie buys a brand new pick-up. When I asked where he got the money, he said, "Don't worry about it." So obviously, I figured Eddie was into something shady.

That's not the worst part. One Saturday afternoon I asked him to watch the baby while I went grocery shopping. When I got home, Eddie and Destiny were gone. I called his cell. He got mad and said, "Can't I take my daughter for a ride without you acting like a bitch?" The thing is, Mel, he's not a hands-on father. In fact, he's pretty much ignored Destiny since she was born. And suddenly, he wants to spend time with her? Doesn't make sense.

I went into deep denial and tried to convince myself Eddie was finally bonding with his daughter. Then something happened yesterday that freaked me out. Destiny's birth certificate is gone. When I asked Eddie if he'd seen it, he blew me off. "You're such a ditz, you probably lost it." I know I didn't. I'm real careful about stuff like that. Tomorrow, I'm going to the house in the picture, knock on the door and try to get some answers. I'm so scared, Mel. Eddie's up to something bad and I think it involves Destiny. So glad you're coming to 3 Peaks. Between the two of us, we'll figure it out. Don't mess with Danimal...right?

Love you lots. Big hugs,
Dani

Dani's words send a chill through my body and leave me with more questions than answers. Questions she'll never be able to answer. Had she gone to the big house in the picture? If so, what did she find? Or, had Eddie put a stop to it? Does Eddie have the baby's birth certificate? Why? The obvious answer is so horrible I can hardly bear to let it float across my mind. Would a father sell his own child even if he had to get rid of his wife to do it? I've never liked the look of Eddie's soul; but mostly, I thought he was a dumb shit, not truly evil. But souls can change. Dani's for example.

I gather up the pictures and letter and get back to

work. For the first time since I arrived in 3 Peaks, I know what I'm meant to do. Dani's gone. Nothing will bring her back. But, I *will* find the answers to her questions and if my suspicions are true, God help the person who has her baby.

Such is my state of mind when my shift is over. We catch a break because the place empties out before closing time. I'm deeply immersed in my thoughts of revenge as I trot through the courtyard toward Number Twelve. As I approach the door, a tall, lanky figure steps from the shadows of my doorway.

Billy.

As promised.

Chapter Twelve

My hand is shaking when I try to insert the key into the lock. Billy, close on my heels, notices and can't let it pass.

"Nervous?" His mouth is next to my ear. The warmth of his breath curls through my body like a slow-moving fire.

With a little snort of derision, I say, "Why would I be nervous? You said earlier you want to see my moves. Well, get ready. I've taken down guys twice your size."

This is a bald-faced lie. There are no guys twice Billy's size. Plus, I've never grappled in a motel room with a guy whose clothes I want to rip off. But, Billy doesn't need to know *any* of that.

He chuckles. I feel the vibration in his chest as he presses against my back. I push the door open. He follows me in and turns the deadbolt. I switch on the light and remove my apron. The bed looms large. Billy leans against the door, arms folded across his chest, amusement dancing in his eyes.

Because I hate long, awkward silences, I decide to proceed with our playacting. In a slight crouch, I begin advancing toward him slowly, arms relaxed and ready. Weight forward on the balls of my feet. Maintain eye contact. (I try not to get distracted by the red-hot embers I see smoldering in his soul). My coach's words echo through my mind. *Show no fear. Make your opponent lose focus and you will prevail.*

"So," I inch closer. "You were a football star in high school. Since you're a big guy, you probably played basketball. Right?"

"Nope." Billy pushes away from the door. "Wrestler." He winks at me. "You want up or down?"

I take a step back. "Huh?

"In wrestling, there's a coin toss. If you lose, you start the match on your knees. If you win, you get to be on top. Since I'm a gentleman, I'm giving you a choice. Up or down?"

Damn! Now I'm getting flustered. Who would have thought Billy, with a perfect build for basketball, would have wrestling experience.

I stand up straight, put my hands on my hips and glare. "Neither one. I'm not a wrestler. I grapple."

Billy frowns, playing his role. "So, am I allowed to defend myself or not?"

I hold up a hand. "Maybe we need a few ground rules, like—"

Before I can finish my sentence, Billy lunges at me. My training kicks in and I react instinctively, ducking under his outstretched arms. I slam into his right leg and wrap both arms around his knee. I get my feet under me for leverage and yank his knee sideways, a move that should result in Billy toppling over. It doesn't. He's as immovable as a giant redwood and grinning down at me like I'm a Chihuahua nipping at his ankles.

"Well, damn," I mutter.

"Are we done?" Billy says.

"We're just getting started."

"You're wrong." The heat in his eyes ignites a firestorm that touches every nerve ending in my body. My grip on his knee loosens.

His voice lowers to a husky rasp. "No way have we started. Let go of my knee and I'll prove it."

I still have my pride so I hold on tighter. "Do you submit?"

"Hell, yeah. All you had to do was ask, Minnie."

He leans over and bumps the top of his head against mine. "Now, let go of my leg. Please."

I release him, get my feet under me and bounce up to a standing position. In doing so, the top of my head smacks into his chin. His head snaps back and he yelps in pain.

"God damn," he mutters, rubbing his chin. "I thought we were done proving how tough we are."

Embarrassed, I stare at the floor. "Sorry. I didn't mean to do that."

Have I ruined the moment? Probably. And here I stand, weak with wanting him.

"No worries." He cups my face in his palms and tilts my head back until I meet his gaze. "Honor Melanie Sullivan also known as Minnie Mouse. I want to take you to bed."

I shiver with anticipation.

He smiles. "Promise you won't hurt me?"

I wrap both arms around his neck. "Not intentionally."

Then, I'm scooped up and deposited on the bed. Billy lands beside me and the world shrinks to our five shared senses. Trembling hands fumble with buttons and zippers. My field of vision is filled with the sight of Billy's bare muscular body poised over mine. The

77

sound of our breathing ebbs and flows like breakers crashing onto a beach. I moan with pleasure as his silky tongue slowly traces every inch of my body. I gasp and breathe in his scent like it's oxygen. He smells of motorcycle leathers overlaid with a touch of minty toothpaste, menthol shaving lather and gasoline. I could pick him out of a lineup with my eyes closed.

I feel a sense of loss when Billy gently pulls away. I see that he's trembling in an effort to control himself.

Lying beside me, he strokes my hair. "I don't want to hurt you. It's just that you're so small and I'm..." His voice fades away.

I brace myself on an elbow and take a look at the organ in question. Whoa. I'm beginning to see the problem. Not that I'm an expert on the subject of male genitalia. My prior carnal experiences all took place in darkened cars and ended fast. I never got a good look at the one-eyed monsters.

Now, here I am, all worked up and wondering if it will fit.

I guess my doubt shows in my face because Billy says, "Here's the deal, Minnie. You're in charge. Whatever you want, that's what I'll do."

Empowered by his words, I take a moment to think it over. I'm in charge, so I give him a shove and order, "Lie on your back."

Smiling broadly, he sprawls on his back, arms outstretched in surrender. "I'm all yours, baby."

I pop up, throw one leg over his midsection and straddle his body. I feel like a bull rider coming out of the chute. Ladies and gentlemen. Next up, we have Minnie Mouse aboard Billy the Kid for the ride of her life. Can she stay on or is the Kid too much for her?

"Now what?" Billy pants.

"Now this," I say, trailing kisses across his chest, up the side of his neck until I reach his mouth. His beautiful, glorious, sensuous mouth. I slide my tongue across his lower lip. He thrashes and moans as I part my legs and slide down his body until I feel the tip of his erection press against me.

I'm trying to figure out my next move when I see him extend his right arm. He's trying to reach his pants. Does he plan to get dressed and leave? Am I doing something wrong?

"Rubber," he gasps. "In my pants pocket."

"I'm on the pill."

"Better use it anyway." He grips me around the waist with one arm and rolls us sideways. Our bodies stay mashed together while he gropes through the pocket of his jeans. He leans out a little too far and we crash to the floor.

Billy goes, "Oof!" I'm still on top. How can that be? It defies the law of gravity. He must have executed a slick maneuver to keep from crushing me, which would have spoiled the moment for sure. I try to fight it, but a hysterical giggle bursts from me like an arrow released from a forty-pound bow.

Billy gives me a weak smile. "Wanna start over?"

I get my hilarity under control and nod. I watch Billy slip on the rubber. I can't help but notice his manly organ seems a bit smaller than its former awesomeness. We climb back on the bed and resume our former positions. I feel laughter bubbling up again and pinch myself. Hard. Billy looks deadly serious. I fear I've lost my way and he knows it.

"How can I help," he says.

I stare into his eyes and, once again, see the fire smoldering in his soul. "I'm not sure."

"It's okay," he says. "I just want to make you happy."

He lifts me off his body, places me on my back and proceeds to make me happy. Very happy. Ecstatically happy. And, everything fit just fine.

****

Bang, Bang, Bang.

Consuela's signature knock.

Before I'm fully conscious, I'm dragged from the bed, tossed onto the floor and covered with Billy's body.

"Down! Stay down!"

His head swivels back and forth across the room. His eyes are wild. After a few moments, the tension leaves his body. He takes a shaky breath and helps me back onto the bed. "Sorry. I was dreaming. Thought I was back in the barracks. In Afghanistan."

I open my arms, inviting him in. "You're right here in good old Number Twelve." I wrap my arms around him and snuggle into his warm chest. The thudding of his heart reverberates through my body.

Our tender moment is blown to smithereens by Connie's nerve-grating screech. "Rosa no here. You help me now!"

"Shit, shit, shit," I mutter. My lips are pressed against Billy's neck. "Nick should fire that Rosa bitch."

I roll out of bed and slip on Billy's T-shirt, long enough to cover the bare essentials. When I open the door a crack, Connie bumps it with her hip. She peers in, her bright eyes checking out the man in my bed and the rumpled sheets. Her eyebrows go up and down like an elevator on speed.

She cackles and wags a finger in my face. "Ha. I see Billy's bike parked here. You a naughty girl, Mel. Connie likes naughty girls. Billy the Keed is macho man. You get tired of Billy, you let me know. Connie will take him for a ride."

Looks like Connie and I have bonded.

"You'll be the first to know." I glance over at Billy who gives Connie a sheepish grin and a salute.

"Now," Connie claps her hands. "You leave thees big, hot man. Come help me. Hokay?"

I dress quickly and tell big, hot man I'll see him later. Before I leave the room, I hand him Dani's letter and pictures.

He studies the pictures first. "Can I take these with me?"

"I guess so. Why?"

"I think I know where these pictures were taken. I'll check it out."

I have a smile on my face as I trot out the door wondering what the day will bring. The night was damn good!

Chapter Thirteen

The next few days pass in a blur. My days are filled with work and I earn my pay. I spend my nights with Billy. One day, I overhear a couple of guys talking about me. What they say slaps me upside the head and makes me think. Apparently it's common knowledge I *belong* to Billy. One guys says, "That new waitress? Hands off. She's with The Kid. Touch her and he'll kick your ass."

I can't deny Billy's presence makes my work shift easier. And, I'm enjoying our nights together. A lot. But, the notion of *belonging* to somebody? The loaded word slips into my cerebral stew and floats around, surfacing now and then to gnaw away at my sense of self. Not when I'm in bed with Billy, though. Then, all rational thought is gone and I'm lost.

Billy returns Dani's things and tells me he's located the medical clinic. It belongs to Dr. Jarod Breen, a fertility specialist. In order to discover this, Billy made an appointment to leave a donation to the sperm bank. In the future, there may be a shitload of little Kids running around 3 Peaks. Not sure how I feel about that.

Dani's graveside service is at eleven a.m. on Tuesday. I dress in my finest thrift shop outfit and take the bus to the cemetery since Billy has yet another interview with the 3 Peaks P.D. A question nibbles at the back of my mind. Will Billy's sensitivity to loud noises impact his future as a detective? Does Billy have PTSD? I guess time will tell. We plan to meet up at the gravesite in the Pilot Butte Cemetery, located in the heart of 3 Peaks.

I step off the bus into a brisk wind that carries a hint of snow. It seems the weather gods are not smiling on Dani's final resting place. As I've been told since I arrived, "It's May in 3 Peaks, Oregon. Anything's possible."

The cemetery is lined with huge pine trees that shelter grassy acres of graves, some with elaborate above ground statuary, complete with heavenly beings carved in stone. I stop and read an inscription. *Elizabeth Marie Hanson. Born September 15, 1910. Died July 20, 1914. Our Sweet Betsy. God's Littlest Angel.* My emotions, held in check since the day of Dani's death, spring to life and begin chipping away at the brick wall I built around my heart.

In the distance, I see cars parked along the long drive that winds through the cemetery and a cluster of people gathering at a gravesite covered by a canopy. By the time I make my way there, all three rows of white folding chairs are occupied. I join the throng standing behind the last row of chairs. Eddie, tugging at the collar of his dress shirt, stands next to a solemn-faced man in a black suit. Mortician or minister? I spot Dani's father, Gil Johannson, front row center. Kendra is on his left, a baby on her lap and a fidgety little boy on the chair next to her.

Black suit guy fiddles with a portable sound machine and *Amazing Grace* blasts from the speakers, startling the gathered crowd. A woman yips in surprise.

Several people clap hands over their ears. When the volume is lowered, I hear a baby cry. My gaze follows the sound to a blond-haired baby who's in the lap of a woman clad in a full-length black leather coat. She murmurs something to the man seated next to her and hands him the kid. During the hand-off, I get a good look at the baby's face. It's Destiny.

The man rises, clutching the squalling baby awkwardly between outstretched hands. The woman settles herself back in the chair, fluffing her hair and smoothing the wrinkles from her coat. Apparently these are Eddie's so-called *friends,* the ones he's entrusted with his daughter's care. They don't look like they hang with Eddie's crowd. The man wears a pricey gray business suit, pale blue dress shirt, cuff links, silk tie and polished black loafers. I know this because he walks by me, holding Destiny away from his body like he's afraid she's going to puke on him. I hope she does.

Now, I'm torn. I want to stay for Dani's service, but I also want to know where the guy is taking Destiny. If I hurry, maybe I can do both. I peel away from the crowd and stroll toward the cars. The man reaches the driveway and turns left, trotting down the line of cars until he reaches a dark blue BMW hybrid with tinted windows.

I step to the other side of the parked cars, pause by one close to the Beemer and dig through my purse like I'm looking for my keys. The man raps on the side rear window of the sedan. The door opens and a pair of hands reaches for Destiny. The man closes the door and hurries back to the service.

Now what, Mel? Approach a total stranger and ask about the baby's living arrangement? I know what would follow: a 911 call and my description on the five o'clock news. I decide to play it cool and see what Dani's dad has to say. I start back toward the gravesite.

"Mel? Is that you?"

I turn toward the BMW and see a pregnant blond girl in stretch pants and oversized T-shirt standing next to the car. She's holding Destiny close to her body and smiling at me.

I freeze in my tracks and stare at her. My brain is having difficulty making sense out of what I'm seeing. "Aida? You're here? With Destiny?"

Aida walks toward me. Destiny's squalls have diminished to pitiful whimpers. "They tell me to call baby Addison. Not Destiny."

****

Remember the brick wall around my heart? It crumbles to the ground brick by brick. "What?" I screech. "Addison's a horrible name. Her name is Destiny. What right do they have to change her name? She's not even their kid. She belongs to Dani. I mean Dani was her mother and she named her Destiny. This is just *wrong*. This sucks!"

I'm furious. I'm sad. I want to squall louder than Destiny. I want to march over to the couple now in possession of my friend's baby and slap them into next week. I want to grab the kid and run. The sane part of my mind says, "Then what, Mel? Catch the bus back to Number Twelve with the baby tucked under your arm? Remember the incident at the hospital?"

Aida observes me calmly during my meltdown. Finally, she shrugs and says, "I'm just the nanny."

When I regain my senses, I realize Aida might have answers I need. I shiver and rub my arms. "It's cold out here. Can we get in the car?"

Aida casts a nervous glance at the funeral party. The crowd is still gathered around the gravesite. "We must be fast. I don't want no trouble with the Missus."

We scramble in the back seat of the car. I hold my arms out to Destiny and whisper, "Hi baby girl. Can I hold you?"

Destiny draws a shuddering breath and studies my face like she's trying to decide if I'm friend or foe. It's like looking into Dani's beautiful blue eyes and I tear up. Then, I get mad. The poor little kid just lost her mother. Her father basically turned his back on her and now she's in a strange house with strange people and a different name.

I must look nonthreatening because Destiny dives into my arms. She pats my wet cheeks with both hands and smiles, revealing two tiny white teeth on her bottom gum.

Aida approves. "Baby likes you. You must be good person. She good judge of character."

I know our time together is limited so I pepper Aida with questions. Name of the couple she works for? She was told to call them Mister and Missus. How long has she been in their home? Not long. Just since baby comes. Where did she work before? With her sister, Larissa, at another big house. Also pregnant.

I wish I had the photos Dani sent me. I want to show them to Aida, see if the house in the picture is where Destiny ended up. What about Aida's pregnancy? Does she have a boyfriend? No boyfriend, she insists, blushing. She claims she has never been with a man in *that way*. I'm dying to say, then how the hell did you get pregnant? But, she's uncomfortable. I know I won't get any more answers. So instead, I take a good long look into her soul.

Aida's getting increasingly nervous and I see the service is breaking up. I whisper a silent apology. *Sorry, Dani. But I bet you'd rather have me hold your baby than mourn your ashes.*

I thank Aida and tell her to call me if she has a day off. I drop a kiss on top of Destiny's head and step out of the car. Ms. Leather Coat is striding toward me, her hubby trailing behind. She doesn't look happy. Time to beat feet. But then I realize Aida will be facing the wrath of *The Missus* all on her lonesome, so I stand outside the car and wait.

The woman's eyes glitter with suppressed rage. "Were you inside my *car*? With my *baby*?"

I realize now is not the time to point out Destiny is not actually *her* baby. Besides, what I see in her soul scares the hell out of me. "Actually," I say. "Aida and I are old friends. I just popped in to tell her hi." *So please don't yell at her.*

Her eyes narrow in suspicion. "How do you know Aida?"

I scramble for a plausible answer. "Through her sister, Larissa." I put a hand on my hip and cop a little attitude. "Why? Is that a problem?"

The Missus thinks it over and gives me a phony smile. "Not really. I just don't want the baby around strangers. Germs, you know."

I meet her fake smile with one of my own. "I assure you I have very few germs. Now, I'll just tell Aida goodbye and be on my way."

I lean into the car and whisper, "We met through Larissa. Stick to the story."

She nods. I close the door and walk toward the crowd, hoping to catch Dani's father. As I approach the gravesite I think about the woman who claims to be Destiny's mother. Her soul is ice blue with a thick black border like a clunky picture frame. That particular combination indicates a total and complete lack of human warmth, as well as an obsession with self. In other words, Destiny's new mother is cold, calculating and a self-centered bitch.

I scan the crowd and see Dani's dad walking with Kendra who is lugging her baby and a diaper bag. Her free hand is latched onto the little boy who's struggling to break free.

Gil Johannson's face is drawn and tired but he manages a smile. He greets me with a hug. "Melanie. So glad you're here. Dani would be glad."

I snuffle into his chest for a moment, unwilling to admit I'd missed the service. When I pull away, I ask him, "What about Destiny?"

Kendra's gaze darts back and forth between Gil and me. It's obvious she's got something to say but doesn't want to break into our conversation.

Gil says, "She's with Eddie's friends. He told me to come over to the house before I catch my flight. He said Destiny would be there."

Kendra can't stand it any longer. "You know Destiny was here…right? With *those people*." Her last two words are dripping with venom.

Gil's face tightens. "Yeah, I saw her. She's the image of Dani." He swipes at his eyes. "I can hardly look at her. It's too painful."

Kendra and I exchange a glance. It's not what we want to hear from Destiny's grandfather.

Kendra's son, Aaron, takes advantage of her distraction and makes a break for freedom. He scampers onto an in-ground marble slab and launches into what looks like an Irish jig, laughing and waving his arms.

Kendra sighs. "I should make him stop."

"Don't worry about it," I say. "This place could use a little joy."

"You coming to Eddie's?" Gil asks me. I can tell he's itching to take off.

I shake my head. "Not invited."

"I've gotta run. It was nice seeing you again, Mel."

As Gil hurries toward his rental car, I tell Kendra about my encounter with Aida. "And," I say, "She doesn't even know their real names. She calls them Mister and Missus. How lame is that?"

"I know who they are," Kendra says. "Ethan and Nina Rockwell. He's a big shot lawyer in 3 Peaks and she's a doer of good works. Assholes, both of them."

"Do they have kids?"

"They do now," Kendra's voice is tinged with bitterness. "Looks like they bought one from Eddie."

I look into Kendra's teary eyes and see the purity of her soul. No wonder she was Dani's friend.

"What about law enforcement? Maybe Billy can get some answers."

"Maybe," Kendra says, but looks away.

Hmm, what's that about?

Chapter Fourteen

Billy tools up on his bike a few minutes later. Little Aaron's face lights up and he dashes into his uncle's arms. Billy puts him on his shoulders and walks over to us.

"How did it go?" Kendra says.

"Okay," Billy says. "Gotta do a few more things at the Vets' Center and then I'm good to go."

Kendra's brows shoot up. "What things?"

He waves a hand. "Just this and that."

"Like what?" she persists.

Billy ignores his sister and turns to me. "Sorry I didn't make it to the service. Need a lift home?"

Before I can open my mouth, Kendra says, "It's too cold on that damn bike. She's riding with me. In a car."

Billy, looking preoccupied, helps load the kids into Kendra's van. He gives me a hug and murmurs, "See ya tonight."

As we pull out of the cemetery, Kendra says, "You in a hurry to get back?"

"Not really. I've got a couple of hours before my shift starts."

She glances at the kids in the back seat. "If I drive around for a while, they'll fall asleep and we can talk."

Within five minutes, both kids conk out. Kendra says, "I hear you and Billy are getting pretty cozy."

Embarrassed, I can't look at her. "Yeah, I guess

you could say we're cozy."

Kendra snickers, turns onto a side street and parks. When I glance at her face, I see the laughter has stopped and the concern in her eyes.

"It's Billy," she says. "Ever since he got back from Afghanistan, he's different. He saw a lot of bad shit over there. Fire fights. Guys getting blown up by roadside bombs." She shakes her head. "Too much bad stuff. Have you noticed anything?"

I tell her about his reaction when Connie pounded on the door

"You heard what he said about the Vet Center...right?"

I nod.

"When I asked him about it, he gave me a non answer. I think Billy has PTSD. And, I think 3 Peaks P.D. wants to make sure he's okay before they hire him as a detective and hand him a gun."

I think about what she said and my first instinct is to defend him. But how can I? I didn't know him *before.* "You think they're making him go for counseling?"

Kendra stays silent for a few moments and then pounds a fist on the steering wheel. "Dammit, why won't he talk to me? I'm his sister and I love the big jerk."

"If it makes you feel any better, he hasn't said anything to me either."

Kendra heaves a huge sigh and suddenly, her mood changes again. She flashes a mischievous grin. "Maybe he'll open up after you guys, uh, get it on. A little pillow talk."

Flames lick at my cheeks. I mumble, "Maybe."

"Okay," Kendra says. "I've got something else to tell you. It's kind of about Billy but not exactly."

I give her a questioning look.

"Don't get mad, but Dani told me about you. That you can read souls."

I flinch in surprise and, despite Kendra's warning, feel angry and betrayed. "I can't believe Dani told you. It was our secret."

"Dani and I were close, like sisters. When she found out you were coming to 3 Peaks, she said maybe you could read Billy's soul and figure out what's wrong with him."

"I've read his soul. Guess what I see? Me. My own face. That's never happened before."

Kendra's forehead wrinkles in confusion. "That's weird. Anything else?"

"I saw fire and smoke a couple of times, but it happened when we were about to get, um, *cozy*. I figured it was reflecting our feelings."

Kendra thinks for a moment. "Maybe not. Maybe the smoke and fire has something to do with his deployment."

"I guess it's possible."

"So, you think you can talk to him about it?"

I can't meet her eyes. "Actually we don't do a whole lot of talking. But, I'll try."

Kendra tries, unsuccessfully, to hide a smile behind an uplifted hand. "Good enough," she says. "Okay, enough about Billy. What are we going to do about Destiny?"

"Go to the cops?"

"And say what? That the Rockwells call her Addison instead of Destiny? That they kidnapped her?

Eddie would jump in and call us liars."

"Is there anybody in the 3 Peaks P.D. Billy can talk to? Ask about the Rockwells?"

Kendra says, "Yeah, he's got a buddy there. Helped him get his job interview."

"Good," I say. "Plus, I'd like to know what's up with the Russian girls. Aida and Larissa. Both pregnant. Both say they never had a boyfriend."

"Oh, please. Do you believe that crap?"

I gnaw on my lower lip before I answer. Kendra knows I'm a soul reader. But I'm so conditioned to guard my secret, I can barely form the words. Still, I look around before I lean toward Kendra and whisper, "She's not lying. I looked into her soul. It's absolutely beautiful. Pure as the driven snow, so to speak. I'm sure she's not lying."

Kendra perks up. "How do you do it? It sounds kinda fun."

I shake my head. "Not fun. Too much information."

"What do you see?"

"Basically, I see colors, or color combinations. It started after my twin sister, Hope, was killed. I was six at the time. I had no idea what the colors meant. Over the years, I've figured it out."

Kendra takes my hand and gives it a squeeze. "Dani said you and your sister were really close. You say this soul reading thing didn't start until after she died?"

I swallow the lump in my throat. "Right."

"So maybe this is Hope's way of staying connected to you. Maybe she's guiding you. Protecting you from bad people."

The very same notion floats through my mind every now and again, but thinking about Hope is so painful, I suppress it. Even now, it makes me uncomfortable. "Maybe."

I turn away from Kendra and stare out the window. If Hope *is* guiding me, wouldn't I feel her presence? I've had a hole in my heart ever since her death. My mother sent me for counseling, but I refused to talk. Basically, I buried my grief until it morphed into anger and came out in inappropriate behavior. Maybe it's time to re-think the soul-reading thing and *ask* Hope to help me. Brand new concept.

Kendra interrupts my thoughts. "So, maybe you can talk to this Russian chick, Aida. See what you can find out."

"She's scared to death. I don't want to get her in trouble."

"I have a friend who's in a hot yoga class with Nina Rockwell. She says the *Missus* is at her fitness club every morning for hours. After yoga, she works out with a personal trainer."

"Do you know where the Rockwells live?"

"No, but we'll put Billy on it. He'll know."

The kids in the back seat begin to stir and fuss. Kendra glances over her shoulder. "Gotta get these guys home."

We exchange cell phone numbers and Kendra drops me off in front of Number Twelve. Before she pulls away, she opens the window and calls, "Remember, pillow talk. Catch him when he's weak."

I grin and wave.

****

I look for Billy all evening, but he doesn't show.

94

Back in my comfy little room, I shed my work clothes, brush my teeth and flop down on the bed. *So what if he's not here. You got along just fine without him before. Don't be a clingy wimp.*

I'd just drifted off to sleep when a rap on the door jolts me awake. "Minnie, it's me. Open up." His tone is urgent.

Clad in sleep shirt and panties, I fling the door open. "What?"

Billy's face is drawn and pale. He steps through the door and locks it behind him. "Aw, dammit Minnie," he says, raking a hand through his hair. "I am *so* fucked up."

He looms over me, clenching and unclenching his fists. His face is in shadow, all sharp edges and angles. A stab of fear knifes through me and I take an involuntary step back. He steps into the light, closes the distance between us and grabs my shoulders. I stiffen; place my hands flat against his chest and push. "I don't know what's up with you, Billy, but I won't let you hurt me."

He gazes down at me, breathing hard, struggling for control. I look into his eyes, hoping his soul will reveal what he's unable to express. The inferno in his soul is so intense, so violent, I can't bear to look.

His hands are shaking as he loosens his grip on my shoulders and cups my face in his palms. He tilts my head back. "Look at me, Minnie. I won't hurt you. I need you. Tell me to stop if I get too rough. I promise I will."

Reluctantly, I look into his soul, expecting to see shooting flames but the fire has burned down to glowing embers. I know his violence is barely under control and I should be scared. But the honesty in his voice and the heat in his eyes ignite an answering spark deep within me. It roars to life, burning bright and hot. Fear vanishes; replaced by a need I didn't know I had. My arms soften; slip around him and I press his hardness against my body, hungry for his touch.

He lifts me in his arms and strides to the bed, kicking a chair over in his haste. I land on my back with Billy beside me. His eyes are wild and hot with desire.

For a brief moment, sanity prevails and fleeting thoughts scurry through my mind. Is this the same guy I've been having sex with? The gentle, solicitous Billy who takes great care not to crush me under his muscular body? The Billy who makes sure I climax before he does? The Billy who always asks, "Are you okay?"

No, it isn't the same Billy, but his fierceness excites me. He grips the back of my neck with one hand and uses the other to unbutton his Levis. He kicks his jeans away and strips off my clothes.

Once again, he sweeps me up in his arms. Two steps and I'm pressed against the wall. He drops to his knees, his hands gripping my hips. His mouth is hot, wet and heavy against me. I take hold of his head, pulling him closer. Lost in sea of sensation, I no longer care which Billy I'm with. I throw my head back, gasping with pleasure. Now, his mouth is moving, touching every sensitive part of my body. I feel his teeth on my neck, nipping at the tender skin. I claw at his shoulders, urging him on with little yips of encouragement. He lifts me off my feet, pinning me against the wall with his body. My legs part. He slams into me and I scream.

"Sorry, sorry," he says, his lips moving against my

neck.

"It's okay," I murmur. I wrap my legs around him and we move together. Then, I lose all track of time. Adrift in a world of rough-around-the-edges pleasure, I hold on tight, my excitement building as wave after wave of ecstasy washes over me.

Later, when the thinking part of my brain kicks in, I realize we're on the floor. How did that happen? We climb onto the bed, both breathing hard. Both exhausted. Billy cradles me against his body. Again, he says, "Sorry, Minnie."

I breathe into his chest and assure him I'm okay. After a long silence, I say, "It's pretty obvious you were in a bad place when you knocked on my door. Want to tell me what's wrong?"

I feel his body tense. He says, "I have some stuff to take care of before I get my badge."

"Like what?"

He props himself up on one elbow and stares down at me. The wildness is gone from his eyes, but the flames are still burning in his soul.

"About my time in Afghanistan."

Looks like Kendra was right about the smoke and fire reflected in Billy's soul.

"You want to talk about it?"

"No."

"Okay. What is it you have to do?"

"3 Peaks P.D. wants me to get counseling at the Vet Center."

Neither of us has uttered the PTSD word, but its presence hangs over us like a ticking time bomb.

I pat his chest. "Counseling could be a good thing. You need to talk to somebody who understands."

When I utter the words, I realize I sound exactly like my mother.

He jerks away from me. "Jesus, Minnie, I don't *want* to talk about it. Okay?"

I think about what I went through when Hope died and totally understand where he's coming from. It's not my place to judge him. "Yeah, it's okay, Billy. Just do what you have to do."

He stares at the ceiling for a while, then gets dressed, sets Dani's letter and pictures on the table and leaves without another word. Looks like I flunked Pillow Talk 101.

Chapter Fifteen

My cell phone wakes me shortly before nine a.m.

"Mel?" It's a woman and her voice is tinged with panic. Because she pronounces my name, "Meal," I know it belongs to Aida.

I sit up and swing my legs over the edge of the bed. "Aida? Something wrong?"

What follows is a burst of rapid-fire broken English. I catch only a few words. One of them is Larissa. And, I can't ignore the urgency in her voice.

"What?" I say, rubbing the sleep from my eyes. "Has something happened to Larissa?"

"Larissa's gone," she says. "You come to house. Missus not here."

Even though I'm exhausted, I write down the directions to the Rockwell's house and promise Aida I'll get there somehow.

I'm pretty sure the bus doesn't go to Broken Top, the most exclusive neighborhood in 3 Peaks. Then, I remember the bike I saw at the thrift shop. I get dressed, grab my backpack and head out.

It's a boy's bike, on the smallish side, but fits me just fine. Adorned with shooting orange flames and knobby tires, the bike sports the name, Blazing Saddles. After some dickering with the clerk, I get a twenty-five percent frequent shopper discount and Blazing Saddles is mine for twenty-four dollars and ninety-nine cents.

I soon discover why Broken Top is an exclusive neighborhood. It's situated on view property, aka, a big friggin' hill. By the time I peddle up to the impressive house set well back from the street, my legs have turned to jelly. The lawn is manicured, the flowerbeds weed free and the long, curving driveway lined with massive trees and perfectly shaped round shrubs. It is the house in Dani's picture. I stash Blazing Saddles behind a bushy, flowering shrub, in case the gardener spots it, and assumes it belongs in the trash.

As I approach the house, the door flies open. Aida flaps her hands at me. "In, in," she says as I hobble up to the front porch. We step onto the gleaming marble floor of a foyer far bigger than my humble home. Silently, Aida grabs my arm and marches me into a kitchen with stainless steel appliances, granite countertops and floor to ceiling windows overlooking the Deschutes River. Beyond the river, I see a stretch of emerald green fairway dotted with an occasional golf cart. Apparently, this is how the rich and powerful live.

While I catch my breath, Aida tells me the baby is sleeping, pours me a glass of water and leads me to a stool parked next to an expansive, curved breakfast bar. She settles in next to me, her hands cradling the bulge in her belly. Her eyes are red-rimmed and swollen.

She waits until I drain the glass before she pulls a photo from her apron pocket. "This is me and my sister. For three days now, I call and call but no Larissa. I have bad feeling. Larissa's time is now. For baby, I mean."

I study the photo of the two girls. Both natural blonds. Both beautiful. Heads together, smiling into the camera. Both wearing identical silver charm bracelets. "And she always answered before?"

Aida nods. "Yes, always. We have system. I call, let it ring three times then hang up. She calls back. Maybe not right then, but soon."

"And you say her baby is due now?"

"Yes, little boy. Larissa very happy for little boy."

I chew on my lower lip, trying to figure out how to politely ask for an explanation of the obvious. "Aida," I begin. "Please don't take offense, but you say you and your sister were never with a man and yet, you're both pregnant. How can that be?"

A flush rises in Aida's cheeks. "Our parents very strict. No boyfriends. Big man comes to Kazakhstan from U.S. Gives money to parents. Says Larissa will have good job in your country. Parents take money, say okay. Few months later, same big man comes back for me."

Apparently Aida gathers from my shocked expression I don't approve, because she lifts a hand and insists, "No, no. Parents good people. Just poor."

I bite back the words, *Yeah, real good people who sell their daughters to strangers.*

"Larissa and I talk about this." She points at her belly. "Only one way it could happen."

Actually, I can think of a couple of ways, but I give her an encouraging nod. "How?"

"Both of us are taken to doctor when we arrive here. Big man tells us we very lucky to get free health care. Doctor give us exam. For one part—you know the part—where he look between our legs, he give us pill to relax. Says he don't want to hurt us. I go to sleep. Wake up a little later. Very next month, no bleeding."

I feel fury building inside my brain and hope my skull won't explode into a bajillion little angry bone bullets. I want to scream, *Shit, shit, shit!* Obviously the girls had been artificially inseminated. This is even more evil than I imagined. I pull Dani's pictures from my pocket and hand them to Aida. She studies them carefully and then points at the photo of the medical clinic. "Yes, that is where we see doctor."

"You said you've only been with the Rockwells for a little while. Where were you before you came here?"

Aida shrugs. "With Larissa at another big house. Another Mister and Missus. I help with cooking and clean the house."

"When they found out you and Larissa were pregnant, what did they say?"

Aida's eyes spark with anger. "They make us feel shame. Say they will do us favor and take care of us."

"Did you ask to go home? Back to Kazakhstan?"

Aida flinches. "No, no, can't go home. Would shame parents."

"Did they give you money? Pay you?"

She shakes her head. "No. They say they do us big favor. Take care of us and babies."

I pound my fist on the expensive granite countertop, causing the empty glass to dance along its surface. Aida grabs it before it falls to the floor.

"Dammit, Aida. This isn't *right*. We need to find you another job, one that pays you money for the work you do. The Rockwells can't make you stay here."

A single tear rolls down her cheek. "Yes, my friend, they can. I have no papers. They say they will call immigration if I try to leave. Or, even worse, give me to big man."

I mull over Aida's information. Is Eddie the big man she refers to? Probably not. Eddie's muscular but not that big, so maybe he's involved in a different capacity. Like selling his baby daughter to the Rockwells.

I slip off the stool and take Aida's hand. "I'll try to help you, Aida. I'm not sure how, but I'll talk to some people I know and we'll figure something out. Okay?"

But Aida's not listening to me. Her head is cocked to one side and her eyes roll in panic. "I hear garage door going up. Missus home. You must *hide*"

She grabs my hand with an amazingly strong grip and drags me across the kitchen to a closed door. She flings it open, revealing a large L-shaped pantry. The shelves are lined with enough canned and packaged goods to feed the entire city of 3 Peaks. She shoves me into the pantry, flaps her hands and, in a harsh whisper, orders, "*Go, go*, behind the brooms and mops."

She slams the door and I'm plunged into darkness. Brooms and mops? I can't see my hand in front of my face. I pull the cell phone from my pocket and search the home screen for the flashlight app. I switch it on and the interior of the pantry is bathed in brilliant light. Aida hisses, "Turn it *off.* She will see."

I aim the light at the back of the pantry and spot brooms, buckets and mops hanging from hooks on the wall. I slither to the back, turn left past the cleaning implements and tuck into a small corner, bumping up against a plastic bin laden with empty aluminum cans that clatter noisily. I hold my breath, praying I'm out of sight if the door opens. I switch off the flashlight and listen.

A door opens and closes followed by the sound of footsteps. "Aida?" A woman's voice.

"In the kitchen."

"Addison sleeping?"

"Yes, Missus."

Something heavy hits the floor. Her gym bag?

"When she wakes up, bring her to me. Dr. Reynolds says we need to bond."

She says the word *bond* with scorn in her voice, like a teenager facing burdensome homework for which she sees no purpose. A wave of pity for Destiny washes over me and my hands curl into fists. Is it possible to bond with an iceberg?

I hear the clink of glassware, footsteps approaching the pantry and the sound of a hand twisting the doorknob. "Is there more Perrier water in the pantry?"

I shrink back into my hidey-hole as the light flicks on, my heart banging like a kettledrum. I wait for Nina Rockwell to march into her pantry, on a mission for her expensive water and, instead, find me among the mops and brooms. I have no script for this scenario. Spring from my hiding place and yell, "Surprise?" Punch her in the face and run? Short of making myself invisible, I'm shit out of luck.

Aida's voice holds a tinge of panic and I sense she's pushed her way into the pantry. "I look for special water, Missus. You go sit down. Rest. You look very tired after work-out."

"I do?" Nina Rockwell says, a note of insecurity in her voice. "Maybe I *should* go lie down. When you find the Perrier, bring it to me."

"Yes, Missus."

At the sound of her receding footfalls, I resume breathing, gasping like I'd just run a marathon. A few seconds later, Aida pokes her head around the corner. Her face is pasty white, her eyes wide with fear. She holds a six-pack of Perrier water in one hand and grabs my arm with the other.

"We wait one minute to make sure she stays upstairs then you go. Okay?"

I nod vigorously, unable to form words. Though I want to burst from the pantry and run like the wind, I listen to my pounding heart for the allotted time period and then tiptoe to the front door followed by Aida.

I whisper, "Stay strong. I'm going to help you."

Aida sets the Perrier water on the floor and pulls me in for a hug. Both of us are shaking. Her belly is pressed against me and I feel the baby move.

"You good friend, Mel," she says and gives me a push. "Now, *go*."

She didn't have to tell me twice. I retrieve Blazing Saddles and pedal away from the Rockwell house like my hair's on fire and my ass is catching. As I coast down the hill away from the mansion I try to figure out what to do next. Who ya gonna call, Mel?

Have I made a promise I can't keep?

Chapter Sixteen

When I get back to Number Twelve, my legs are wobbly with fatigue. I flop down on the bed and mull over Aida's situation. My first instinct is to go to the cops. Surely the Rockwells and the others involved in bringing the girls to the U.S. are breaking all kinds of laws. How did they get the girls into the country? Commercial flight? Private plane? Is it possible Aida and Larissa are only the tip of an iceberg? Are there more foreign girls in Oregon, pregnant and in servitude?

The girls would have to present passports and work visas. Could the documents be forgeries? Rockwell's a lawyer and a smart guy. He probably has all his bases covered, his ducks in a row, paper-wise. He knows important people. Judges, etc.

When I go over the scenario in my mind, I realize Aida, the missing Larissa and possibly others have been neatly trapped. They're scared, pregnant and alone, afraid they'll be deported. There's no way they'll cooperate with the police. Proof. I need proof.

I look outside and see Nick and Myron unloading cases of food from the back of his pick-up. Nick usually knows what's up in 3 Peaks. Plus people under the influence of adult beverages tend to talk a lot. Maybe he's heard something. I scamper outside and catch him at the back door to the restaurant. Myron holds it open with his foot.

"Quick question, Nick," I say. It turns out to be anything but quick when I realize he needs at least some of the back-story. I don't mention names, but tell him there are at least two foreign girls working as housemaids/nannies for wealthy families in 3 Peaks. Both pregnant. Both claim they have no boyfriend.

Myron snorts. "Yeah, right. Two little Virgin Marys right here in beautiful 3 Peaks, Oregon."

"Have you heard anything?" I ask Nick.

He sets the box down and scratches his head. "Not a word. You friends with these girls?"

"Sort of," I say.

He grins and cuffs the side of my head. "Whatever it is, I hope it's not catching. Don't turn up pregnant. Ya hear?"

A flush warms my cheeks when I think about my recent encounters with Billy. I'm comforted by the following equation. Birth control pills + rubbers = no babies. Better safe than sorry.

"No worries, boss." I say, walking away.

My cell phone chirps. I dig it out of my pocket, press *on* and hear, "Do you ever get a day off?"

I recognize Kendra's voice even though she doesn't identify herself.

"Yeah, but I haven't been taking them because I need the money."

"We need to talk. I'll pick you up in a half hour."

She clicks off before I can ask "Why?"

I stagger into the shower and stand under a stream of hot water until I feel the strength return to my legs. When I wipe the steam from the mirror, I see the mark on my neck where Billy nipped me last night. That whole scene now seems surreal; I'm unable to process it. I decide to file it away under, *Things I'll Think About Later.* Yes, denial is my friend.

Kendra pulls up next to my front door and taps the horn. I lock up and jump into the mini-van. The back seat is empty.

"Where are the kiddos?"

"My husband's working from home today. Craig's a CPA. He manages accounts for a bunch of different businesses. Tax season's over so he's got a little more free time."

"Where are we going?"

"I'm taking you to lunch. Someplace other than Nick's."

"Is this about Billy?"

"Among other things."

Despite my persistent questions, Kendra clams up, so I fill her in on my visit with Aida. We get to the restaurant, a nice one with white tablecloths, cloth napkins, heavy, ornate silverware and a live pine tree in the middle of the dining room. Once we're seated, she checks her watch, murmurs, "It's five o'clock somewhere," and orders two strawberry margaritas in gigantic fishbowl-like goblets.

After a few slurps, the alcohol hits my empty stomach and shoots through my body like a bolt of lightning. I push the drink away and try to focus my eyes. "Why are we here?"

Kendra holds up a finger and takes one more sip. "I've got an idea, but after what you just told me, I'm re-evaluating the plan."

"Which is?"

"How to get solid information about the Rockwells

and their apparent takeover of baby Destiny."

"And your plan?"

Kendra uses her napkin to dab at the strawberry foam mustache on her upper lip. "Craig does the books for a catering service, one the Rockwells use when they entertain, which is frequently. The caterers often hire experienced waitresses looking to make extra money, and since you're an experienced waitress, well, I thought maybe you could work one of Rockwell's parties. You know, snoop around a little. See what you can find out."

"But Nina Rockwell knows who I am. We met at Dani's service. She might think it's a little weird when I show up at her house." *Again.*

Kendra nods. "I have a blond wig and glasses you can wear. Trust me, rich people don't look at the help. To them, you're just part of the landscape, the faceless hordes whose sole purpose is to make their lives easier."

The idea of snooping around Rockwell's house tickles my fancy. Tickles it a lot.

I take another slurp of the margarita. "Sounds interesting. But won't I have duties? Waitressing duties?"

"Once people get liquored up, there will be some slack time. You're a smart girl. You'll figure it out."

I remember my time in Nina Rockwell's pantry and suppress a shiver. Something about the vibe in that house gives me the creeps. Then, I remember the mission. Destiny. "I'll give it a try, but don't expect miracles."

Kendra offers me a fist to bump. "Right on."

After I suck down a little more tequila (knowing

I'll regret it later), I recall her previous statement. "You said you were re-evaluating *that* plan, so you must have another option."

Kendra grins. "Craig also does the books for the people who clean the medical clinic. And since you have experience cleaning motel rooms…"

"So I have a choice. I can either be a waitress or cleaning lady?"

"Or both."

"Your husband's okay with this?"

Kendra winks. "He likes to keep me happy."

"So if there's an incident, it won't blow back on him?"

"Probably not. Those companies are always looking for good help. They don't need to know I told you about it."

Suddenly Kendra frowns and leans over the table, pointing at the bruise on my neck. Instinctively, my hand flies up to cover the mark.

"Did Billy do that?"

A flush warms my cheeks. I can't meet her gaze. "He was, um, a little upset last night." I glance up at her and try to smile. "Afterward, I tried to get him to tell me what was bothering him, but he took off. Guess I'm not very good at pillow talk."

Kendra's eyes sparked with anger. "Not your fault, girlfriend. He bottles up all those bad feelings and, *boom,* they erupt in a huge friggin' mess. Inappropriately. I've seen it happen. That's why he needs to go to counseling, even though he's fighting it."

She reaches across the table and takes my hand. "Believe me, I never dreamed he'd hurt you. I'll talk to him."

"*No*." I snatch my hand away and duck my head, embarrassed. "We got a little carried away. I probably left some marks on him too."

Kendra stays quiet for a long moment. I feel her studying my face. "You sure?" she says. "I can usually get him to listen."

"I can handle it."

When Kendra drops me off at Number Twelve, the man in question is leaning against my front door, looking relaxed. I thank Kendra for lunch and open the door of the mini-van. Kendra points at Billy and calls, "You be good to this girl or I'll kill ya. You hear?"

Billy quirks a half grin. "I hear ya, sis. No worries."

As she pulls slowly away, I see her looking in the rearview mirror.

Billy follows me through the door. "Let me guess. Strawberry margaritas and lunch."

I nod and check out his expression. His eyes are red-rimmed but calm. The tension is gone from his body.

He touches the bruise on my neck with his forefinger and follows up with a brush of his lips. I sense he's about to apologize again. "It's okay, Billy. I'm fine."

He wraps me up in his arms and presses his cheek against the top of my head. "Damn, Minnie. Sometimes shit, uh, I mean stuff gets to me. Didn't mean to take it out on you."

Since I never seem to say the right thing, I remain silent. This is Billy's journey and all I can do is hope he'll be able to rid himself of the anger and pain residing in his soul. I know a little about that journey since I'm travelling the same road.

He releases me and sits on the end of the bed, still rumpled from last night's workout. "Got some good news today, though."

I pick up the chair he kicked over last night and sit. "What?"

He runs a hand through his brush cut and stares at the floor. "Guess you already know I've been diagnosed with PTSD." He glances up at me. "Not that I agree."

Looks like I'm not the only one with denial issues.

"Okay."

"I thought I had to go away to a treatment center, but they told me I can do outpatient here. So, I can stay in 3 Peaks and take care of it."

"Sounds good, Billy."

He stands. "That's why I'm here right now. To tell you. I don't know a whole lot about what lies ahead, but I might not be around as much. You okay with that?"

A stab of alarm steals the breath from my body. *Why does this feel like goodbye?* I manage to stammer, "Um, sure. Do whatever you have to do. I'll be fine."

He folds his arms across his chest and gazes down at me. "I know you and Kendra aren't going to rest until you know more about Dani's death. You need to be careful. There are some real bad dudes in 3 Peaks you don't want to mess with. I'll help when I can."

"Kendra says you have a buddy in the 3 Peaks Police Department."

He nods.

I tell him about Aida and Larissa's situation.

His eyes widen in surprise.

"Do you know this person well enough to see if anybody's filed a report about these girls?"

"I'll check it out. Anything else?"

"Yeah, what about Dani? Did anybody question Eddie? He claims he wasn't there when she fell. That he found her when he got home. Seems kind of convenient."

Billy steps up close, cups my face in his hands and drops a kiss on my forehead. It feels like a brotherly sort of kiss. Is this what the future holds for our relationship? Not the time to ask, of course.

He says, "I'll see what I can find out."

After another brief hug, he's out the door. I sink down on the bed and wonder if last night's blaze is now a pile of dead ashes. Or, is it still smoldering and waiting for the right time to burst to life. Too many questions. Not enough answers.

My cell phone chirps. I glance at the screen. Sandra. I'm not in the mood for a mother-daughter chat, but why put off the inevitable?

When I answer, I hear truck sounds in the background. Uh oh.

"What time do you go to work tomorrow?" Sandra says.

"Same time as always. Half past three. Why?"

"I'm in a truck on my way to 3 Peaks. Abel is driving the Godmobile. I'll meet up with him there. He plans to preach at a truck stop tomorrow morning at eleven. We'll pick you up at ten."

Knowing she won't take *no* for an answer, I murmur, "Okay."

So, unless the world stops spinning tonight, I know exactly where I will be at eleven o'clock tomorrow morning. In the Godmobile. With my mother. Terrific.

Chapter Seventeen

My stepfather, Abel, is a successful businessman. He owns a fleet of trucks that cruise around the western half of the United States delivering goods. His books are in order. He provides a nice living for his family and donates money to his favorite charities. But running a trucking firm and making money is not his calling. He would much rather spread the gospel. So, once a year, he embarks on a crusade.

What my mother calls the Godmobile is actually an eighteen-wheeler retrofitted with an altar and permanently affixed benches for the congregation, mostly truck drivers. Abel pulls into a truck stop, usually on a Saturday night, and begins a campaign of what some would call harassment. He prefers to call it "recruiting for Jesus." I'm not sure why, but something about his technique works and, come Sunday morning, the Godmobile is packed with hung-over truck drivers, more than willing to dig into their pockets to support Abel's ministry.

But, this is where Abel deviates from the norm. He refuses to pass the collection plate. He wants nothing more than the privilege of preaching to the stalwart men and women who deliver the goods and services we take for granted. When I picture Jesus, he's dressed in jeans and a work shirt and looks a lot like Abel.

The next morning, I'm showered, dressed and

ready to roll when I hear a semi rumbling through the motel parking lot. It's exactly ten o'clock. Consequently, I'm sure one of the passengers in the semi is my mother. My instinct is to leave my room, lock the door and hop into the truck, but I know it would be a waste of energy. Sandra will want to inspect my living quarters and, more importantly, inspect *me.* Because I know her agenda, I make sure Number Twelve is scrupulously clean and sweet smelling, with no obvious signs of the sexual activity recently visited upon the premises. I'm fresh from the shower and the shirt I'm wearing covers the mark on my neck. Anything else? Oh yeah, nutrition. Orange juice and microwave popcorn sound healthy.

I brace myself and open the door. Sandra is on the other side, one hand raised, ready to knock.

"Baby," Her eyes fill with tears. "I miss you so much."

In spite of my intent to appear mature, independent and not in need of mothering, I dive into her arms. I bite my lower lip to hold back answering tears. "I miss you too."

She grips my shoulders, pushes me slightly away and gives me a thorough visual examination. "Maybe I should move to 3 Peaks."

I suppress the urge to scream, "No."

Instead, I frame my words carefully. "Actually, I think it's time for me to take care of myself. So far, I'm doing a pretty good job."

She peers around me. "This is where you live?"

"For now," I say. "Maybe I'll get an apartment later. After I save up some money."

"About that," she begins. "Abel and I would be

glad to—"

"No," I interrupt. "I need to do this on my own."

In the process of checking out Number Twelve, Sandra spots Blazing Saddles parked next to the wall behind the door. A horrified look blooms on her face. "Is this how you're getting around? On a kid's bike? Do you have a helmet?"

I confess I do not.

After my mother finishes her inspection, we climb in the truck where I'm relieved to see the driver isn't Brett. Yes, that Brett, who's wasted no time narcing me out about my relationship with Billy. She pumps me for information on our way to the truck stop.

"When will I meet this guy?"

"Not sure. He's pretty busy prepping for his new job." *Also known as, getting treatment for PTSD.*

We pull into the truck stop under bright Oregon sunshine. A soft breeze carries the scent of pine. I see the Godmobile. It's open for business. The back hatch is up. A wide rubberized ramp spans the space between the ground and the cargo area. A bunch of drivers clutching super-sized coffees are milling around, shooting the breeze.

Abel spots us and comes running. First a hug for Sandra. Then me. He brushes the hair back from my face and whispers, *"Te amo, hija."*

I smile and kiss the bristly cheek of the only father I've ever known. "I love you too, Abel. Looks like you've got a good crowd."

He places a hand over his heart and then points to the sky. "Recruiting for Jesus."

The service starts precisely at eleven to an overflow crowd. After an opening prayer followed by a hymn blasting from the state of the art sound system, Abel launches into his message of God's grace, love and forgiveness. From my vantage point in the back, I see a number of people pull kerchiefs from their pockets and swipe at their eyes. One guy blows his nose so loudly; the honking sound reverberates through the cargo area like a blast from Gabriel's horn. Nobody laughs.

I feel the cell phone in my pocket vibrate and walk down the ramp to answer.

"Mel? It's Billy."

It's only three words but, at the sound of his voice, heat spirals through my body and lingers in all points south. *Damn.*

I strive to keep my voice neutral. "Hi, what's up?"

"I talked to my friend at 3 Peaks P.D. Asked if there had been any reports filed about foreign girls coming here and working as nannies and maids. If any of them had come to the cops looking for help."

"I seriously doubt if any of the girls would go to the police. They're scared to death. But there's a chance somebody else might have noticed these girls and reported it."

"My friend said the guy in charge of human trafficking is a waste of air. He sits on his fat ass and looks online for prostitutes to bust. Human trafficking. That's what they call prostitution now. But, my contact will check with him and get back to me."

As I listen to his voice, I try to figure out his mood. Tense? Calm? Angry? Ready to explode? It's impossible to tell. Finally, I remember it's my turn to talk. "Thanks, Billy."

After a long silence, he says, "I couldn't sleep last

night so I checked out the medical clinic."

His frame of mind is what concerns me most, so I zero in on the first part of his statement. "Why couldn't you sleep?"

I hear an irritable sigh. "Guess I have a lot on my mind right now. But that's hardly the point."

Oh really? I decide not to push it, so I zero in on the second part. "Looking to get your sperm back?"

"Nah, they can have my little swimmers. I parked across the street and watched the place for a while. Guess what I saw?"

My hand tightens on the phone. "What?"

"A couple came out, carrying a baby. They loaded it into the back seat of their car and took off. California plates on the car."

I search my mind for a logical explanation. "Maybe it's an urgent care clinic and their kid was sick."

Billy says, "No, it's strictly a fertility clinic. They keep business hours, nine to five."

"What the hell? Did you see anything else?"

"Yeah, I followed them. They're staying at the Fairfield Inn. Room 223."

"Where are you now?" I ask.

"In the Fairfield coffee shop. They just came in with the baby. Looks like they're ordering breakfast."

"I'm sensing there's more."

"Might be a good time to check out their room. I'll call you later."

He clicks off before I can ask him. H*ow?* And, *Are you nuts?*

I wander back into the truck although my mind is somewhere else. Since it's a church service, it seems appropriate to offer up a prayer for Billy's safety. What if he gets caught? Arrested? His future employment plans would be down the drain, all because I asked him for help. Guilt takes me away from the present, so I'm startled when a group rises and gives Abel a standing ovation. Some people pull money out of their pockets. Apparently they don't know about Abel's mission.

I trot down the ramp, still thinking about Billy when my phone buzzes again. I tuck in around the corner from the Godmobile to answer.

"Billy? You okay?"

"Yeah, I'm good. Are you home?"

I explain about my mother, Abel, the Godmobile and the truck stop. Billy chuckles. "This I gotta see. Be there in a few."

Abel and Sandra are still pressing the flesh, so I trot to the espresso stand adjacent to the truck stop and snag a grande Americano with a shot of chocolate. After a few sips, I feel the caffeine race through my system like rocket fuel. When I get back to the Godmobile, the crowd has thinned out. Sandra and I help Abel collect the hymnals and pick up trash.

A few minutes later, Billy tools up on his bike. I tap my mother on the shoulder and, in the Biblical spirit say, "Ask and you shall receive. Come and meet Billy."

Her eyes sparkle and she practically runs down the ramp. I hurry after her. Only God knows what Sandra might say to my sexy yet sensitive, PTSD-afflicted boyfriend. And, who knows which Billy will show up today? Good old boy, Billy or stressed out semi-violent Billy?

I needn't have worried. Billy steps up to the plate and hits a home run. He grins at me and then gives Sandra a big hug. "I'd know you anywhere. You and

Mel look just alike. Are you sure you're not sisters?"

Sandra blushes and pats his cheek. "Well, bless your heart! Aren't you a sweetie pie?"

Billy and Abel shake hands. The meeting-of-the-boyfriend-and-family is totally awesome, but I'm dying to hear what Billy found at the Fairfield Inn. I wish I could hop on the back of his bike, zip away to a private place and make him spill the beans. But, as Sandra is fond of saying, "If wishes were horses, beggars would ride."

The pleasantries are winding down when I hear the unmistakable rumbling sound of Harley Davidsons motorcycles. A bunch of them. The sound grows steadily louder.

Sandra stiffens and puts one hand over her eyes to block the sun. She whirls around and barks at Abel. "Is that who I think it is?"

Abel gives her a sheepish grin. "Motorcycle gangs need God, too. They were trying to get here in time for the service. They must have got a late start."

Sandra rakes Abel with a squinty-eyed glare and speaks through clenched teeth. "You should have told me he was coming."

She starts to march away. But then, she looks at me and changes her mind.

Billy throws an arm around my shoulder, pulls me close and whispers, "What's going on?"

I smooch his cheek. "Brace yourself. You're about to meet Uncle Paco."

Chapter Eighteen

Genetics are weird. If you stood Abel and Paco side by side, you'd never guess they are full-blood brothers. Abel is slight of build, maybe five feet eight inches on his tippy toes, well groomed and law abiding. Paco stands six feet four and weighs close to three hundred pounds. His shoulders are wide. His body is heavily muscled and slabbed with a thin layer of fat due to his fondness for Mexican beer. His hair is pulled back in a ponytail and he sports a droopy Fu Manchu mustache. He rides with Los Habaneros, whose insignia is a chili pepper in the shape of a knife dripping with blood. The same image is tattooed across his chest. He always has plenty of money. Early in life, I learned not to ask how he acquired it. It's a *don't ask, don't tell* situation.

Fifteen Harleys, driving in a single file, pull into the truck stop. Paco is in the lead. His current old lady—I think her name is Roxy—rides behind him. They remove their helmets and park the bikes in a long, gleaming line. Everyone but Paco heads for the restaurant in the truck stop.

Abel calls, "Hey, little brother. About time you got here."

Sandra snorts her disapproval as the two men embrace. Wrapped in Paco's massive arms, Abel very nearly disappears. Paco spots me, flashes a smile and bellows, "Baby Girl. Come give your Unc a hug."

I know what's coming, so I'm prepared. After a quick squeeze, he tucks me under one arm and musses my hair. From my position dangling over Uncle Paco's arm, I catch the puzzled expression on Billy's face and realize how ridiculous our greeting ritual must look. "You can put me down now, Uncle Paco. Come meet my boyfriend."

He sets me gently on my feet and scowls down at me. "Boyfriend? You're too young for a boyfriend."

"I'm twenty-two."

"No way. How did that happen?"

I can't hold back a smile. It's the same every time we connect. I'm still a baby to him and he's still my shady though protective uncle. His soul is unique. I've never seen another like it. It appears in shades of green, a color I've come to realize reflects harmony and balance. Somehow, this seems at odds with what is surely his life of crime. But, who am I to judge?

I take hold of his sleeve and pull him over to Billy, who extends a hand. "Nice to meet you, Paco. I'm Billy McCarty."

I hold my breath while Paco checks him out and then tips his head toward Billy's Harley. "That your bike?"

"Yeah."

"Nice."

The two then engage in a conversation totally foreign to me, using terms like giggle gas, baffles, drag pipes and blips.

Sandra sighs and drags me away. "This could go on for hours. Let's go have lunch."

Another hour goes by before I'm able to get Billy

alone. Before we cruise out of the parking lot, my extended family informs me they will catch me later at Nick's, so I'd better be on my toes.

Back in Number Twelve, Billy fills me in on his sneak peek into room 223. "The maid was across the hall. Spoke very little English. I told her my key card wasn't working. Could she please open my door?"

"And she did?"

Billy shakes his head in disbelief. "Yeah, she did."

My cynical mind collates this quickly. Cute hunky guy needs key to his room. Young, vulnerable motel maid can't wait to oblige.

Billy goes on. "The place was a disaster. Baby stuff everywhere. I knew I'd better get in and out fast, so I looked through their suitcases. One suitcase had more baby things, clothes and blankets. Nothing in the other two suitcases but clothes. Then, I looked under the bed and found the briefcase."

"And?"

"I found a file folder with a bunch of papers on how to care for a newborn, even when the umbilical cord is supposed to fall off. Maybe everybody with a new baby gets one."

"Were the instructions printed on plain paper? Was there a logo in the header?"

"Plain paper."

In my former life as a nurse's aide in a hospital, I'd wheeled about a bajillion new mothers and babies outside to where the proud daddies were waiting with their cars. All of the mothers clutched a handful of papers describing how to care for their new babies. All the instructions included names and phone numbers of people to call if more information was needed. And, all of the instructions were printed on paper with the hospital's name and logo.

"No call back numbers?"

"No."

"That's weird. What else did you find?"

"That was pretty much it. At the bottom of one page, somebody scribbled BC, tomorrow's date, 9:30 a.m. and an address."

He pulls a scrap of paper from his pocket. "423 Bond Street."

"I wonder if they bought themselves a baby."

Billy says, "Can't prove it by what I found. Still, it seems pretty strange they'd pick up the kid in the middle of the night."

I remember Aida's panic when she couldn't locate her sister and a chill snakes down my spine. Could this be Larissa's baby? If so, it will likely be in California by the end of the day tomorrow. "What did the baby look like?"

He shrugs. "Like any other baby. Red face. Waving its fists in the air. Making that wah-wah sound new babies make."

"Pink blanket or blue?"

"Yellow."

"What color hair?"

"Dunno, it had a hat on. A blue one."

"Then it's probably a boy," I say. "Aida's sister was about to give birth to a boy. It could be her baby. But, if it is, where's Larissa?"

"Good question," Billy says.

"No birth certificate in the briefcase?" I ask.

"No."

I think for a moment and then fetch the phone book

from the bedside table. On a hunch, I look up the business address for Ethan Rockwell's law firm. 423 Bond Street. I point it out to Billy. "Maybe that's why they're going to Rockwell's office tomorrow. To get the birth certificate. BC. Birth certificate. I'd like to be a fly on the wall for that meeting."

Billy grimaces and his eyes spark with anger. "Just when things get interesting, guess where I'll be tomorrow? In *counseling.*" He uses his fingers to make air quotes around the word that angers him.

I'm beginning to understand Billy's mood swings. Lurking beneath his rage, I suspect there's a big, ugly mess of fear crashing into his psyche like a wrecking ball. Fear of what he might find if he lets his guard down.

Previous attempts at sweetness and understanding have been a miserable failure. I decide to switch gears. I fold my arms across my chest and stare up at him. "Hasn't this pity party gone on long enough? If you want that job as a detective, you better suck it up and deal with it. I can think of worse things than *counseling.*"

Billy blinks in surprise. Uncertainty replaces the anger in his eyes. "Well, I…"

"Look Billy, Kendra told me about your tours of duty in the Middle East. She told me about the medals you earned. You're one of the bravest people I've ever met. But you need help with your anger issues. Can't you see that?"

He mimics my pose. Arms folded across his chest. Stares down at me. "Maybe we're both wounded warriors. You need to take a look at yourself. I know about your twin sister dying, that you couldn't speak for a while. I know about the soul-reading thing too, even though you don't trust me enough to tell me."

My mouth drops open in surprise. Not a good look for me. Damn Kendra. Part of me has to admire how neatly Billy had deflected the conversational ball coming at him and batted it back, directly at my head.

Even though I'm seriously pissed about the switcheroo, I try to hold it together. "Okay, fair enough. I guess we both have issues to work on."

His lips twitch. I can tell he's trying not to smile. "Oh, Minnie, if you could see your face."

He opens his arms. I hesitate for a moment before I slip between them. My head is pressed against his chest and I hear the rumble of his laughter. My anger disappears as quickly as it arrived. I hug him tight and decide it's okay if I laugh too. Laughing is better than crying. Right?

His lips brush my ear. "So, what do we do about the baby?"

The touch of his lips distracts me for a moment. Then, I step away from him. If I don't, we'll end up naked. "I'll call Aida and see if she's heard from her sister. I wonder if Rockwell keeps anything of interest in his study."

Billy says, "I doubt it. If he's involved in this, he'd be careful not to leave anything incriminating lying around."

I glance at the clock on the bedside table. Time to get ready for work.

Billy swallows hard and takes my hand. "I'm supposed to go to Kendra's tonight for dinner, so I probably won't be back. Not sure what tomorrow will bring, but whatever it is, I'll deal with it."

"That's good, Billy. You know where to find me if you need to talk."

He grins at me. "Sure thing. I'll do that. Then, you can tell me everything you see in my soul. Deal?"

He did it to me again. Damn, he's good. "Deal."

I walk him to the door and watch him drive slowly from the parking lot. Before he rounds the corner and disappears, he stops and raises a hand in farewell.

Chapter Nineteen

It's six o'clock when Sandra and Abel show up at Nick's for dinner. Abel is trailed by three of his converts who sheepishly order beer. Abel doesn't care. He orders a beer too. Sandra orders white wine and a Reuben sandwich. After I take her order, she pops up and trots over to Nick who, as usual, is on high alert behind the bar.

Sandra perches on a barstool, gets Nick's attention and points at me. It's obvious from her body language the interrogation has begun. She leans over the bar, her eyes focused on Nick's face. I see her lips move as she fires questions at him like bullets from a semi-automatic rifle. Nick's eyes widen in surprise. Finally, he lifts his hands in a *hold it, lady,* gesture. Sandra takes a breath and leans back. I don't know what he tells her, but when he's done, they shake hands.

My mother hops off the barstool and motions to Nick to follow her. She leads him to her table and introduces him to Abel and the others. When Nick walks back to the bar, he looks over at me and gives me a big thumb's up. I smile my thanks.

Paco and the rest of Los Habaneros stroll in at seven. Once through the door, they stop and scan the place. Let me paint a picture. Fifteen riders; ten of them trailed by their old ladies. Count 'em. That's twenty-five scruffy, heavily tattooed, scary-looking people entering a neighborhood sports bar in 3 Peaks, Oregon on a Sunday night.

Helen, who's usually unflappable, lets a tray of food slip from her hands and crash to the floor. I see Nick's eyebrows shoot up to the stratosphere. I dash over to him realizing, too late, I should have warned him.

"It's okay, Nick. The big guy with the Fu Manchu? That's my Uncle Paco. He'll keep the rest of them in line. Plus, they'll drink lots of beer and order double everything from the kitchen. Think big bucks."

I turn to Helen who's scooping up French fries from the floor. "They're good tippers, too."

Nick says, "That's your uncle? No way he's related to the guy I just met. Your stepdad."

"Yep, they're brothers."

Before he can question me further, I trot over to Paco. "Follow me, Unc."

I lead them into the Corral, practically empty on a Sunday night. Before he sits down, Paco clamps his meaty hand around my neck and says, "Hey, little girl, you remember Roxy, my old lady?"

He turns me around. My eyes are at boob level with Roxy's ample cleavage. Her left breast sports a heart tattoo, inscribed with the words, *Mi Amo, Paco.* I lift my gaze to the top of her bleached blond head, sporting a half-inch of dark roots, before I glance into her eyes. "Hi Roxy."

Her eyes are black as sin and she doesn't look glad to see me. "That's me," she says. "And you're Mel, Paco's precious little niece. Good for you."

Paco growls something at her in Spanish. She gives me a phony smile. "So good to see you again."

Her voice drips with sarcasm but Paco doesn't get it.

"You too," I purr. "What can I get you to drink? Maybe a nice Mountain Dew Me?"

Roxy blinks rapidly. Paco erupts with laughter and slaps her butt. "She gotcha good, girl."

He grabs both of us around the neck and smushes us against his chest. As a result, Roxy and I end up forehead to forehead. I try not to look into her evil eyes. God only knows what lurks in her soul. Probably a burning desire to kill my ass.

Once I'm released from Paco's powerful grip, I start taking orders. My prediction proves to be right. Fry cook, Sammy, is on duty tonight and Los Habaneros keep him hopping. Helen and I do our best to keep the food and drinks coming.

I'm in the Corral when I hear, "Kid."...the familiar, welcoming cry from Billy's fan club. But wait, he's supposed to be at Kendra's, doing the family thing before he starts counseling. Gripping the empty tray, I whirl toward the sound and see Billy walking toward me. Even from a distance, I feel the heat of his intense gaze. It swirls through my body like molten fire. Part of me enjoys the sensation. The other part, the thinking part, wonders how this man has the ability to turn my legs into jelly with a single look. Should I be worried about losing myself or just enjoy the feeling?

No brainer. I smile up at him as he approaches. He cups my face in his palms and brushes his lips across mine in a quick kiss. Paco and his gang erupt in whoops of delight peppered with lewd suggestions.

My cheeks are on fire as I take a step away. "Skip out on the family?"

"Ate dinner. Decided to come here. See what's going on. Maybe we can spend some time together when you get off work."

As much as I want this man, the presence of my mother looms large. Kind of like an automatic sprinkler system triggered by a flash fire, squelching the flames before they can spread.

"Um," I say. "My mom and stepdad are staying here tonight."

Billy cocks his head to one side and narrows his eyes "In your room?"

"Well, no. But, knowing my mom, she'll want some girl talk later."

He grins. "I get it. You can't do it if your mom's close by…right?"

I give a little snort of disdain to mask my surprise at his intuitiveness. "I need to get back to work."

He's still grinning when he joins Paco and his group. Apparently he's decided to hang around in case I get the hots for his big sexy bod in spite of Sandra. Who am I kidding? It could happen.

At nine, Sandra seeks me out. "Abel's doing his thing." She points to their table where a throng has gathered. "I'm bushed and he wants to leave at o dark thirty tomorrow. Can I crash in your room for a while?"

"Sure." I hand over the key to Number Twelve.

I'd just delivered a loaded tray of food to the Corral when my mother bursts through the door, her face the color of wallpaper paste. Her eyes are wild and frantic as she gazes around the restaurant. When she spots me, she lifts a hand, staggers to a chair and collapses. The room goes silent as Abel and I race over to her. Nick joins us.

I crouch next to her, "What is it? What happened?"

She takes a deep, shuddering breath, unable to speak. Abel kneels in front of her and takes both her hands in his. "Tell us what happened, love."

"Blood," she whispers. "All over the bed. On the floor too." She pulls free of Abel's grip and points at her white sandals, now streaked with red. "I stepped in it."

Abel's face tightens. "Whose blood? Yours? Are you hurt?"

She covers her face with her hands and rocks back and forth. "No, no," she moans. "Not my blood. Just— just blood—everywhere. And that thing on the bed…it looked so real."

Filled with dread, I ask, "What thing?"

She lifts her head and swipes at her eyes with the tail of her shirt. "It's—It's a dummy or manikin— whatever you call it. And she has a knife buried in her chest."

I clap a hand over my mouth, unable to speak.

I feel the presence of others and look up to see Billy standing next to Nick. Billy's eyes glitter with anger. A grim faced Nick says, "I'll go check it out."

I pop up. "I'm going with you."

Abel says he'll stay with Sandra. Helen assures us she can handle the restaurant. Paco joins us as Nick, Billy and I dash out through the kitchen and cross the courtyard to Number Twelve. The door is ajar. The lights are on. Followed by Billy, Nick pushes the door open, steps in and curses. "*Son of a bitch.*"

Billy turns to me and barks, "Don't come in here, Mel."

I don't listen and dart past the men. Billy makes a

grab for me but misses. The images slam into me like a punch in the face. I gasp and double over. For a brief second, colors are all I can take in. The grisly picture painted in crimson and beige somehow seems more obscene in the soft glow of lamplight. A naked female dummy is sprawled on my bed, a large hunting knife embedded in her chest. I close my eyes, open them again, take a deep breath and try to make sense of what I'm seeing. At some level I'm aware Paco is cussing a blue streak, Nick is muttering under his breath and Billy is clenching and unclenching his fists.

I force myself to look and see a scarlet river of dried blood where it streamed across the beige coverlet topping my bed and dripped onto the floor. A cry escapes my lips and I bury my face in my hands. Number Twelve, my very first home, my cozy refuge, has become a scene from a horror movie.

Nick says, "Wait for us outside."

"*No*." I cry. "This is my home. I'm staying."

Paco slips an arm around me and presses me against his massive chest. His words rumble like thunder in my ear. "Don't you worry, little girl. Uncle Paco's here. I'll find out who did this. I promise."

I nod and pull away from him. Billy's standing in the open doorway, using his cell phone to call 911. Nick is assessing the damage. I force myself to look around, try to see if anything is missing. Taking care not to step into the pool of blood on the carpet, I walk to the bathroom. When I flip on the light, the message on the mirror leaps out at me. Scrawled in big black letters are the words, "You're next, bitch."

My quivering legs collapse and I slump against the wall. Gulping air, I try to fight off the blackness closing in on me. When my vision clears, I grab the doorframe to steady myself. Paco peers over the top of my head, spots the message on the mirror and yells, "*Hijueputa. Cara de monda. Percanta.*"

I'm not sure what the words mean. It's probably better I don't.

Billy shoulders his way around Paco, wraps his arms around me and braces my body with his. For a brief moment, I let him hold me. The strong beat of his heart is like an infusion of much-needed courage.

When the cops arrive, I'm standing outside the room, still reeling from the shock. They take pictures of the scene and use their radio to call for a tech to dust for fingerprints and collect blood samples. One of the cops is a woman, an Officer C. Talbot, who exchanges a few words with Billy and then questions me gently about disgruntled boyfriends, spurned suitors, people I may have pissed off at the bar. My answer is *no* to all of the above.

"Is anything missing?" she asks.

I've already checked the dresser drawer where I stash my money in a sock hidden beneath my panties and it was untouched. It's really all I have of value.

"My money's still there," I tell her. "Maybe I better take another look around."

Then I discover the intruder has taken only two things from my room. My newly purchased thrift store bike, Blazing Saddles and the letter and pictures from Dani.

Chapter Twenty

Sandra pulls herself together and appears shortly after. She and Nick take charge. She scoops up my personal belongings while Nick leads me to my new home, Number Ten. It is laid out exactly like Number Twelve except the coverlet and carpet are blue instead of beige. I perch on the end of the bed while Sandra fusses around. Nick goes out to talk to the cops. Billy hangs around until my mother runs him off, saying, "Thanks for your help, Billy, we've got it covered now."

Although I try to fight it, my mind keeps flashing back to the gruesome scene. The blood-splattered female manikin positioned for maximum shock value. Blotches of crimson splashed on the neutral coverlet like some grotesque work of modern art. The hateful words scrawled on the mirror. The fact some sick perv is capable of creating such a scene as a warning scares the crap out of me. It also makes me damn mad. Yep, scared and mad pretty much sums up my feelings at the moment.

But, underlying those emotions, runs a powerful river of resolve. I may be scared, but I'm not leaving. I come from strong stock. Sandra, younger than I am now, gave birth to twin baby girls and managed on her own for years. As for my *damn Spaniard* father, it's possible he has some good qualities too. A long time ago, I decided not to hate someone I've never met.

Nick pops back into the room. "The cops think whoever did it brought along containers of blood to splash around, you know, make a stronger statement. The lab will test the blood and let us know if it's human or animal."

"Sick," Sandra mutters.

"Majorly," I add.

Nick rubs his eyes. I've never seen him look so tired. Suddenly, I'm consumed with guilt. He's been a rock and now, one of his motel rooms is now completely trashed.

I jump up and give him a quick hug. "Nick, I'm so sorry. Do you want me to move out? Looks like I've brought you a shitload of trouble."

He pats my cheek. "No way. I've got a stake in this too."

Sandra bustles over. "Abel and I would be glad to pay for the damages."

Nick waves her away. "Forget about it. Your daughter didn't cause this mess. We'll throw out the mattress, put in new carpet and Number Twelve will be ready to go."

He turns to leave, then pauses. "Almost forgot, Mel, they found your bike. It's in the dumpster all smashed up. Looks like somebody ran over it."

"Well, damn," I murmur. "I just got that bike."

Now I had one more thing to add to my revenge list. No more Blazing Saddles.

Fortunately it's Sunday night and the motel is mostly empty. The police presence only attracts a few of the guests. A patrol officer stands outside Number Twelve to keep them from peeking in. No sense in scaring off the remaining clientele.

After the cops leave, we troop over to the restaurant. Since everyone's gone but Paco and crew, Nick decides to close up early. While Helen and I finish cleaning up, Sandra and Abel's whispered conversation grows louder and blossoms into a major fight over— guess who?

Sandra: "I can't believe you still want to leave at five a.m. after what happened. I can't leave Mel here by herself."

Abel: "You underestimate your daughter."

Sandra: "What the hell does that mean? She needs me."

I know better than to interfere, trusting Abel will talk sense into my mother. But, it's Paco who saves the day.

He clamps one hand around the back of Sandra's neck, the other around Abel's. "Hey, you two. Knock it off." He tilts his head toward me. "There's a kid in the room."

Despite the grimness of the evening, I have to smile.

Paco gently bumps their foreheads together. "Now, here's the plan. You both go on home tomorrow. I've got business in Idaho, but the boys can take care of it. Roxy and I will stay in 3 Peaks until we find out who did this and I beat the crap outta him. Mel will be safe. I promise."

Unless Roxy kills me. The thought remains unspoken.

Abel agrees immediately. Sandra is harder to convince. "Dammit, Paco, I'm her mother. I should be staying here, not you." Paco keeps his big paw clamped on her neck until she gives in. Reluctantly. Paco releases her. She rubs the back of her neck and shoots daggers at him with her eyes.

Sandra insists on staying with me until morning. I breathe a sigh of relief knowing she'll be leaving early. Why? Because I have an agenda.

I sleep very little that night. First off, I try to fend off my mother's interrogation. I tell her (truthfully) the incident probably has something to do with Dani and Destiny, but omit a few pertinent details, like the bizarre situation with Aida and her sister, Larissa. Sandra is far from satisfied with my answers but finally, completely exhausted, falls asleep gripping my hand.

Later, listening to Sandra's gentle snores, I stare at the ceiling and try to make sense out of the chaos in Number Twelve. Once the shock and fear subsides, my wits return. I begin to see a clearer picture. Basically, it was an act of terror. Nothing of value was taken. The person (or persons) wanted to scare the hell out of me and chase me out of 3 Peaks. The destruction of my bike was an afterthought. A simple act of meanness.

The fact they took Dani's letter and photos is significant. Dani poured out her heart in the letter, clearly stating her worries and suspicions. She'd followed Eddie and taken photos of the places he went. She must have thought it was important. Whoever made off with her things now knows *I* know at least as much as Dani did. And look what happened to her. Obviously, somebody doesn't want me snooping around. All the more reason why I should. Fatigue finally gets the best of me and I drift into a brief but dreamless slumber.

The next morning, Sandra's already gone when I

hop on the bus in front of Nick's. Fifteen minutes later, I'm standing inside a three story brick building on Bond Street. The directory tells me private practice doctors occupy the first floor, everything from cosmetic surgery to psychiatric counseling. Floor number two holds the legal offices of Rockwell, Smyth and Verstrate. Various and sundry small businesses, including an actuarial, are located on the third floor. This strikes me as very convenient. It's one-stop shopping. If your plastic surgery is botched, the shrink is right next door. Counseling doesn't help? Make an appointment with the boys on the second floor to sue the surgeon. After you collect your dough, the actuarial can tell you how many years you have left to spend it. Sweet.

But now, I'm hoping to get a look at the couple from California and their baby. I'm not sure why, but it seems like the next logical step.

There's a small waiting area tucked into one corner of the lobby. I plop down in a chair and wait. The door creaks open and a tall, dark-haired man wearing mirrored sunglasses enters. He gives me a brief glance and walks to the directory. The hair on my arms bristles with alarm. I'm still spooked from last night. I grip the arms of the chair, ready to spring up and dash out the door.

The man turns to face me and lowers his glasses. He stares at me with a penetrating blue gaze. "Guess I'm in the wrong place. I'm looking for Dr. Johnston, not Dr. Johnson." His voice is deep and carries a slight accent. He makes no move toward me. I'm too far away to read his soul.

My heart is pounding so hard I'm unable to form words. My gaze swings over to the door as I estimate the time and distance it would take for me to dash outside. If I run really fast, can I get out of the building before he grabs me? I slide to the edge of the chair, poised for flight.

He looks like he's waiting for me to respond. When I don't, he pushes his sunglasses up, pivots on his heel and exits the building. I resume breathing and watch through the window as he strides away. I take a shaky breath and wonder how long it will be before I feel safe again.

Unable to sit still, I walk to the window and peer out. A car with California plates pulls up and parks across the street. The male driver climbs out and opens the back door of the car. The upper half of his body disappears inside the car. He emerges carrying a baby in a padded infant car seat and a briefcase. He bumps the car door shut with his hip. A woman hustles around the back of the car. She's lugging an enormous diaper bag and has a leather handbag hanging from one shoulder.

I step away from the window and stand by the elevator like I'm waiting to board. Juggling the baby, briefcase, diaper bag and purse, the two fumble through the door. They look to be in their mid-forties. Both are clearly exhausted, particularly the woman. Her eyes are puffy and bloodshot, her dark blond hair mussed. The man's shoulders droop slightly and he's unshaven. Looks like their little bundle of joy kept them up all night. They walk to the elevator. He sets the baby in its comfy car seat on the floor and shifts his briefcase to his other hand.

Usually, I'm reluctant to talk to strangers. In this case, I know I have to. I tap into my inner Sandra. My mother's never met a stranger, so, what would Sandra do?

I glance at them and smile. "Wow, you two have your hands full. Can I help?"

The guy eyeballs me for a moment and then looks at his wife who gives me a grateful smile. Apparently they decide I'm not going to snatch the kid and run. Lucky for me they don't know my past. The woman sighs and hands me the diaper bag. "I guess we look like we need help."

"Baby keep you up all night?"

"Every two hours, like clockwork," the man says with a chuckle. "But look at him now. Sound asleep. Wish he'd sleep this good at night."

I lean over the car seat and check out the baby. They have him bundled up like we're in Siberia. A fluffy yellow blanket is pulled up to his chin. I zero in on the only visible part of his body, the tiny red face beneath a knitted blue cap. "Oh, what a cutie." I gush. "A little boy. Right?"

"Yes," the woman says, pride in her voice, "This is Michael Junior. He's just two days old."

"I bet he has your blond hair."

The woman carefully pulls the baby's cap back to reveal blond fuzz. "Yes," she says. "He has blond hair."

I run an appraising eye over her slim figure. "You look great. Can't believe you just had a baby."

The couple exchanges a glance. I stand there, grinning like an idiot, hoping my expression says: *you can trust me*.

The woman leans close and says, "Thanks for the compliment, but I wasn't pregnant. We tried for years to have a baby." Her eyes fill with tears. "And now we do. Michael is adopted."

In my heart, I feel the pain they've suffered. Now, I see their souls overflowing with joy. These are good people. If this baby was stolen from Larissa, she's not the only victim.

I swallow the lump in my throat and try to think of something to say. "I'm happy for you," is all I can come up with.

The guy presses the button for the elevator and picks up the baby carrier. The doors open and we all pile in. "We're going to two," he tells me. I reach around him and hit the button for three.

The tiny elevator lurches to a stop at the second floor. The doors open to an expansive carpeted lobby. It smells like money. A receptionist guards the door to the inner sanctum where I'm sure Ethan Rockwell is waiting with the birth certificate for baby Michael.

I hand over the diaper bag and, in keeping with my new friendly-as-a-puppy persona, chirp, "If you ever need a baby sitter, I'm available. I have references." *Or I will after I contact Sandra.*

Before she steps through the open doors, the woman digs around in her purse and hands me a card. "We live in San Francisco. But if you're in the area and need a job, give us a call."

I take the card and, as the doors are closing, call, "I don't have a card, but my name is Melanie Sullivan. Good luck with baby Michael."

On the bus ride home, I pull the card from my pocket and discover I've just met Michael and Pamela Kruger. The embossed card includes their address, their home phone number and a cell phone number for each of them. I think about their joy at welcoming a child into their lives and my heart aches for them. I can't prove this is Larissa's baby, but my gut tells me it is. If I'm right, there will be no happy ending for the Krugers.

And, where the hell is Larissa?

Chapter Twenty-One

Back at Nick's, a white panel truck emblazoned with the words Bio Clean-Up blocks my view of Number Twelve. I peer around the truck and see the bed is already gone and two guys are tearing up the carpet. Looks like Nick meant business when he said the room would be ready to rent in record time.

Second surprise. Paco, straddling his Harley, is parked outside my new home and he's shooting the breeze with Connie, Captain of the Motel Maids. As my mother would say, Connie is no spring chicken. In fact, she's probably close to the half-century mark. Her hair is usually pulled back and secured with an elastic band. Now, freed from its bonds, it tumbles around her face in a cascade of dyed black ringlets, as if she's been tossing it flirtatiously. She stands with one hand placed on her plump hip, shoulders back, ample breasts thrust forward for Paco to enjoy. And, judging by the look on his face, he is. Enjoying them.

Oh my God, I think, as I visualize a hissing, scratching catfight between Roxy and Connie. My fervent prayer is, if it happens, it won't be at Nick's.

As I approach, Paco tears his fascinated gaze from Connie's bountiful attributes and growls at me. "I was looking for you. You're supposed to call me when you want to go someplace."

"I am?" I walk past him and unlock the door to

Number Ten. "Guess I didn't get the memo."

Connie's screech is gone. Her voice is sexy growl pitched two octaves lower than normal as she purrs, "Aye, Paco. I get to work now. You know where to find me, big man."

I glance over my shoulder and see Paco grin and give her an enthusiastic thumb's up. He follows me into the room. We settle into chairs next to the table. He folds his arms across his chest, tilts the chair back and frowns at me. "It's what your mother wants."

I suppress an annoyed sigh and choose my words carefully. "I appreciate the offer, but the bus stop is right out front. If I need you, I'll call. You mentioned you have—um—business in Idaho. If you have to go, it's fine with me. Really. I can take care of myself. I won't tell Sandra you're gone."

His eyelids slip to half-mast as he mulls it over. Finally, he stands and stares down at me. "Nope, I'm going to hang around a while. At least until that boyfriend of yours has more free time. Looks like counseling will keep him tied up for a while."

Say what?

He starts for the door.

"Hold it." I spring from my chair. "You know about that?"

He turns to face me. "Yeah, he told me about the PTSD yesterday."

I'm speechless with shock. Billy, my Billy, who can barely utter the PTSD word to me, his girlfriend, had wasted no time unburdening himself to a total stranger. How did that happen? Is it a man thing? A bromance? Had they bonded over their Harleys? Part of me is slightly pissed off.

"Well, damn," I mutter.

Paco plants his big paws on my shoulders and squeezes. "Look, kiddo. I'll try not to get in your way. Just call if you need me. You've got my cell number. Right?"

I assure him I do. He tells me he and Roxy have pitched a tent in a campground south of 3 Peaks.

"How does Roxy feel about staying in 3 Peaks?"

Paco shrugs. "If she's not happy, tough shit. Like they say, lots of fish in the sea."

I get a sudden visual of Paco riding off into the sunset with Connie clinging to his back. Will Connie be my next aunt?

Paco and I hammer out the details of our agreement. As far as Paco is concerned, unless I think he needs to know something, he promises my business is my own. He won't ask for details about where I'm going, what I'm doing, or whom I'm doing it with. That way, he tells me, he has little or nothing to report to my mother. Sounds good to me.

After Paco leaves, I gather up my dirty clothes and head for the laundry room, taking care to avoid Connie in case she's found a particularly nasty room for me to clean. I'm sitting cross-legged on top of the washer, trying to figure out my next move, when my cell phone rings. The display says *Aida*.

I step outside. "Hi, Aida. What's up?"

She's crying so hard she can barely speak. When she does, her speech is mangled and I have a hard time making sense of the heavily accented words. When I do, a cold chill forms at the base of my neck and slithers down my spine.

"You come. Now. Missus gone. Police come. Tell

me Larissa is dead. Say nothing about baby." Her voice breaks and she sobs, "How can that be? Where is baby? You come. Please, Mel."

I promise I'll be there soon and search for Paco's number in my phone. Go figure. I just told Paco I don't need him. Now I do.

****

When we get to Rockwell's house on Broken Top (much easier on a Harley), I try to convince Paco to drop me off and skedaddle until I call him to pick me up. He doesn't agree. He's all about serve and protect. Finally, I say, "Paco. You're a 300-pound Mexican man wearing a leather jacket with gang insignias. And, you're in the most exclusive neighborhood in 3 Peaks. Think you don't stand out just a little?"

Fortunately, he doesn't take offense. Before he motors away, he pats the top of my head. "Call if you need me."

Aida meets me at the door, Destiny in her arms. The baby is fixated on Aida's face as if she's trying to figure out what is causing her distress. As I step into the foyer, Destiny glances over at me and buries her face in Aida's neck.

Once inside the house, the memory of being trapped in the pantry comes flooding back. I'm acutely uncomfortable. Even though we're alone in the house, I whisper, "Are you sure Mrs. Rockwell won't surprise us again."

Aida waves a hand. "No, no. Missus tell me she go to lunch with friends after work-out. She take lunch clothes. Come with me. Baby tired. I put her to sleep."

She leads me through the kitchen and into the adjoining family room with leather furniture and a gigantic flat screen TV extending across one wall. A portable crib is tucked into the corner. Aida plops down in a rocking chair and pats Destiny's back, murmuring softly to her. Her charm bracelet jingles rhythmically, in time with her pats. The baby relaxes as she snuggles against Aida's body, her chubby legs splayed wide over Aida's growing tummy. Afraid I'll interrupt the process; I'm reluctant to speak even though I want to get the hell out of Rockwell's house as fast as possible.

After a couple of minutes, Aida places the sleeping baby into the portable crib and covers her with a blanket. She joins me on the leather couch and takes my hand. She's fighting tears and her lower lip quivers. "Oh, Mel. I don't know what to do. My sister is dead. "

I wrap my arms around her and pat her back; trying to comfort her in the same manner she comforted Destiny. I'm dying to pepper her with questions, but stifle the urge. In time, the sobs subside and she pulls away from me. I pull a wad of tissues from my pocket and hand them to her. She wipes her face and takes a deep breath.

"How did the police make the connection between you and Larissa?" I ask.

Aida fumbles with her charm bracelet. Her hands are shaking, but she manages to unclasp it. "I show you how she did it. Larissa very smart." Aida uses her thumbnails to open a small silver charm shaped like a heart. "She fold up tiny piece of paper with my phone number and put inside heart. Police find it and call. I answer phone. They tell me they find my number in silver heart, they coming over to show me picture of dead girl. I know right away it is Larissa. Mister and Missus very upset. They tell me, 'Be careful. We send you away, to place they treat you very bad.' They tell me to say, 'Yes, this my sister,' but say nothing more. Ask no questions. So, I'm too scared to ask about baby."

I'm unable to speak, sickened by her words and the Rockwell's threats. They'll send her to a place where she'll be treated badly? The term human trafficking once again rears its ugly head. What happens to these foreign girls after they give birth? Are they forced into prostitution?

Aida swallows hard and continues. "They show me picture. I see it is Larissa and try not to cry. I tell police her name. Mister and Missus are watching me. Police say, 'Where did your sister work?' I tell them I don't know, 'cause I really don't know."

When I find my voice, I try to think of a tactful way to phrase my questions. Not possible. "Did the police say how she died? Was she shot? Had someone beaten her? Were there marks on her body?"

Aida shudders. "They say will tell me more after they do…what you call it?"

"Post mortem?"

"Yes. That. But, Mel, what about baby? Where is baby?"

I'm caught in a moral dilemma. Do I tell Aida I believe Larissa's baby is now Michael Kruger Junior and on his way to San Francisco? Or, do I keep my mouth shut until I have more proof? I decide to do a little of both.

I take her hands in mine. "When is your baby due?"

Two worry lines appear on her smooth forehead. "End of summer. August. Why?"

"I think Mr. and Mrs. Rockwell are involved in something very bad. But, you mustn't say anything to anybody. I'm trying to find out what they're up to. With any luck, we'll have it figured out before you have your baby."

Aida pulls her hands free and glances over at Destiny. "What you mean, something bad? Something about babies going missing?"

"I don't have any proof yet, but I'm working on it," I say. "Remember when I told you Destiny's mother, Dani, was my best friend?"

She nods.

"She died in a fall and now the Rockwell's have her baby. Dani would never have agreed to give the baby to them or anyone else."

"So, what we gonna do?"

"I have a couple of people I trust who are helping me figure things out."

"I mean," Aida says, "What do *I* do?"

I think for a moment. "Do the Rockwell's talk about things in front of you."

She nods. "All the time. They think I'm a stupid girl who doesn't understand."

"Excellent. Keep your ears open and if you hear anything about the medical clinic or babies, let me know."

Aida puts two and two together and her face blanches. "You think they want my baby?"

I place a hand on her arm. "That's what we need to find out. But, don't worry. I won't let 'em."

Sandra is fond of saying, "From my lips to God's ears."

Amen.

Chapter Twenty-Two

Paco is true to his word. When he drops me off at the motel, he asks me no questions and repeats his previous statement. "Call if you need me."

I'd just fitted my key into the door of Number Ten when I hear a car pull up behind me. I glance over my shoulder and see it's fry cook Myron in his big old Impala. Beads of water dot the hood. Looks like he'd just come from the carwash. He leans across the wide front seat, cranks the passenger side window down and a blast of country music pours out. He calls, "Hey, kid. Hear you had a scare last night. You okay?"

I glance into his flat gray eyes and lie. "Couldn't be better."

"That's good. I see you have a new place to crash."

"Yep. Number Ten is my new home."

After a long, awkward pause, he says, "Anything I can do to help, let me know."

"Okey dokey."

I watch him pull away and think about the strangeness of our conversation. In the past, Myron barely acknowledged my existence. Now, he's suddenly Mr. Helpful? I try to remember if Myron was working last night, but I'm drawing a blank. No, I'm sure it was Sammy in the kitchen. But, why would Myron want to hurt me? Should I add him to my list of suspects along with Eddie and his sleazy buddies?

I finish up my laundry. The mindless task gives me time to think about the events of last night and Larissa's death. I'm certain there's a connection but I have no proof. If I go to the police with my story, they'll think I'm a nut job. I have to do something. But what? Then, I remember what Sandra always says when frustration gets the best of me. "You can't control other people, but you can work on yourself."

Since arriving in 3 Peaks, I've been obsessed with making a living. And with Billy. I've neglected my physical training. Time to get back in shape. I change into shorts and a tee, clear off a space on the floor and go through the warm-up drills I learned in Brazilian Jiu Jitsu. Blessed with a flexible body, I find I haven't lost much since I've been idle. I finish with a long stretch, legs wide apart, arms reaching forward, forehead touching the floor. I grab my key and trot out the door for a run.

At first, my feet feel leaden and my breath is labored. After I cover ten blocks, everything smooths out and I pick up speed. A feeling of euphoria rushes through me. My feet have wings as I circle around a pocket park and head back home. A block before I reach Nick's, I hear a car coming up behind me. When it doesn't whiz past like the rest of the traffic, I peek over my shoulder. A late-model gray sedan rolls along, keeping pace with my stride. I stop and turn to face it. That's when I see the driver is wearing mirrored sunglasses. My breath hitches in my chest. The guy sees me checking him out, hits the gas and zips away.

Aw, come on. Twice in one day? Can't be a coincidence. Wasn't the bloody scene in Number Twelve good enough? Have they sent a hit man after me?

I'm still feeling paranoid when I trot across the motel parking lot. I look behind me, making sure there's no sign of the gray car. Before I duck into Number Ten, I remember Nick has a copy of today's paper in his office. I angle away from my front door and jog to the back of the restaurant. Myron glances over his shoulder as I dash through the kitchen.

I find Nick in his office, his feet on the desk.

"Can I borrow your paper?'

I'm sweaty and breathing hard. His gaze roams up and down my body. "Hell, you can have it." He grins and hands me the paper. "You look intense, like you're getting ready to kick somebody's ass. Don't want it to be mine."

I force a smile. "Once was enough?"

"You got that right."

I wander back through the kitchen and step outside. As I walk by Myron's car, something catches my eye. A tiny red fragment clings to the inside rim of the left front fender. I stop to take a closer look, but a quick glance over my shoulder tells me Myron is standing at the screen door, watching me walk away. What's up with that? Is Myron just a horny guy who enjoys looking at women's butts, or is there another, more sinister reason?

Back in Number Ten, I lock the door, flop down on the bed and start going through The 3 Peaks Tribune. I find what I'm looking for in the local news section under the heading, *Woman's Body Found in 3 Peaks Motel.* "The body of a young woman identified as Larissa Doroshenko was discovered Sunday morning at the local Rest Inn. According to motel manager, Jeffrey

Tomlison, a maid entered the room after knocking and getting no response. The cause of death has yet to be determined. However, law enforcement officials stated it appears the woman had recently given birth. Anyone with information about Ms. Doroshenko is encouraged to contact the 3 Peaks Police Department."

The sickness I felt earlier today returns, but this time it's different. Today, I've experienced the Trifecta of worrisome events. 1. The Kruger's and their newly adopted baby who surely belongs to Larissa. 2. The newspaper's factual account of Larissa's lonely death in a motel room. 3. The guy with the mirrored sunglasses following me to the lawyer's office and skulking behind me as I jogged. Thinking back on these events ignites a blaze of fury that burns away the sickness in my belly.

Unable to stay still, I throw the paper down and jump to my feet. Pacing back and forth across my room, I mutter enough swear words to curl my mother's hair and wonder what to do next. Billy is unavailable. Paco is an awesome bodyguard. But unless I want him to beat someone senseless, he probably can't help me. It's totally up to me. Melanie Sullivan, whose name used to be Honor. Is it time to reclaim my name? It gives me something to ponder while I shower and get ready for work.

It's seven p.m. and Helen and I are practically running to fill orders when Kendra and her hubby arrive at Nick's for what she tells me is "date night." She rolls her eyes when she says it. Her husband, Craig, is sandy-haired and wears wire-rimmed glasses, as befitting a certified public accountant. Clad in tan khakis and a dark blue golf shirt, he has the slim, wiry build of a long-distance runner. He obviously adores his wife. As she introduces us and jabbers away like a jaybird, he smiles and reaches for her hand.

I find a booth for them in my section. Kendra says, "When's your break?"

I glance at the clock. "When the food orders slack off. Maybe a half hour?"

"Join us then. I've got something to tell you."

"Is it about Billy?"

Kendra gives me an exaggerated wink. "Could be."

While I'm busting my buns delivering food and drink, I spot Kendra at the bar, interrogating Nick. I'm obviously the focus of their conversation. Not hard to figure out since Kendra points at me and then leans over the bar and pokes a finger in Nick's chest, her lips moving a mile a minute.

It's eight o'clock before I catch a break. Before joining Kendra and Craig, I slip into the kitchen and grab the special of the day, fish and chips. Kendra slides over so I can sit next to her.

While my mouth is full of grease, she says, "I stopped by to see you today and guess what?"

I assume it's a rhetorical question and keep on chewing.

She places a hand on my arm. "Why am I the last to know about what happened in your room?"

I swallow a bite of fish. "I'm sure you're not the last. If the past is any indication, now that *you* know, other people will also know. And, I figured Billy would fill you in."

"Well, he didn't." Kendra scolds. "Why didn't you call me this morning? I would have come right over."

Craig follows the conversational ball bouncing back and forth between Kendra and me. His head is cocked to one side as if he's trying to understand a foreign language.

I finish my last bite of fish and smile my thanks. "I appreciate it, Kendra. But my mother and stepfather were both here. They left this morning. My uncle is here too."

"Yeah, Billy told me he met your family. He says that uncle of yours is something else."

"He's that all right," I say. "Stick around. He'll be here later with his evil old lady, Roxy."

Kendra gets over her mad quickly and grins at me. "Wouldn't miss it."

It's then I realize I have a lot of catching up to do, Kendra-wise. "Have you read today's newspaper?"

"No time. Too many kids."

Craig says, "I did."

"Did you see the article about the young woman found dead at the Rest Inn?"

Craig nods.

I tell them about my visit with Aida and the fact Larissa is, without a doubt, dead.

Kendra's eyes are huge. She lowers her voice to a whisper, like she can hardly bear to utter the words. "What about her baby?"

"I think her baby is now Michael Kruger Junior." I then fill them in on my encounter with the Krugers. I omit all information about the man with the mirrored sunglasses. Enough is enough.

Kendra's eyes fill with tears. "This is awful. Just awful. Poor Larissa." She swipes her eyes with the back of her hand, blows her nose on a napkin and drains her wine glass.

Craig leans over the table and takes her hand. "You

okay, babe?"

Kendra kisses the back of his hand and nods. "It's just—just so *wrong*. Something has to be done. Tell Mel about the Rockwells' thing."

Craig releases Kendra's hand and lowers his voice. "The Rockwells are having a party on Thursday night. Rumor has it they're celebrating the adoption of their new baby."

Once again, anger sparks to life. "*Their* new baby?" My voice is squeaky with outrage.

"I hear ya, girl," Kendra murmurs.

Craig continues, "If you want to work the party, I can arrange it."

Kendra snaps to attention. "Sign me up too," she says.

Apparently this is news to Craig whose eyebrows shoot up to his hairline. "Um, Kendra, do you think that's a good idea?"

"Yes, I do," she says. "I think it's a dandy idea."

Her eyes are bright with excitement when she turns to me. "We'll do it together."

Chapter Twenty-Three

Before my break is over, Kendra and I plan our strategy. I don't have to worry about Nick. Kendra guilted him into giving me a night off. She told him, "You're working that girl to death. She needs a day off. Thursday would be good."

On Thursday, I'll catch a ride with Paco to Kendra's house. We'll put on our waiter garb—black pants and long-sleeved white tops—and then, work on our disguises.

Kendra says. "Once I do my thing, those assholes won't have a clue who we are."

I fervently hope she's right, since I still have residual fear and trepidation when it comes to the Rockwell estate.

Shortly after my break is over, Paco lumbers in. Roxy limps along behind him. I glance over at Kendra and Craig, point my finger at Paco and nod. Kendra's mouth drops open in surprise. Craig smiles and nods. I follow Paco and Roxy into the Corral. Roxy winces as she perches on a chair. In the spirit of fake kindliness, I say, "What's wrong, Roxy? You seem to be in pain."

She orders a double JD on the rocks and glares at me through slitted eyes. "What's wrong? I'll tell you what's wrong. I slept in a sleeping bag on the goddamn ground last night. That's what's wrong."

I whisper to Paco, "You need to buy her an air

mattress. Wal-Mart's still open."

Paco shrugs off my suggestion. "Just bring the bottle and two glasses," he says, "If I get her drunk enough, maybe she'll stop her bitching."

I turn around and bump into Kendra whose wide-eyed gaze is fixed on Paco. She says, "Aren't you going to introduce me to your uncle?"

I make the introductions. Paco springs to his feet, knocking his chair over in the process. He takes Kendra's hand in his and kisses it. "Any friend of Mel is a friend of mine."

Kendra's face turns bright pink.

Roxy's upper lip curls into a sneer. I can tell she's dying to say something nasty, but Paco gives her a look and she settles for, "Whatever."

After I deliver Paco's bottle of Jack, I see Kendra and Craig heading for the door. She waves and calls, "Call you tomorrow."

Stalker guy comes in as Kendra and Craig are leaving. Even without the mirrored sunglasses, I know it's him. Once inside the door, he stops and looks around. His gaze comes to rest on me. My pulse kicks up a notch. He strolls over to Helen and engages her in conversation. I see her glance over at me.

On impulse, I dig my cell phone from my apron pocket and dial Billy's number. It goes to voice mail. I say, "Hi, um, just called to say hi. No big deal. Whatever. Gotta get back to work. See ya soon."

At nine, the serious drinkers arrive, including Dani's husband Eddie and my old friend, Darrell. A third man, unfamiliar to me, trails behind. His blond hair is long and swept back from his face, spilling down onto to his shoulders. His eyes are pale blue and wary as he glances around the restaurant. He's clad in faded jeans and a short-sleeved navy T-shirt hugs his impressive biceps and well-developed pectorals. Doesn't hurt to look, right?

Darrell and his buds head for his usual table. I take a deep breath and step up to take their orders. The new guy looks me over. His eyes linger on my chest for a while before moving south. I don't roll my eyes. I guess he enjoys looking too.

"The usual?" I ask Darrell.

He nods.

The new guy clears his throat and says, "You have wodka?'

Darrell and Eddie crack up at his accent.

Darrell says, "Hee, hee, by all means, bring the boy some *wodka*. It's on me."

I ignore the laughing hyenas and tell the new guy, "Yes, we have vodka. How would you like it?"

"Oh, yes," he says. "How I like it?"

This gets the boys going again.

When they settle down, I turn to Eddie. "Who's your new friend?"

"Oh, yeah," Eddie says. "Sorry, Mel. This is Mikhail. We call him Mick. Mick, this is Mel. She is, um, I mean, she was a friend of my wife."

"Nice to meet you, Mick."

"Mel. Nice to meet you too," Mick says. He pronounces my name, *Meal,* exactly like Aida does.

"So, I'm guessing you're from somewhere in Russia?"

"You guess right," Mick says. He smiles, revealing a set of perfect white teeth. "And," he says, "I like my wodka with water."

Darrell says, "Don't you mean *wodka* with *vater*?"

I wait until the hilarity dies down before asking Eddie. "How's the baby?"

"Destiny's fine."

I wait for more info but he's all done talking.

"I'd like to see her."

He shifts in his chair. "Sure. Anytime."

Oh, really?

"How about Thursday?"

"Sorry, Mel. Thursday won't work."

Probably because her new parents are getting ready to throw a big party. Are you invited, Eddie? After all, you are the birth father.

When I deliver their drinks, I take a good, long look into Mick's eyes, expecting to see something grubby and faintly disgusting, like the souls of his drinking buddies. I'm surprised to see his soul is predominately blue. Not ice blue bordered with black like Nina Rockwell's chilly soul, but a soft sky-blue streaked with wisps of white. In my limited experience as a novice soul-reader—I wonder if there are professionals—I've found people with souls the color of Mick's are calm, intelligent and trustworthy. What on earth is he doing with these guys?

The crowd thins out a little after eleven. I spot Billy sitting at the bar, shooting the breeze with Nick. He sees me looking and raises his beer in greeting.

Paco and Roxy head for the door. Paco gives me a hug and shows me the key to Number 22. "Gotta get Roxy on a soft mattress or there will be hell to pay tomorrow. So, remember, I'm close by if you need me."

I wonder if his decision has anything to do with the voluptuous Connie. *Not your problem, Mel. You have enough on your plate.*

Like Sunglasses Guy. I've been keeping an eye on him and notice he's taking care not to look my way. When he rises and walks to the men's bathroom, I know what I have to do. It probably defies logic. It most certainly defies common sense. Chalk it up to the fact I'm sleep-deprived, cranky, paranoid and suffering from PMS. And, I'm tired of being victimized. And, I need answers. And, I have the element of surprise.

I scurry over to the bar and get Nick's attention. "There might be a slight commotion in the hall. Pay no attention. Okay?'

Nick's brows draw together. "Say, what?"

Billy stands and frowns down at me. "What's going on, Minnie?"

"Nothing I can't handle it." I turn and take off at a trot.

Billy catches up with me as I step into the hall. He grabs my arm, spins me around and grips my arms. "You're not going anywhere. Not until you fill me in."

Breathing hard, I push at his chest. "I need to kick somebody's butt when he steps out of the bathroom. Let me go or I'll lose the element of surprise."

Billy doesn't budge. "Who and why?"

"Dammit, Billy, let me handle it. This guy's been following me. I need to find out why."

Billy's grip tightens. Before he can question me further, Mr. Sunglasses steps through bathroom door into the dimly lit hallway. I inhale sharply.

"That guy?" Billy asks.

I nod. Billy bristles up, releases me and takes a step toward my stalker. I dart around him. No way will I let Billy steal my thunder. Since the element of surprise is now a non-issue, I opt for a full frontal attack. With a shriek of fury, I launch myself at the guy, ramming my shoulder into his midsection. The air whooshes from his lungs. He grunts with pain and folds in half, gripping his belly with both hands.

Billy is not to be denied. He pushes me to one side, grabs the man's shoulders and slams him against the wall. I slide in close and whisper in his ear, "You've been following me all day. I want to know why."

When he doesn't respond, Billy shakes him. Hard. The man's head bangs against the wall and he moans in pain. His eyelids flutter and he pants, "Please…please, release me so I can explain."

A couple of guys peer into the dim hallway. Somebody yells, "Hey, Nick. Your barmaid and the Kid are kicking somebody's ass."

Nick shows up and announces, "The excitement's over, folks. Just a little misunderstanding." He grins and adds, "Just remember. Don't mess with Melanie."

After the onlookers drift back to their tables, Nick gives me a look. "I don't know what this is about but, whatever it is, you need to work it out. Right here. Right now. My office. Go."

He walks us down the hall to his office and points at the chairs. "I'll be right outside if you need me." He closes the door behind him and the three of us take a seat, Billy taking care to sit between the stranger and myself.

The guy's face has lost its color. He lifts a trembling hand to smooth his hair and winces as he touches the knot on the back of his head. I bite back the urge to apologize. "Who are you? Why are you following me? Is this about what happened last night?"

His eyes widen in surprise. "Last night? I know nothing about last night."

I look in his eyes and search his soul for clues. For the truth. His soul is clear and shimmers like sunlight reflecting on a mountain stream. No ugly brownish streaks. No telltale sign of duplicity. Now what, Mel?

"Okay," I say. "What do you want?"

"You don't know who I am, do you, Honor Melanie Sullivan?"

An eerie feeling creeps through my body and I stiffen. How does he know my full name?

"No. Why don't you enlighten me?"

He takes a deep breath. Lets it out. "I am Estefan Delgado. Your father."

Chapter Twenty-Four

For a few seconds, it feels like the world stopped spinning. I stare, speechless, into blue eyes, so like my own. I've been totally clueless. Remember my permanent tan? My blue eyes? They are the genetic gifts bestowed on me by the man Sandra always refers to as *that damn Spaniard who knocked me up and split?* Now, here he sits with a big goose egg on his head, compliments of his daughter and her over zealous boyfriend. Not that I regret it for a minute.

I have a bajillion questions and start with, "How did you find me?" I would save *what do you want* for later.

"I hired a private detective agency. First, they found your mother. I knew she would not speak to me, not after I abandoned her. Somehow, the detective found out you lived in 3 Peaks. Don't ask me how he did it. Perhaps it wasn't even legal."

I sigh. "And here you are. Why the sneaking around? Why not just come up and introduce yourself? Would have saved you a world of hurt."

His hand is still shaking as he rakes it through his dark hair. I notice a few threads of silver among the black. "I had to make sure it was really you. I'm sorry if I scared you."

I glance at Billy who is looking as shell-shocked as I feel. I place a hand on his arm. "Maybe I should talk to, um, Mr. Delgado by myself. You okay with that?"

Billy stands. "I'll be in the hall. Leave the door open."

I look into my father's eyes again. He'd impregnated my mother with twin girls and never looked back. How can his soul look so pure when he'd done something so utterly without scruples?

I blurt, "Did you know there were two of us?"

"Yes. The detective told me your twin sister was killed at age six. I am so very sorry."

"Seems like you have a lot to be sorry for. Why did you leave?"

His eyes fill with tears. Fake or real? I don't know him so I can't tell.

"Because I was young and a damn fool. My parents insisted I return to Spain and marry the girl they'd picked out for me years before."

"People still do that?"

He nods. "Yes. Certain families still believe in the old ways. My mother and father were among them."

I brace myself on my elbows, lean over the table and glare. "I want you to know it wasn't easy for Sandra. You never gave her a penny in support. She had a rough time until she married my stepfather."

He flushes. "I am very ashamed. Would you tell her for me? And, that I would like to make amends?"

"No. That's on you."

He avoids my eyes and sighs. "Yes, you are right."

After an uncomfortable silence, I ask the biggie. "Why did you hire somebody to find me? What do you want?"

He lifts his hands helplessly. "I very much fear you will not be sympathetic to my situation."

"What situation?"

He glances at the ceiling as if looking for an answer from above. When he finally speaks, his gaze is over my head. "After many years of unhappiness and denying who I am, I recently divorced my wife."

"And, who are you?"

"Among other things, a man who has much to atone for. You are the beginning of a new life for me."

I stare at him like Wile E. Coyote whose eyes pop out on stems when the Roadrunner appears.

I choose my words carefully. "So, you're on some journey of self discovery and I'm supposed to give you my blessing? Is that about right?"

He beams. "Exactly right."

I'm torn between laughter and tears. Is he really that clueless? I slide out of my chair. "Well, good luck. Have a nice life."

I start for the door when I hear, "Wait."

I turn to face him. "Why? You asked. I answered."

"I have something else to offer."

"If it's money, no thanks."

He says, "It's not money."

Intrigued, I take a step closer. "Then, what?"

He glances at the open door and lowers his voice. "I believe we have something in common. Something you've inherited from me causes anxiety and confusion in your life."

I return to my chair. "Go on."

"I see the way you look quickly into someone's eyes and then down at the floor. Almost like you're afraid of what's behind their eyes. I recognize you for what you are. A soul reader. I call it a gift, but I sense you do not. I've had many years to, shall we say, hone my skills and have much to teach you. If you're willing to learn."

My poor brain is ready to explode. Does he really think I can forget his abandonment and twenty-two years of neglect? No friggin' way. On the other hand, he may be the only person in the world who knows how bewildering and scary it can be to read people's souls. His offer to help me navigate through the rough seas to calmer waters sounds sincere. Color me intrigued.

Then, reality hits. He must have an agenda. To test my theory, I boil it down to a simple equation.

"So, if I forgive and forget, you'll teach me to be a better soul reader."

He raises his hands in denial. "No. I am happy to teach you all I know. As you Americans say, 'No strings attached.' It's true, I have not been a father to you. I know I cannot make up for missing twenty-two years of your life. But, I can help you understand your gift. If you will allow me to."

I still don't trust him. How can I trust someone whose main goal is to make himself feel better? I slide out of the chair again. "I'll think about it," and quickly add, "Not the forgiveness thing. The soul reading thing."

He scrawls his phone number on a napkin and hands it to me. "Fair enough. Call if you want to talk. Goodbye, Honor."

"Mel," I correct. "Call me Mel."

We lock gazes for a long moment. I feel the magnetic pull of his soul and look away. "Okay, then, I guess I'll see you around, Mr. um…" What do I call this man who claims to be my father?

He grins and the change in his expression is

startling. His blue eyes dance with amusement and crinkle at the edges. The corners of his mouth turn up, just like mine. Well, damn.

"Just call me Steve," he says. "Easier that way."

After he leaves, it's closing time. I climb aboard the stool next to Billy and prop my elbows on the bar with my chin resting in my palms.

Nick is doing an inventory of the liquor bottles lined up on glass shelves behind the bar. He scribbles something on a pad and turns to face me. He gestures at the liquor display. "Want something to drink? Looks like you could use it."

"Water sounds good."

He fills a beer mug with water, adds a couple of ice cubes, tops it with a slice of lemon and places it in front of me. "What was that all about? The ruckus in the hall. Do you know that guy?"

I take a big slurp of water and glance over at Billy. "You didn't tell him?"

"Not my place."

"The man says he's my father."

Nick blinks in surprise. "You never met your father?"

"No, he took off before my sister and I were born."

He frowns. "Quite an introduction. Beat up by his daughter and her boyfriend."

I explain about the stalking, about my paranoia after last night.

Nick blows a disgusted sigh. "Why didn't you tell me he was following you? You didn't have to attack him physically. We already know how tough you are, Mel."

Then Billy chimes in. "You know what, Minnie?"

170

The irritation is obvious in the tone of his voice. "You've got a big problem when it comes to asking for help."

I grip the edge of the bar and rake them both with a slitty-eyed glare. "I don't recall asking either of you for an opinion. I can take care of myself, thank you very much."

Nick reaches across the bar and fake punches my shoulder. "Guess I can't blame you after what happened last night."

Billy doesn't cave as easily. "But, still…"

Suddenly, I'm too tired to move. I lay my head on the bar and close my eyes. Billy slips an arm around me. "Come on, I'll walk you home."

"Almost forgot," Nick says. "Your mother called, said she'd been texting you and you haven't answered. I told her you're fine."

I pull the cell phone from my pocket and see ten messages from Sandra. Each one says, "Are you all right?"

I dash off a quick text of reassurance and tell Nick. "Smother mother is now in the loop."

"One more thing," he says. "I got a message from the lady cop who was here last night. She said they should have results from the blood samples tomorrow and she'll give me a call when that happens."

"Okey dokey."

Billy guides me to the door, one arm wrapped around my shoulders. When we step outside, one big hand slides down my back and latches on to my right bun. Sliding inward, his fingers are like a heat-seeking missile, searching and exploring until they zero in on the tender bit of flesh beneath the center inseam of my pants. His gentle strokes spark a wave of heat that spirals outward from his touch and coils deep in my belly. I bite my lip to keep from moaning my pleasure. Trust me, his ego needs no inflating.

"Tired?" He murmurs.

Hmmm, maybe not so much.

When we get to Number Ten, I fit the key in the lock and open the door. Billy follows me in and starts yapping again. "Nick's right, Minnie. You don't have to handle everything yourself. You—"

I whirl around, grab his shirt with both hands and shove him toward the bed. "Shut the fuck up, Billy."

A slow grin spreads across his face. He raises his hands in surrender. "I'm all yours, baby."

Another hard shove and he's spread-eagled on the bed, right where I want him. "Talk, talk, talk," I murmur, my fingers fumbling with the metal fasteners on his jeans. "Way too much talking."

He lifts up and reaches for his fly. "Need some help?"

I push him down again and clap a hand over his mouth. "Swear to God, Billy, if I had handcuffs, I'd use them on you."

Laughter rumbles deep in his chest. When he speaks, his breath is hot against my hand. "When I get my badge, I'll keep that in mind."

After my threat, he becomes the poster child for cooperation. He lifts each foot so I can pull off his boots. Raises his hips so I can remove his jeans and boxers. Arches his back and groans with pleasure when my tongue slides along the length of his erection. Amazing what a threat can do.

I pin his wrists to the bed and warn, "Don't move.

Don't speak. I'm getting undressed now. Nod if you understand."

He doesn't speak, but his eyes crinkle in amusement and he nods. His gaze follows my every move as I whisk my clothes off and toss them toward the chair. I straddle his body, cup his face in my palms and gaze into his eyes. The fire still burns in his soul, but I catch a glimpse of something else. It's the silhouette of a woman, standing at the edge of the flames. I blink and look again. She's gone. Me? Or somebody else?

Right now, I have more pressing concerns. Hot and eager, I slide down Billy's body until I reach the tip of his penis. Downward, downward, until he fills me up. With my hands braced against his body, I throw my head back and find the rocking rhythm that creates a delicious friction in all the right places. His hands go to my breasts. I cover his hands with mine and hang on, enjoying the ride.

It's later, much later. We're hovering on the edge of sleep when it occurs to me I haven't told Billy about my interaction with the Krugers and baby Michael. Because, according to Billy, I'm already skating on thin ice in my determination to go it alone, I know I need to clue him in. "Guess what I found out today?"

With a snort, Billy jerks back to consciousness. "What?"

I tell him about baby Michael Kruger Junior and Larissa's death. His inner detective rises to the surface. He peppers me with questions and tells me he'll talk to his cop buddy to see if he can ferret out any more information.

Our conversation winds down. Billy wraps me up

in his arms and pulls me into the spooning position. I'm just drifting off when he murmurs, "You going to see your dad again?"

"Probably not. Why should I? Other than the soul reading thing."

Billy stiffens and lifts up on one elbow, staring down at me. "Hold on. Are you saying your dad's a soul reader too?"

"Yes. He offered to help me with it."

"Then you need to see him again."

When I don't answer, he says, "I know you have a king-sized grudge. I don't blame you. But, don't turn your back on his offer out of spite. Think about it. Who else do you know with that kind of knowledge?"

Actually, his advice makes a lot of sense. I mutter, "I'll think about it."

"Good."

Considering the matter settled, Billy falls deeply asleep. I listen to his gentle breathing and glance at the red numbers on the bedside clock. Strangely, it brings to mind the red fragment clinging to the fender of Myron's Impala. My exhausted mind connects the dots and I'm wide-awake. That tiny red fragment is the exact same color as the racing stripe on my bike, Blazing Saddles. Did Myron run over my bike? If so, why?

Chapter Twenty-Five

A loud bang on the door awakens me at ten a.m. Billy is long gone. I drag myself out of bed and peek through the blinds. It's Paco. I check to see if Connie is lurking around. She's not and slacker maid Rosa is wheeling her cleaning cart across the parking lot. Grateful for the reprieve, I fling the door open.

Paco steps in. "Get dressed. I'm taking you to breakfast."

A little more sleep sounds inviting, but know what sounds better? Crispy bacon and pancakes drenched in maple syrup. I grab some clothes and head for the bathroom to get dressed.

I leave the door open a crack so we can talk. "What about Roxy?'

"Still asleep," he says. "You know the saying about letting sleeping dogs lie?"

"I do."

His gusty sigh almost blows the door open. "Honestly, kiddo, when love's burning embers grow cold, it's time to get the fuck out of the relationship."

I'm not quite sure how to answer, even though this is a recurring episode in Paco's life. It happens approximately every two years. I do, however, have an appreciation for his gift of language. Half romance novel. Half motorcycle gangster.

The best I can come up with is, "Exactly how cold

is it?"

"Colder than a penguin's pecker."

"Sounds over to me, Unc."

"How should I do it? Buy her a bus ticket and send her back home? Give her money? Rent her an apartment in 3 Peaks?"

Paco is asking me for advice? I try to wrap my head around his options, but the last one makes my blood run cold. Roxy living in 3 Peaks? Hanging out at Nick's every night, giving me the stink eye?

I step out of the bathroom. "I think the only fair thing to do is give her money *and* a bus ticket. What do you think?"

Paco is sitting at the table, holding his shaggy head in his hands. He lifts his head and looks up at me. "She just turned *mean* and I can't figure out why."

"*Just* turned mean?" The words leap out of my mouth before I can stop them.

Paco squints at me. "You think she's always been mean? That I didn't see it?"

"You want the truth?"

He nods.

"Well, yeah," I say. "She's always been a bitch. Guess you didn't notice. Maybe she had other, um, attributes that blinded you from the truth."

Paco thinks it over for a full minute. "If you're right, then I don't feel bad about dumping her."

Suddenly, I get scared. "Paco, please don't bring me into it. Okay?"

He promises not to mention my name. We leave my room and climb on the Harley. It brings back memories of the past. After my mother married Abel, Paco came into my life. I soon became his favorite niece. He'd appear out of nowhere, plop an oversized helmet on my head and seat me behind him on the Harley. Breakfast was our thing. His current old lady was never invited. It was just Uncle Paco and me. To keep Sandra happy, Paco always fastened my little body to his with a long strap and buckle.

At breakfast, Paco quizzes me about Billy. "You guys serious?"

Good question. I shrug. "I guess."

"Take a lesson from Uncle Paco," he says. "Play the field. You're too young to settle down."

I hide a smile. Uncle Paco, the king of short-term relationships, is giving me advice. I know he wants the best for me so I opt for a non-specific reply. "You could be right."

He waves a fork at me. "Some of my boys have PTSD. Damn, but they have some fuckin' hellacious nightmares. One time my buddy, Tito, heard a bike backfire and went ape shit. Billy ever do that?"

I slosh my last bite of pancake into a puddle of syrup and pop it into my mouth. "Sometimes."

Paco leans across the table. "Thing is, relationships are hard for these guys. They have to get over their heebie jeebies first. Just so you know."

I think about what Paco said and decide it's not all bullshit. Instead of staying in denial, I need to at least entertain the thought Billy and I may not live happily ever after. I reach over and squeeze Paco's giant paw. "Thanks for the advice. I'll take it under advisement."

As I wait for Paco to finish his Lumberjack Special—steak, three eggs, hash browns, sausage and toast—I make a decision. Why not share my current problems with my favorite uncle? After all, he's been on the shady side of the law for years. Can't hurt to get another perspective.

"I want to tell you something, but you have to promise not to tell Sandra," I begin.

He lifts two fingers. "Scouts' Honor."

I laugh. "As if."

I lower my voice and fill him in on my suspicions about Aida, poor dead Larissa and her missing baby.

He mops his face with a napkin and shakes his head in disgust. "So that explains what happened in your room. They're trying to scare you off."

"If they didn't suspect me before, they do now. Somebody stole Dani's letter and pictures."

Paco grimaces. "Big money in selling babies." He shakes his head sadly. "Dirty business."

Then, I tell him about the red fragment inside Myron's fender.

"You kidding me?" he says. "Myron, the fry cook?"

I nod. "Might be a coincidence."

"No such thing," Paco says. "He working today?"

"No, it's his day off."

"I'll check it out."

He doesn't tell me how he's going to do it and I don't ask. Remember don't ask, don't tell?

When Paco drops me off, I remind him of his solemn oaths. He means well but sometimes runs off at the mouth. "*Do not* utter my name when you dump Roxy. And, don't forget to give her money and a bus ticket."

Promise number two: "When Sandra calls you—and she will call you—*do not* say a single word about the human trafficking/baby selling thing I told you

178

about while on a sugar high from pancakes and syrup."

Paco chuckles. "Sandra's pretty scary, but I'll try."

"Try really hard. And, thanks for breakfast."

He heads out toward the highway. I fervently hope he's on his way to the Greyhound station to buy a ticket.

Before I unlock my door, I hear, "Hey, Mel."

It's Nick and he's striding across the parking lot. "The lady cop just showed up. You want to join us?"

Of course, I do. Officer C. Talbot is waiting in Nick's office. She offers her hand, asks how I'm doing and tells me to call her Candace. I take a good look at her. She's a willowy blond and attractive. The night of the incident, I'd been too stressed to notice her appearance.

We settle into chairs, Nick behind his desk. Candace reaches into a briefcase and pulls out a wad of papers. She finds the one she's looking for and clears her throat. "Thought you'd want to know about the blood." She pauses and makes eye contact with both of us. "Right?"

I nod and Nick says, "Yeah."

"It's a little strange," Candace says. "Some of the blood was animal. Possibly feline. You know, from a cat."

Yeah, lady. I'm not an idiot. I know the word feline has to do with cats. I keep my snarky attitude to myself and cock my head in what I hope is an inquisitive, intelligent expression.

"Anyway," she says. "There was human blood present as well. And here's the interesting part. The blood contains placental fragments. Our lab guy says the blood is likely from someone who'd just given birth."

I catch my breath. This, I wasn't expecting.

Nick's brows pull together in a fierce frown. "So, where would someone get childbirth blood? From a hospital?"

"There's more," Candace says. "Our tech said the woman was more than likely suffering from placental abruption. It's a condition where the placenta peels away from the uterine walls. It can be extremely dangerous for both the mother and the baby."

Nick still looks puzzled. I feel sick. Is this Larissa's blood? Is this why she's dead?

I decide to take the bull by the horns. "Could this be connected to the woman who was found dead at the Rest Inn? The paper said she'd recently given birth."

Candace avoids my eyes and stuffs the papers back into her briefcase. "We're looking into it."

"Jesus," Nick says. "What kind of weirdo are we dealing with?"

"A sick one," Candace says. "I'll be in touch."

Nick stands and tucks his chair close to his desk. "Thanks, Candace. Gotta run. I'm expecting a delivery."

He dashes out of the room. I'm left with about a bajillion questions, but since I don't know how to phrase them, I zip my lip.

Candace starts to follow Nick through the door. Then, she turns and gives me a curious look. "Billy called me. He asked the same question you did. About the dead woman at the Rest Inn."

I feel my mouth drop open in surprise. This statuesque beauty is Billy's cop buddy? When I gather my wits, I say, "You know Billy?" I want to say *my*

Billy but sense I would regret it.

She flashes a brilliant, gleaming white smile. "Of course I know Billy. Everybody in 3 Peaks knows Billy the Kid."

I'm dying to ask, "Do you really *know* him? Like, in the Biblical sense?" Fortunately, my internal censor kicks in at precisely the right time. I'll save that question for later. For Billy boy.

Chapter Twenty-Six

The next day, Wednesday, I spend a great deal of time thinking about all the moving parts of my life and try to make sense of them. Dani and Destiny. The Rockwells. The bloody scene in Number Twelve. Larissa. Aida. The Krugers. Billy's cop buddy, Candace. Uncle Paco's love life. My nosy mother and the damn Spaniard who knocked her up. Myron's fender. I think so long and hard I sense my brain is overheating. I look in the mirror to see if smoke is pouring out of my ears. I need help but don't know where to turn. What to ask?

Then, I remember Billy's comment about my fath—fath—um, Steve's offer to help me out with the soul-reading issue. Billy's precise words were, "He might be the only person in the world with that kind of knowledge."

Like most people in a relationship, I want to be right. It's an ego thing. But, my recent heavy-duty cerebral workout resulted in the following conclusion: Billy is right and I am—choke, choke—wrong. I need all the help I can get, especially since Kendra and I will be in the lion's den, also known as the Rockwell house, tomorrow night.

So, considering all of the above, I locate the napkin upon which is scrawled the phone number of Estefan Delgado.

He picks up on the first ring. "Melanie?"

"Just checking to see if the offer still stands. You know, the lesson on soul reading."

His voice rises in excitement. "Yes, yes, of course. Just tell me where and when."

We decide on a neutral place. I don't call Paco for a ride since I still haven't filled him in on the bio father bit. Hopefully, he's putting Roxy on a Greyhound bound for wherever the hell she came from. Instead, I take the city bus to a coffee shop in downtown 3 Peaks. Before I dash from my room, I impulsively grab the picture of Hope and me and tuck it into the pouch of my hoodie.

Steve is waiting for me. We collect our coffee drinks and head outside into the bright sunshine. A gentle breeze ruffles my hair as I follow Steve through the outdoor patio to a table well away from the crowd.

I'm acutely uncomfortable, not knowing how and where to begin, so I sip my latte and try to act like I don't give a damn. Steve lowers his sunglasses and studies my face before slipping them back on.

"Did you call your mother about me?"

I am *so* not expecting this question. "Oh, God no," I blurt. "She's already worried about me. If she knew you were in town, she'd freak."

"Why is she worried about you?"

I don't know this man, much less trust him, so I shrug off his question. "Just mother-daughter stuff."

He sighs and leans back in his chair.

I wait until a couple with a dog walk by. "I'm not here to talk about my mother. I'm here to learn about soul reading."

The corners of Steve's mouth lift in a broad smile.

"Very good."

"So, where do we begin?"

Steve taps his fingers on the tabletop and ponders my question. He removes his sunglasses and gazes into my eyes. "You might not like what I have to say. Are you ready to hear the truth?"

"Yes."

"First of all, you must rid yourself of fear. It clouds your judgment and inhibits your ability to read souls. You must think of yourself as a clinician, a scientist looking for evidence upon which to base a conclusion. Your emotions are getting in your way."

I feel heat rising in my cheeks. Who the hell is he to judge me? "Well, dammit," I sputter. "Maybe there's some stuff I'd rather not see and…"

He lifts a hand to stop me. "I asked if you were ready to hear the truth."

Oh, yeah. That. I take a big breath and mutter, "Sorry. Please continue."

He reaches across the table and takes my hand. I want to pull away but his touch feels warm and somehow *right*.

"Melanie," he says. "The last thing I want is to hurt you. Like you, I was once afraid. I had no one to turn to. No one to guide me."

Unable to speak, I nod.

He releases my hand and pulls a small spiral notebook from his shirt pocket. He slides it across the table. "I've written down everything I've learned in my lifetime. It's yours to keep."

I pick up the notebook and open it. The first page is titled, Elements of the Soul. Below the title, the following words are printed in block letters.

EMOTIONS. ENERGY. PAST. PRESENT. FUTURE.

I turn the notebook and point at one of the words. "I totally get everything but future. How is that possible?"

Steve tilts his head to one side. "Do you not believe a person's past and present is a predictor of future actions? Take yourself for example."

I squirm in my chair. This is getting personal. I lift my gaze to his and, once again, see the shimmer of light dancing over water and something I hadn't noticed before. A tiny dark cloud swirls through his soul, sporadically touching down on the surface of the water, dimming the light.

"What about me?" I ask.

"Would you like to know what I see in your soul?"

Truth be told, I've always wondered what resides in my soul. When I look into the mirror, all I see is a pair of blue eyes looking back at me. I nod.

He smiles. "It's quite unique. In fact, I've never seen another like it. You are the girl with the rainbow soul."

Involuntarily, my lips curl up in an answering smile, as I picture a rainbow arcing across my soul. "No way."

"Oh, yes," he says. "It contains all seven colors present in a rainbow. Red, orange, yellow, green, blue, indigo and violet. But it's not bow shaped." He strokes his chin and peers deeply into my eyes again. "Imagine hovering over the top of a rainbow. And it is illuminated from beneath. It glitters and glows with every color in the rainbow. That's the first image I see."

"There's more?"

He nods. "Much more. I see a jagged black line

bisecting the blue spectrum, indicating a major crisis in your life. Possibly, the death of your twin sister. Sometimes death, either in the past or near future, appears as a black line."

His words tap into grief that sweeps over me like a tidal wave. My fingers close around the picture of Hope and me. If only I could feel her presence. Maybe then I'd be able to say goodbye. I take a shaky breath. "What else do you see?"

"The rainbow is surrounded by a blue background with crimson streaks. This tells me you are somewhat at odds with yourself. That particular shade of blue means you are intelligent, a seeker of truth and a logical thinker. The crimson streaks are the purest of red. They can be interpreted two ways. Red may indicate a certain liveliness, perhaps even friendliness, or…"

He hesitates as if searching for the right words. Maybe I don't want to hear what's coming next.

He clears his throat. "No offense, but I believe, in your case, the red indicates you have streaks of pent-up aggression at odds with your ability to use logic and reason. Of course, my opinion is somewhat influenced by the manner in which you introduced yourself last night."

I try to make a joke out of it. "You mean when I slammed my shoulder into your belly?"

He doesn't laugh. "Yes, Melanie. Exactly what I mean."

I think about the recent events in my life, the anger and frustration boiling up inside me with no place to go. Pent up aggression? Damn straight.

"Okay," I say, trying to sound intelligent and logical. Unaggressive. "Now that you've looked into my soul, what does my future holds?"

He doesn't even pause for reflection. "I see you as an avenger. Someone who is willing to put herself in danger to right a wrong."

I shrug and try to laugh it off. "Guess you can't win 'em all."

"Now, you're lying," he says.

Shocked, I say, "So now you have a truth-o-meter?"

"It's easy to tell when someone's lying."

I've picked up on lies before, but usually from body language, not something I'd read in a soul. When a person lies, they avoid eye contact and turn their body or head away. The fake or forced smile is another clue. The idea I could actually see a person is lying intrigues me. I have to know more.

"Okay," I admit. "It's possible you were right about some things. Now, tell me how you can detect a lie."

"When a person lies, a white-hot flash appears in his soul. It's easy to miss. The best way I can describe it is to compare it to a camera flash. It sometimes appears as fluorescent pink or bright green. Since you're so reluctant to hold eye contact, you've probably missed it."

Now, I'm fascinated. "Show me."

"Ask me some questions," he says. "Some of my answers will be truthful. Some will be lies."

Yes. All my life, I've had questions about my father. Now I have a chance to get answers, providing I can tell if and when he's lying. I rip a blank page from the spiral notebook and borrow Steve's pen.

Hmm, how does a lie detector work? I jot down

five questions, take a big breath and let it out. I know it will be hard for me to maintain eye contact.

"Ready?" he says.

I look deeply into his soul and see the glimmer of light on moving water. The amorphous dark shape peeks out from one edge. "Is your name Estefan Delgado?"

"Yes."

The dark shape touches down on the water and distracts me. I don't see the flash he described, so I write *true* next to question one.

Steve says, "Repeat the question. And this time, don't look away."

"Is your name Estefan Delgado?"

"No."

Faster than the blink of an eye, a white-hot flash flicks across his soul. I gasp in surprise. "I saw it. You're lying."

The corner of his mouth quirks up in a smile. "That's it. No more help from me. Please continue."

Since I've always wondered if I have siblings, I ask, "Do you have children with your wife in Spain?"

"Yes."

Again the brief flash. I write *lie* after question number two. Apparently I'm an only child.

"Do you love your wife?"

Without hesitation, he says, "No, we're divorced."

No flash. Truthful answer.

"Do you still have feelings for my mother?"

"No," he says again.

Lie.

I have one question left, but first I need a break. I drop my gaze and rub my eyes, trying to decide how to phrase the question.

I lift my eyes to his. "Why did you try to find me?"

He hesitates, just for a moment. "It's difficult to explain."

I blow out a disgusted breath. "What kind of an answer is that?"

"A truthful one. Did you see the flash?"

"Well, no. But it's still not an answer." I continue to stare into his eyes.

"I've been living a lie for many years. Not wanting to cause my parents pain, I've stayed in a loveless marriage. My father died two years ago. My mother passed last month. Maybe I'm feeling my own mortality. Maybe I want to meet my only child and make amends for my neglect."

Well, damn. The man is telling the truth. I'm not sure how to answer, so I swallow the lump in my throat and hand him his pen. I want to learn more, but my emotions are getting the best of me. So I do what I always do when I'm in this kind of situation...split. I rise from my chair. "Thanks for the lesson. And the notebook."

"Good luck, Melanie," he says. "Maybe we can meet again and you can tell me what you see in my soul."

Surprised, I can't help but smile. "Guess I'm the only one in the world who can tell you the truth."

He hands me his business card. One side is in Spanish, the other in English. The name of his company is CyberSecure and includes his contact information.

Before I leave, I show him the picture of Hope and me. He studies it carefully, strokes his index finger across the glass, kisses it and hands it back to me.

"Thank you. You are both beautiful."

I tuck the picture back into my pouch and nod my farewell.

He says, "Until next time, *mi hija*."

As I walk to the bus stop, I realize Senor Estefan Delgado, *that damn Spaniard,* just called me his daughter. I'm not sure how it makes me feel. Only time will tell.

Chapter Twenty-Seven

Paco delivers me to Kendra's house at four p.m. Thursday. I'm already dressed in the requisite black pants and white shirt. Kendra said she would need a couple of hours to *fix me,* which I assume means, perfect my disguise before our shift starts at six. Paco drives into their cul-de-sac slowly, taking care to avoid a pack of little kids tooling up and down the street on their Big Wheels.

When I hop off the bike, Paco says, "Need me to pick you up?"

I kiss his bristly cheek. "Kendra will drop me off. How's it going with Roxy?"

He shakes his shaggy head. "Work in progress. I'll keep you posted."

I interpret this as: last night Paco got lucky and he's rethinking his need to rid himself of Roxy. Oh, Connie, Queen of Motel Maids, where are you when I need you? *Stay out of it, Mel.*

Paco points at a Harley tucked in next to the garage. "Looks like lover boy is here."

He no sooner utters the words than the front door opens, filled by none other than Billy the Kid. At the risk of sounding like a sappy romance novel, my heart beats a little faster. Sappy or not, I bid Paco farewell and fly into Billy's open arms. I hear Paco roar with laughter as he turns his bike around and pulls out of the driveway.

I snuggle into Billy's body, and it feels so good I want to drag him into Kendra's house, lock him in the bedroom and rip his clothes off. Guess I've missed him.

"Minnie Mouse," he murmurs into my hair. "How ya doing?"

"Okay," I whisper into his neck. "What about you?"

I push away and check out his expression. He's a bit pale but the fire in his soul now looks like banked coals. "How's the counseling going?"

"Pretty good. Got another session tonight."

"How late?" Hope blooms in my chest.

"Not sure. I'll drop by if I can."

"I really, *really* hope you can."

He cups my face in his palms and brushes his lips across mine. "Me too."

Officer Candace Talbot pushes her way into my mind. I *so* want to ask Billy about her, but pinch my lips together to keep the words from spilling out. Before I can break my vow of silence, Kendra turns up. She's in her waiter's garb and sporting a massive amount of black hair pulled back into a gigantic bun. Good God, if that thing falls off, the earth will move. Am I willing to put myself in Kendra's hands? What choice do I have?

"Hi, girlfriend. Ready for a makeover?"

Billy and I grin at each other. He leans close and whispers, "Go for naughty nurse."

"Don't think a naughty nurse will cut it for catering a party. How do you feel about sexy waitress?"

He presses his lower body against me and I know *exactly* how he feels.

"Hold that thought." I pat his cheek and follow

Kendra into the house. Billy trails behind.

Craig is on the floor pushing toy trucks around with Aaron. The baby is sitting in a contraption hung from the doorjamb. When he sees Billy, he crows with delight, pushes off the floor and begins to bounce, his chubby little legs working like pistons.

"Hey, Mel," Craig calls. "What do you think of my new wife? Shall I keep her?"

"Sure, if you like big buns."

Craig's and Billy's laughter follow us out of the living room. Kendra leads me upstairs to the master bedroom and waves me into a chair in front of a small dressing table. It's piled high with cosmetics, several pairs of glasses and a platinum blond wig.

I point at the wig. "Is this one for me?"

She positions herself behind me and plops the thing on my head. "Yep, and it's human hair."

"Ick. Whose hair?"

"You're missing the point. Human hair is the best kind of wig. Looks real because it is."

She studies my face in the mirror, then picks up a styling brush and begins tinkering with my new hair. "Close your eyes. I want to surprise you."

Obediently, I follow her order. I'm pretty sure I'll be surprised. I feel her tugging, fluffing and rearranging. At one point, she slides a pair of glasses on my face.

"Okay. Open."

I open my eyes and stare into the face of a blue-eyed stranger wearing dark-framed glasses. My new hair, parted on the side is straight and silky and just touches the top of my shoulders. One wavy strand drapes across my left eye. I push it back.

Kendra slaps my hand away. "No. You're ruining the look."

"But I can only see out of one eye."

She frowns. "Oh, yeah, the soul-reading thing."

"Which is kind of the point."

She pulls it back over my eye. "Okay, just push it back when you need to. Otherwise, leave it there."

An eye roll would be wasted since she can only see my right one, so instead, I mutter, "Yeah, yeah, you're the boss."

She fusses over me some more, adding eye shadow, eyeliner, blush and lipstick. Finally, I realize she's having way too much fun. When she comes at me with the mascara wand, I slap her hand away. "For God's sake, Kendra. I'm not going to the prom. Enough is enough."

She takes a step back to appraise her handiwork. "You'll do. Let's go see if the boys recognize the new you."

Craig gives me a standing O. Little Aaron scowls at me as if a tacky blond stranger has invaded his living space. The baby stops bouncing. Billy's eyes widen in appreciation. "Whoa," he says. "You look like a super hot librarian. I like hot librarians."

Sounds like he knows a few.

He springs off the couch and makes a beeline for me. Kendra fends him off. "Hands off, cowboy. Mess her up and I'll mess *you* up."

He glances at time on his cell phone. "Gotta go."

He slips around Kendra, grabs my hand and kisses it. "Later. I hope."

"Later," I repeat.

On our drive to the catering company, I quiz

194

Kendra about Officer Candace, even though I'm reluctant to admit the green-eyed monster is alive and well and living in my heart. Probably my soul as well.

She glances at me through slitted eyes and spits the word. "*Her?*"

"Apparently she's Billy's cop buddy."

"She'd like to be more than his buddy. She's one predatory bitch."

"So, did they have a fling or what?"

Kendra nods. "Oh, yeah. She had her claws in him real good. Billy was home on leave, between deployments. I could tell he was trying to figure out how to end it. When he went back to Afghanistan, it died a natural death. At least as far as he's concerned, it is."

"What about her?"

"Honestly, Mel, a woman like Candy Talbot doesn't like to lose. As long as she has breath in her body, she'll try to get him back."

"Great," I mumble. "And she's working my case, the bloody mess in Number Twelve."

We ride in silence for a few blocks while I try, unsuccessfully, to forget about Candy Talbot and her designs on Billy.

"Earth to Mel," Kendra calls. She slings her purse into my lap. "You said Aida couldn't call unless the Rockwells are gone. I got her a pre-paid cell phone. Now, she can call or text when she needs to. I programmed our numbers in. She'll have to hide it from the Evil Ones, of course."

I open her purse, locate the phone and charger and slide them into my pants pocket. "Good idea. Hope I can figure out a way to get it to her." I'm still a little shaky about being on the Rockwell premises.

We arrive at the catering company whose logo is: "2 Busy 2 Cook? Call Carl." Carl himself greets us at the door.

Kendra says, "I'm Linda. This is Annie. We're the servers Craig Harris recommended."

Earlier, we'd agreed using our real names was not in our best interests.

Carl gives us the once-over. Kendra passes with flying colors. I don't.

"Sweetheart," he says, in a kindly fashion. "You're very attractive, but, trust me, people don't want long blond hair in their food. Do you think you can tie it back or something?"

I can tell by Kendra's expression she's bummed. Secretly, I couldn't be happier. "No problem," I say.

Kendra and I find the ladies room. She pulls my blond tresses back and weaves them into a single braid, cussing like a sailor through the entire procedure. I keep my mouth shut.

Once I pass inspection, we help load trays of food and cases of liquor into Carl's van. It's now six thirty. We need to be at the Rockwells before seven to set up for their party. The entire wait staff is sitting in the van. Carl is fuming, fussing and pacing back and forth across the parking lot.

"What's happening?" I whisper to the tiny, grandmotherly-looking woman sitting next to me. I wonder why she's not at home watching re-runs of Gray's Anatomy.

"He's waiting for Frankie, the bartender," she says in a raspy smoker's voice. "He's so goddamn unreliable I don't know why Carl puts up with him."

Five minutes later, Carl marches over to the van, flings the door open and points a finger at me. "You. Annie is it?"

I nod and freeze in my seat.

"I hear you work at Nick's Place. You know how to mix drinks, right?"

"I, um…"

Kendra jabs a pointy elbow into my ribs and hisses, "Yes, you do."

I'm dying to ask *why* but figure there must be a reason Kendra is being so insistent. I do have a vague idea how mixology works, so I won't be totally lying. Still, I don't trust my voice so I nod again.

"Alrighty, then," Carl says. "You're my new bartender. It's a good job. The Rockwells bought all this liquor, plus I have extra. All you have to do is keep pouring."

He hops into the driver's seat, fires up the van and away we go.

I turn to Kendra and whisper, "Are you crazy? What if they ask for something exotic, like sex on the beach? What do I do then?"

She grins at me. "I actually know how to make that one. Don't worry, I'll help."

"But why? I need to be free to snoop around. Now, I'll be stuck making drinks."

"Because," she says, "if you get everyone drunk fast, tongues will be loosened. You're in a position to make the drinks really strong. Get it?"

Now with my hair pulled back, she can see my eyes. I roll them so hard I'm surprised they don't pop out of my head. "This could be a real disaster."

Chapter Twenty-Eight

Carl parks the van next to the Rockwell's front door. Aida opens the door and we lug everything into the house. A portable bar has been set up in the family room next to a counter with a sink and small fridge. When I file past Aida, I wink. I called her yesterday and told her I'd be at the party, but she wouldn't recognize me. When she sees the wink, her eyes widen in surprise. The corners of her mouth lift in a brief smile of recognition. Ethan and Nina Rockwell are nowhere in sight. Neither is Destiny. Last minute party primping?

Carl leads me to my station and hands me a two-pronged wine cork opener. "You know how to use one of these?"

My heart leaps with joy. "Do I ever?"

Early on, Nick schooled me in the use of this device and I was, quite possibly, the fastest wine cork remover on the planet.

"Open three bottles of red and let them breathe. Wait until someone orders white before you uncork it." He shakes his head. "Not my idea. Orders from the boss. Nina Rockwell."

I get busy, opening wine bottles, filling the ice bucket, slicing lemons and limes, opening jars of green olives and cocktail onions and placing them in containers. This part is easy. Not sure what will happen when I actually have to mix a drink.

Shortly before seven thirty, the Rockwells make their appearance. The Mister is casually elegant in pressed jeans and form-fitting black silk tee topped with a sport coat. Nina Rockwell follows him into the kitchen, clickety-clacking in four-inch heels. Her dress has a fitted black bodice with spaghetti straps and a loosely draped skirt patterned in shades of forest green and black. It ends just above her bony knees. I hold back a shiver of apprehension. Her aura screams, "I'm an ice-cold bitch and don't you forget it." She barks an order at Aida who wastes no time trudging up the stairs.

After the Rockwells inspect the food and leave the kitchen, Carl claps his hands to get our attention. "All right, here's the plan. The guests will be guided into the formal living area where you people," he points at the four person wait staff (including Kendra), "will circulate with the food. As you can see, the bar is in the family room, which means people will migrate into this area. If the weather stays nice, the Rockwells will open up the doors and allow the party to spill onto the outdoor area. At precisely eight-thirty p.m. baby Addison will make her appearance. The Rockwells will say a few words and champagne will be poured for the toast. Any questions?"

Silence. My silence is fueled by burning resentment. A champagne toast for the Rockwell's newest acquisition, baby Addison? I want to scream, "Hell, no."

Carl points to a hallway leading away from the kitchen. "Should you need to use the, um, facilities, there is a bathroom you may use next to the laundry room. Be sure to wash your hands."

When the doorbell chimes announcing the first guests, I'm nervously re-arranging liquor bottles while trying to channel Nick and his ability to mix drinks. After Nina greets another set of guests, she makes a beeline for the bar and snaps her fingers in my direction. "Don't just stand there like a dummy. Fill some wine glasses. Half white. Half red. Then, get someone to take them to my guests. They'll have to come in here for mixed drinks."

I suppress the urge to flip her off and respond meekly. "Yes, Ma'am."

To my great relief, she doesn't give me a second glance. She spins on her pricey heels and calls over her shoulder. "Make it snappy."

I get busy with the cork remover and soon have the tray filled. Six red. Six white. Not sure if I should leave my post, I summon Carl who's filling a silver tray with chilled shrimp impaled on toothpicks. "Mrs. Rockwell wants the wine in the living room. Stat."

Carl walks over to the hallway, cups his hands around his mouth and calls, "Gladys. Get your ass out of the bathroom. Please. We need help."

He glances over at me. "Great little worker but she has bladder issues."

I hold up a hand and murmur. "TMI."

Gladys appears, grabs the tray and totters away in her orthopedic sneakers.

The doorbell keeps ringing. People pour in. The noise level goes up and I get my first customer, a silver-haired gentleman with sharp brown eyes and the profile of a hawk. Naturally Kendra is nowhere to be found, despite her promise to help.

"Gin martini, honey." He has a raspy smoker's

voice. He glances at the condiments. "Extra olives."

The word gin, is a huge clue, but what else goes in a martini? I remember Nick asking, "How dry?" Not certain what it means, but I give it a whirl. "How dry, sir?"

"Just a tiny splash of vermouth," he says.

Thank God. Now I know at least two ingredients. I reach for a glass. My fingers close around a short, and squat one which, probably holds eight ounces.

"On the rocks, please," he says.

I scoop some ice into the glass, put in a dollop of vermouth, fill it up with Beefeaters Gin and top it with six green olives.

His hawk face lights up like he's just spotted a wounded rodent. "Wow. That's quite a martini. Where's your tip jar, darlin'?"

"No tip jar. It's on the house."

"That's ridiculous." He reaches past me, grabs a sixteen-ounce beer mug and stuffs in a ten-dollar bill. "Here you go, sweetheart. I'll be back."

More groups of people arrive and the noise level increases exponentially with the heavy slugs of alcohol I'm delivering. I'm doing okay, making whiskey sours, Scotch straight up and margaritas on the rocks, the margarita mix thoughtfully provided by Carl. All of the men place money into the tip jar. The women do not.

A short, plump man with a bad comb over sidles up to me. "Judge Mahoney says you make a hell of a martini."

"Sure thing. You want one of my specials?"

He leans on the bar and looks me up and down. "Sure do."

I almost succumb to the *ick* factor, but manage a

fake smile. "Coming right up."

While I'm mixing his drink, a fortyish couple greets my new customer. The man pats him on the shoulder. "Hey, Doc, how ya doing?"

"Hello, Jared," the woman says. I hear a trace of sadness in her voice.

My mind gets busy along with my hands. *Hmm. Doc. Jared. Could I be serving a giant martini to none other than Dr. Jared Breen from the fertility clinic? I'm all ears.*

Jared pulls the woman in for a quick hug. "So sorry it didn't work out, Abby. Come see me next week. I have another idea that might help. Okay, sweetheart?"

She brightens a little. "I'll do it." She takes her husband's hand and leads him outside to the expansive patio, now filled with people enjoying the view and soft summer breeze.

I deliver the martini. "Here you go, sir."

Then, I take a good long look into his soul, trying to remember what Steve taught me. It's hard not to drop my gaze, but the need to know is a huge motivator.

While I gaze into his pale blue eyes, I chirp, "Oh, are you *the* Dr. Breen?"

His smoky gray soul looks like it's spewing ash from a volcano. No flash indicating a lie. He gives me a smarmy grin. "Why, yes I am. What can I do for you, dear?"

"What kind of a doctor are you? Are you taking new patients?"

"My specialty is women's health."

His eyes flick away but not before I see the white-hot lie flash across his soul. Does that mean impregnating women without their knowledge is his real occupation?

He takes a sip of his martini and smacks his lips. "Excellent drink, my dear. Now, let me amend my statement. Basically, I run a fertility clinic where I try to help childless couples achieve their dream of parenthood."

Whoa, had my expression tipped him to the fact I thought he was lying? Note to self: be careful, Mel. This guy's no fool.

"The last thing I need is a fertility clinic."

He leans even closer and glances down at my lower quadrant, zeroing in on the sweet spot. I hold my ground. "Don't be so sure," he says. "I pay top dollar for fresh eggs." He adds a wink and a leer. "I'll bet yours are extremely fresh."

I bat my eyelashes and manage a flirtatious giggle. "Oh, really? You can tell that by looking at me?"

Dr. Breen hands me his card. "If you want to check it out, call this number and make an appointment."

Nina Rockwell swoops down on us as I tuck the card into my apron pocket. "It's almost eight thirty, Jared. I'm rounding everyone up for the champagne toast." Without waiting for a reply, she dashes outside and begins to herd her guests inside.

Carl summons the wait staff. They fill champagne flutes and arrange them on trays. I've just stepped away from my station to help them when Eddie shows up. He growls, "Gimme a MGD."

I panic just a smidge, wondering if he'll recognize me. I didn't expect to see Eddie here. Not trusting my voice, I nod and hand him a beer with my eyes cast downward. *Just go away, Eddie. Your daughter's about to make her debut as Addison Rockwell, you asshole.*

But, no, Eddie decides to hit on me instead. "I'm Eddie. What's your name?"

Startled, I begin to babble. "It's Annie. Short for Annabelle. I was named for my grandmother." *Shut the hell up, Mel.*

Eddie gives me a seductive wink. "You don't look like a Annabelle. You look more like a Bambi or Cookie. Guess I'm trying to say, you look hot."

"Thank you, sir." I brush by him. "I need to help serve the champagne."

He grabs my arm. I freeze. "Don't I know you from somewhere?"

"I doubt it. I just moved here from Fargo, North Dakota."

"Huh," he releases me. "Annabelle from Fargo. Almost sounds like a made-up story."

I really need to work on my lying skills. I bustle away, calling, "Bye, bye, now. See you around."

The guests gather in the cavernous living room. The champagne has been distributed. I join the wait staff in the foyer, ready with more champagne should it be required. At precisely eight thirty, Aida descends the stairs with Destiny in her arms. Aida looks beautiful in white pants and a blue shirt the same color as her eyes. Her shiny blond hair is tied back with a blue ribbon. Apparently, the Rockwells sprung for new clothes so Aida wouldn't embarrass them. She makes the turn into the living room, hands the baby off to Ethan Rockwell and steps back into the foyer with the rest of us peons where she slips in between Kendra and me. We make eye contact and she whispers, "You come upstairs to nursery. I have much to tell you."

I whisper back, "Don't think I'm allowed up

there."

She slips a baby pacifier into my hand. "You tell Missus you find it. Want to take it to baby. Missus is busy with guests. Plus, she doesn't like baby screeching. Plus, she's a little bit drunk. Will be okay. Trust me."

I nod and tuck the pacifier into my apron pocket next to Jared Breen's business card.

From my vantage point in the foyer, I see Destiny in her new father's arms. Her dress is made from the same material as Nina Rockwell's. Yes, that's right. Mother-daughter dresses. I stifle my gag reflex. Destiny's dress has cute little puffy sleeves and a full skirt. She's wearing lacy white anklets and tiny black patent leather Mary Jane shoes. Her wispy blond hair has been coaxed into a Kewpie doll curl on top of her head.

She looks utterly miserable. I suspect she was sound asleep and jarred awake for her first public appearance. She squirms in Rockwell's arms, twisting around in an effort to locate Aida. When she doesn't see her, her lower lip trembles as if her heart is breaking. Mine is breaking too.

"Ladies and gentlemen," Nina Rockwell trumpets. "May I present our new daughter, Addison Nina Rockwell."

She places a hand on her husband's shoulder and lifts her champagne flute with the other. "Our dreams have come true. Please raise your glasses."

Loud clapping and cheers follow the toast, scaring the heck out of Destiny. She stiffens and howls her outrage. Aida is summoned and Destiny dives into her arms.

Someone yells, "She's not a party girl like her mother."

Laughter erupts as the baby is borne away. I spot Eddie on the edge of the crowd, guzzling his beer, and wonder if he feels any emotion about giving up his only child. His only connection to Dani. Apparently not, because he sees me looking at him and gives me a lecherous smile.

Is disgustipated a word? If not, it should be.

Chapter Twenty-Nine

After the festivities die down, I go back to the bar. Everyone is pretty well saturated with alcohol, so my business slacks off. Carl tells me to take a break. I'm dying to talk to Aida but not at all enthused about asking permission from the Missus. I make an executive decision. I'll try to sneak up the stairs. If someone challenges me, I'll have the pacifier story ready.

While Carl busies himself counting the remaining liquor bottles, I slip into the foyer where I bump into Kendra. Her bun is listing to one side and she has fire in her eyes. She grabs my arm. "Can you believe these people? Poor Destiny. They trot her out like a show pony and then pass her off when she acts like a baby. I'd like to slap Nina Rockwell into next week. And scuzball Eddie's here. Why?"

I'm short on time. I nod my agreement and tell her I'm heading to the nursery to talk to Aida. "Do me a solid and see where the Missus is right now. I don't want her to see me go upstairs."

Kendra quickly checks the living room and pops back into the foyer. Her eyes are wide with excitement. She whispers, "The coast is clear," like she's in a spy movie. I suppress a hysterical giggle. Before I head upstairs, I tell Kendra, "By the way, Eddie thinks I'm Annabelle from Fargo in case anybody asks."

She flaps her hands in a shooing motion. "Go. Hurry."

I run up the stairs like Nina Rockwell is after me with a meat cleaver, an image that raises goose bumps on my flesh. A long hallway bisects the landing at the top of the stairs. Left or right? The hallway to the left is long and mostly dark except for dim light leaking from behind a closed door. Glancing to the wing on the right, I see a door open. Aida's blond head appears. I scamper down the hall and join her in the nursery.

Destiny is fast asleep in an elaborate crib topped with a canopy. Stripped of her party clothes, the baby looks comfy in a pale pink onesy, her butt in the air, thumb in her mouth. Aida puts a finger to her lips and leads me through an open door into the spartanly furnished adjoining room.

We perch side by side on her narrow bed. Aida's hand is shaking when she grabs mine and squeezes it. "I'm so glad to see you, Mel. The doctor is here. The one I told you about. The way he looks at me makes me want to run away and hide. I think he knows what happened to Larissa's baby."

"Yes, I met the creepy Dr. Breen."

"The others are here too," she says. "The men who have been here before."

"Others?"

"White hair gentleman they call judge something. And big policeman. The Mister and Missus make sure I know big policeman is here. They want me to stay scared. So scared I say nothing to nobody."

My heart kicks up a beat. So now we have a judge and policeman involved, along with a lawyer and fertility doctor, very neatly covering all the bases.

"Tell me about the policeman. What does he look like?"

"Big man. Mean eyes. Red hair."

I know the man she's describing. He visited the bar a few times. Beer drinker. Non-tipper.

I hand her the pre-paid cell phone and show her how it works. I caution her to keep it hidden from the Rockwells. Overwhelmed, her eyes fill with tears.

"You give this to me? To keep?"

"Yes," I assure her. "It is yours to keep."

She shakes her head in disbelief. "Nobody ever give me anything before."

I swallow the lump in my throat and change the subject. "Does the Mister have a study?"

I can see the word throws her. "I mean like an office, a place where he does work."

Her hand tightens around mine. Her eyes dilate with fear. "Other end of the hall. I am not allowed."

I gently extricate my hand and stand. "Does he keep the door locked?"

"Maybe. I don't know."

"I'm going to take a look."

Aida's breath hitches in her lungs. "Please, my friend. Be careful."

"Call me tomorrow. Okay?"

My legs are shaking as I slip down the hall. Let me state, up front, I'm no coward, but I've never considered myself a brave person. I'm ashamed to admit I have, upon occasion, actually jumped at the sight of my own shadow creeping up on me. But I can't ignore Aida's plight. I can't ignore the inherent *evilness* of the greed-based scheme I'm only beginning to grasp. I made Aida a promise and I intend to keep it. She has no one else.

I try the door at the end of the hall, fingers crossed it's not Nina's private bathroom. The doorknob turns in my hand and I peek into Ethan Rockwell's personal space. An enormous, cherry wood, L-shaped desk with two matching file cabinets dominates the left side of the room, obviously meant for business. The right half of the room is all man cave and includes a wet bar, a large, wall-mounted flat screen TV and a leather sectional. The heavy drapes are pulled back, revealing French doors leading to a deck that overlooks the back yard.

In and out fast, Mel, I tell myself. And stay away from the windows. Fortunately, a desk lamp casts a low light across the business end of the room. The gleaming surface of the L-shaped desk is uncluttered and holds nothing but leather-trimmed accessories. Pencil holder. Desk blotter. Picture of Ethan and Nina. No computer. Why?

What did you expect, Mel? A folder labeled, *How To Import Foreign Women and Sell Their Babies for Profit?*

I pull the desk chair back and test the drawers in the L-shaped extension. Locked tight. The file cabinets too. Then, I hear a sound in the hall and freeze. Is it a woman's voice? Am I hallucinating? I slither along one wall and risk a peek out the door. What I see scares the shit out of me. Kendra and Aida stand outside the nursery. Kendra is gesticulating wildly. Aida is pointing in my direction. Kendra spots me and leaps in the air, her legs churning like a cartoon character. She dashes down the hall.

She's hyperventilating and can barely spit out the words. "I think Rockwell and his buddies are coming.

We need to split. Fast."

Footsteps on the stairs. Male voices.

"Too late." I cast a frantic look up and down the hall. Not enough time to make it to the nursery. No place else to hide. I grab Kendra's wrist, pull her through the door and shut it. Her eyes are rolling like a panicked horse. I shove her toward the wall facing the back yard. "Get behind the drapes. Make sure your shoes don't show and try not to shake."

She sprints across the room, dives behind the drapes and flattens herself against the wall, her feet turned sideways. I scramble under the desk, pull the desk chair in behind me and curl up in the corner opposite the drawers. Strangely, the feeling of panic subsides. Instead, I'm filled with an eerie calmness totally inappropriate for the situation I'm in. It's hard to put into words but somehow it feels *right*. Like I'm exactly where I'm supposed to be. Maybe I'm cut out for espionage after all.

Seconds later, the door opens and the overhead light flicks on. I hear Rockwell's voice. "Have a seat, gentlemen. What can I get you to drink?"

"That little bar maid fixed me up real good." I recognize the judge's raspy voice.

High-pitched cackle from Dr. Breen. "She's a doozy all right. I offered big bucks for her eggs. She's a little on the shrimpy side, but her tits and ass are great."

Male laughter all around. I pinch my lips together in disgust.

"And that's what's important, right Jared?"

The last statement elicits more laughter and is spoken by a man whose voice I don't recognize. Could it be the big policeman who strikes such fear in Aida's heart?

My only clue to what's happening is through sound. Ice cubes rattling in glasses; manly small talk. I sincerely hope they don't decide to close the drapes.

Footsteps approach the desk followed by a dull thud as something hits the floor. The desk chair is pulled back and a pair of legs appears in my line of vision. My heart kicks up to warp speed. I try to make myself smaller. A key is inserted into a lock. A drawer slides open. Rockwell extracts a thick manila envelope and closes and locks the drawer. I hold my breath until he walks away.

Since I can't see diddlysquat, I press one ear against the front panel of the desk, hoping Rockwell will say something incriminating. I hear the rustle of paper. Rockwell says, "Here you go, guys. Things are looking up."

The acrid scent of cigar smoke drifts to my end of the room and tickles the inside of my nose. I pinch my nostrils together, holding back a sneeze.

Breen says, "Does this include the revenue from Portland?"

"Yes," Rockwell says. "It will increase as the stable gets bigger."

Stable? What the hell? Do they have racehorses? Greyhounds?

Rockwell continues, "We have another shipment coming in next week. Are you ready, Jared?"

Breen cackles again. "I was born ready."

"You using the new guy?" I hear the judge's voice.

"Yeah," Rockwell says. "Both of 'em will go."

"Do we have enough product to meet the demand?" The question comes from the man whose voice I don't recognize.

"No, the demand is always there. But we have to use caution, gentlemen. Especially after what happened this week," Rockwell says.

"Unfortunate loss of revenue there," the judge says. "No way to trace her to us, though. Am I correct, Rusty?"

Okay, Mr. X now has a name. Rusty.

"I've got it covered," he says.

"Good," Rockwell says. "Because I've got another little problem to deal with."

"What?" The judge's voice is sharp.

"We got our hands on a letter and pictures that originated from Eddie Morgan's wife. Turns out she was following Eddie without his knowledge. She took pictures of the clinic and my house and sent them to her friend along with a letter outlining her suspicions. That friend is now in 3 Peaks and working at Nick's Place."

"Do you anticipate a problem with her?"

"Eddie doesn't think so, but I plan to clue the new guy in. He's got the smarts and the balls to take care of it."

An icy chill creeps over me, chasing away the calmness I recently bragged about.

"Keep us informed if anything changes," the judge says.

Rockwell agrees and the subject turns to golf. I start to panic. Just a little. Carl will be looking for us. After what seems like an hour but is probably only a couple of minutes, I hear the door open and Nina Rockwell's voice. "Thought I'd find you here, Ethan. Isn't it time you joined your guests?" She sounds pissed off.

The room empties out. I wait until the sound of footsteps fade completely away before leaving my hidey-hole. Kendra's ashen face, framed by a mass of frizzy black hair, appears through the opening in the drapes. Her eyes are huge.

I hiss, "Hurry, Carl is probably looking for us."

She points toward Rockwell's desk. "Is that his laptop?"

"What?" I follow her line of vision and spot the black leather case propped against the side of the desk. Must have been the sound I heard when Rockwell came to his desk. I'd been in such a rush to leave I'd missed it.

Torn between curiosity and my need to flee, I cross to the desk, unzip the case and take a quick peek. "Yes, it's his laptop."

"Shall we take it?" Kendra says.

"We'd never get out of the house with it. Somebody would see us for sure." I plunge my hand into the case and grope around. My fingers close around a small cylindrical object. I pull it out and smile. "Maybe he won't miss this." I hold up the tiny flash drive for Kendra to see. "Now, let's get the hell out of here."

I open the door a crack. Thankfully, the hall is empty. I want to tell Aida we're okay but there's no time. As Kendra and I head for the stairs, I whisper, "Your bun exploded. You need to fix it."

We're halfway down the stairs when Nina Rockwell appears in the foyer. She glances upward, does a classic double take and pivots to face us, hands on hips.

Kendra whispers, "Oh, shit," and freezes in midstride.

Nina extends an arm and stabs at the air with her pointer finger. "What the hell are you two doing?"

I grab Kendra's arm and drag her down the stairs. Despite my sudden onset of panic, I give Nina my most charming smile and deliver it with subservient downcast eyes. "I found the baby's pacifier. I heard her crying so I took it to the nursery."

Her eyes narrow in suspicion. "It takes two of you to do that?"

"Linda was on break. I asked her to come with me."

"There better not be anything missing upstairs. Don't think I won't check out your story."

"Please do," pops out of my mouth before I can stop it. It sounds slightly smart-ass but I've had all I can take of Nina Rockwell's bitchiness. The comment earns me another visual smack down.

I'm acutely aware of the pacifier burning a hole in my pocket along with the purloined flash drive. I hope and pray Aida has a back-up pacifier in the nursery and that Nina won't be looking through Ethan's computer bag. But in my heart of hearts, I know Nina's first priority will be to make sure the family jewels are unmolested.

The Missus waves us away with a flap of the hand. We skirt the living room and peek into the kitchen. Carl spots us and points at his watch. Before I return to my station, Kendra grabs my arm and leans close. "I saw it all through a crack in the drapes. Rockwell gave each of the men an envelope with money. Looked like lots of money."

Chapter Thirty

Before the evening is over, I get a good look at Aida's big police man, the man the others call Rusty. He visits the bar for one last beer and makes no secret of checking out my body parts so crudely described by Jared Breen. He, like the others in Ethan Rockwell's study, has no problem dehumanizing women. Thinking of them as *product*. I look into his mean, little eyes and try not to shudder at what I see. It's filled with jagged ice blue fragments and is amazingly similar to Nina Rockwell's soul.

I force myself to smile at him. "Enjoying the party, sir?"

He grunts an affirmative and reaches for his beer.

"Lots of nice people here," I chirp. "I just met Dr. Breen and he offered me money for my eggs." I pause and giggle. "Isn't that hysterical?" Then, I inhale sharply and clap a hand over my mouth. "Oh my God, I shouldn't have said that. He's probably a friend of yours."

"Not really," he says. "I know who he is. That's all."

Since I'm gazing into his eyes, it's easy to see the lie flash across his soul. Before I can think of another question, he pivots away and joins a group of men on the patio.

Just before it's time to close the bar, Eddie shows

up again and he's with his vodka-loving Russian friend, Mick. Eddie introduces me as Annabelle from Fargo. I start to reach for a bottle of Grey Goose and then snatch my hand back. *What the hell are you doing, Mel?* There's something about this guy's mesmerizing pale blue gaze that makes me lose my wits. It feels like he's trying to peer into *my* soul, that he sees through my disguise and knows exactly who I am.

I force a smile. "What can I get for you, sir?"

"Grey Goose. On the rocks."

I scoop ice into a glass and reach for the bottle of vodka. Midway to the glass, the bottle slips from my hand. Mick grabs it and sets it on the bar.

"Careful," he says in heavily accented English. "This is how accidents happen. You might get hurt."

Is this the new guy Rockwell mentioned in the study? The one with the smarts and balls to take care of their little problem? Me. Very likely. Maybe I am overreacting, but if he knows exactly who I am, his words take on a whole new meaning. I draw a shaky breath. *Don't think about it now, Mel.*

I pour the Grey Goose over ice and set it in front of him. "Here you go, sir."

Before I release the glass, his hand closes around mine. It's warm and I feel an odd tingling sensation, almost like an electric shock. "You very pretty, Annabelle from Fargo."

I pull my hand free. "Thank you, sir." *Is he softening me up so I'll be easier to kill?*

I turn around and begin to pack liquor bottles into the boxes we'll leave at the Rockwells. I feel the heavy weight of his gaze. I'm afraid to meet his eyes again. Afraid I'll give myself away.

Carl and the rest of the wait staff are cleaning up and covering leftovers with plastic wrap. When I count the money in the tip jar, it's well over $200. I give it to Carl and tell him to divide it up with the others. He nods, but slips me $100. "You earned it."

Back at the catering company, we climb into Kendra's car. She says, "You've got the flash drive. Right?"

"Sure do."

"You want to check it out at my place or go home?"

I know, like me, she's itching to know what's on the flash drive. "Your place. But don't get your hopes up. It probably has nothing to do with the babies. Maybe he's secretly writing a romance novel. And, it's more than likely pass protected."

I tell her about the Russian guy and how he creeped me out.

Kendra reaches over and grabs my hand. "I'm scared for you, girl. What are we going to do to keep you safe?"

I shrug. "I need to be extra vigilant. That's all. And I've got Billy and Uncle Paco."

"They can't be with you 24-7."

The truth of her words sinks in, so I say nothing.

"Why don't you move in with us? At least until this thing gets settled."

I squeeze her hand. "Thanks a million, but I'll stick it out where I am. Please, please, don't tell Billy what they said about me being a problem. He doesn't need to hear it right now. Okay?"

She nods. I make her say it out loud. It requires a sharp jab into her ribs, but after crying, "Ouch," she complies.

"You're fingers better not be crossed," I warn.

"They're not." She stares straight ahead. "I need you to promise something too. You *cannot* tell Craig we got trapped in Rockwell's study. He'd freak out."

"Then, how did we get the flash drive?"

Kendra thinks for a minute. "Okay. You went upstairs to return the baby's pacifier and sneaked into Rockwell's study. You saw the laptop case and couldn't resist opening it. You snagged the flash drive and took off."

"Will Craig believe me?"

"I hope so."

"What about the stuff we heard in the study?"

"*Damn*." she says. "We don't make very good spies. How about this? We saw a bunch of people there who might be in cahoots with Rockwell. The police guy. The judge. Dr. Breen."

"That's a little vague. How would we know they're in cahoots or whatever?"

She risks a glance at me. "The soul reading thing. You looked in their souls and figured it out."

I stiffen in outrage. "You told Craig about me?"

She holds out a hand in supplication. "I had to, Mel. He's my husband. You can trust him. He won't say a word to anyone."

I'm still not over it. "So, who else have you told?"

"Nobody. I swear."

"Well, shit," I mutter. "Guess we don't have any other options.

We do a mutual pinkie promise as we pull into Kendra's driveway. Craig is still in the family room, snoozing in his recliner. The TV is muted and the house is quiet. Kendra creeps up behind the recliner and drops a kiss on a tiny bald spot blooming on the crown of Craig's head. He jerks awake and practically levitates out of the recliner. Kendra and I crack up laughing, our only honest to God laugh of the evening.

Craig wraps her up in his arms and nuzzles her cheek. "What happened to your hair, babe?"

Her bun has pretty much given up the ghost. Freed from its bindings, her fake hair hangs in limp tendrils down her back. She pats his cheek. "Long night. Don't think I'm cut out to be a server."

She goes on to tell Craig the story we've concocted and I produce the flash drive. He frowns at both of us. "So, you stole this from Ethan Rockwell?"

Kendra nods.

"Look, Craig," I say. "If you don't want to get involved, no problem. I'll take it with me and try to figure it out."

Craig's facial expression reveals his moral dilemma. Clearly, he disapproves of our theft but he's also curious. Curiosity wins. He sighs and reaches out for the flash drive. "Let's see if we can get into this thing."

We can't. Turns out Ethan Rockwell is more security conscious than we hoped. We try every permutation of Ethan, Nina, Rockwell and Addison we can think of. Craig even pays for access to a people finder website in order to get Nina and Ethan's birth dates. Nothing works.

Finally, Craig ejects the flash drive, hands it to me and mutters, "We need a twelve year old boy."

Kendra says, "What about Paco? You said he's on the shady side. Does he have hacking skills?"

"I'll check." I yawn and stretch. The flash drive will have to wait until morning. "Can you run me home?"

On the drive home, I get a text message from Billy. "Sexy librarian, I wanna check u out. At your place."

I text back. "On my way. Hope u don't have overdue books. If so, no service."

He then sends me a message, describing in explicit terms, exactly how he intends to pay his fine. Once again, I'm no longer tired.

Chapter Thirty-One

I'm in front of the bathroom mirror, still in my catering clothes. Billy stands behind me, his body pressed against mine. His eyes are intense and focused. I look into his soul. The fire still burns. He slips off my glasses and pushes my blond braid to one side. His lips are warm against my neck. I tilt my head to one side to give him better access and relax into his body. His hands get busy unbuttoning my blouse.

I attempt to focus. "I have a lot to tell you. About what happened tonight."

He nibbles my ear lobe. "Later."

I take a shaky breath. My *no* button seems to be on the fritz. Halfheartedly, I say, "It's really important."

"Mmm hmm."

Since he will not be deterred, I decide to enjoy the moment.

"I guess you like blonds," I murmur. Naturally, my hyperactive mind takes it a step further and I visualize Billy and Officer Candace Talbot naked in bed. *Don't go there, Mel.*

He removes my blouse. "What I really like is this." With deft fingers, he unhooks my bra and cups my breasts in his hands. His thumbs gently stroke my nipples. They grow rigid in his touch. His tongue is hot and moist in my ear. He whispers. "I want you like I've never wanted another woman. It's different with you, baby, and I don't know why. Did you cast a spell on me?"

Even though it's the most romantic thing Billy's ever uttered, his words snap me out of my altered state. My hands close over his, stopping the action. "Look at me, Billy."

He lifts his head and stares at me in the mirror.

"Do you really think I'm capable of casting spells?"

"Aw, come on, Minnie, of course not." He slides his hands downward to circle my waist.

I hold his gaze and see the lie flash across his soul. Hmm. Why is he lying to me? I decide not to make an issue of it. Not now when he's in a critical place with his counseling and, selfishly, my body is really into what he's doing. But, I will not forget.

I don't want to see any more lies, so I close my eyes. He fumbles with the buttons and zipper on my pants and peels them off along with my little pink panties. His breath is hot against my skin. His hands slide over my hips.

I feel his lips against my ear. "Open your eyes and see how beautiful you are."

I look in the mirror. The erotic image slams into me and I gasp at the sight.

One of Billy's hands is stroking my breast. The other is buried between my legs, his thumb stroking the little button of flesh that brings me such pleasure. My head is thrown back against his chest, my eyes are half closed, my lips parted. I arch my back, reach behind me and circle his neck with my arms, completely surrendering to his touch.

"Jesus, Minnie," he pants. "I'm gonna die if I'm

not inside you right now."

He lifts me in his arms and three steps later, I'm on the bed and he's ripping off his jeans. His erection is huge. Once again, I think how awesome nature is; despite the difference in size and plumbing, it all works so damn well.

He eases into me, struggling for control. "Oh God, you're so tight. I can't hold off much longer."

I wrap my legs around his waist and push against him. "It's okay. Go for it."

With a grunt of pleasure, he explodes and collapses beside me. He pulls me close, his big, warm hand stroking my belly. When he catches his breath, he says, "Don't move."

I hear him in the bathroom, running water and then he kneels on the bed beside me. He says, "My turn to make you happy."

He holds a washcloth over my naked body and squeezes. Droplets of warm water splash down on my belly followed by soft, circular strokes with the washcloth. Billy takes his time, making sure every inch of my body receives his attention. By the time he works his way up from my feet, calves and inner thighs, I lose control, thrashing and moaning with need.

The washcloth sails to the floor. He uses his hands to part my legs and I feel his mouth on me, hot and wet and knowing. I stifle a scream and break into a million crystalline pieces of pure pleasure. Just for a moment, my troubles are forgotten and I float away to a special place, where my only reality is pure sensation. I want to stay there, where life is simple and nobody is trying to kill me. But that isn't possible.

Reality sucks.

Billy and I don't spend a lot of time talking that night. I sense he's trying to avoid anything heavy and I'm too tired to form a sentence. Feeling safe wrapped in his arms, I sleep better than I have for a long time.

The scent of coffee wakens me at eight a.m. Billy flips on the lamp and sets a mug of coffee on the bedside table. He sits on the edge of the bed, studying a business card.

"Good morning," I scoot up to a sitting position and reach for the coffee.

"Is this your dad's card?"

"Yes. I took your advice and met with him. Actually, he taught me a lot about soul reading."

"Like what?"

How to tell if someone's lying, like you did last night.

"Oh, just this and that."

"So," he says, casually, "Is it about mind control?"

This surprises me. "My mind or someone else's?"

Is this what he's worried about? That I'll somehow control him?

"Well, both."

"It's about *my* mind, Billy. I've been afraid to look into people's souls, afraid of what I might see. He's helping me get over that fear. That's all."

He leans down and drops a kiss on my forehead. "That's good. Now, what were you trying to tell me last night?"

I use the edited version Kendra and I concocted and fill him in on the pertinent information.

His eyes light up. "So you actually have the flash drive?"

"Yes, but we can't break the password."

"Can I try?"

"Sure. My laptop is on the table. The flash drive is still in my pants pocket, the pants you ripped off me last night."

Billy stands and stares down at me. "Hope I made it worth your time."

"You did."

While I sip my coffee and try to wake up, I think about the strangeness of our relationship. I've never seen where Billy lives. Neither one of us has ever spoken the L word. Do I love him? I know I care about him. He's the first man who has ever given me sexual satisfaction. I like being with him. Is that love? I'm not sure.

Billy tries to break into the flash drive for at least twenty minutes but finally gives up. He turns to face me, straddling the chair. "You should call your father."

"Why?"

"Because of what he does. His business is called CyberSecure. Obviously, he knows about computers."

He walks to the bed and hands me his cell phone and Steve's card. "You want to get into that flash drive? Call him."

Steve answers on the first ring. I give him a sketchy back-story and tell him I *found* a flash drive that might contain pertinent information I need and would he be willing to help?

"Of course, Melanie. I'll be there soon."

I wonder why Billy's still here. "Don't you have counseling or something?"

"Not until eleven. My counselor has a thing at his son's school."

He looks evasive when he says it. I think he's lying

again but he's not meeting my eyes so I can't tell for sure. But, I do wonder if he's blowing off something important.

Twenty minutes later, Steve shows up. Moments later, I hear, *Bam, bam, bam.*

I open the door. Paco looms large. He invites himself in, nods at Billy and glares suspiciously at Steve. "Who's he?"

Paco, in full-out protective mode, can be pretty terrifying.

Panic robs me of my speech as I look back and forth between Paco and Steve. Billy's presence is understandable, but how do I explain my bio father's presence? To the brother of the man who raised me? Beads of perspiration pop out on my forehead. The walls of my tiny room feel like they're shrinking as the testosterone level rises.

Thankfully, Billy comes through behaving like he's known Steve all his life. He does some sort of a complicated gang handshake thing (who knew?) with Paco who responds with a slap on Billy's back that almost takes him to the floor.

Billy gathers himself and says, "Hey, Paco, this Estefan Delgado. He's been helping Mel with some computer stuff. He's a good guy. No worries."

Whew. No mention of the bio dad thing.

Steve thrusts out his right hand. "Call me Steve."

Paco looks Steve over. "Okay. Just so you know, I'm not a hater and I make sure my guys don't beat up gay guys. To each his own, I say. Trust me, I've had a lot of issues with *women*."

What?

"But—but," I sputter. I look over at Billy who

grins and shrugs.

I check out Steve. He looks totally at ease and shakes Paco's hand. I see their lips moving as they exchange pleasantries, but don't ask me what was said. My mind is reeling. *My father is gay? Is that why he left my mother? Is that why his marriage ended in Spain? My God, am I really so clueless? Paco and Billy knew instantly.*

I clear my throat and attempt to speak. "Well, um…"

Paco wraps a meaty arm around my neck. "Judging from the look on your face, I'd say your gaydar is seriously malfunctioning."

Hearty male laughter all around. I sink down on the bed and try to figure out my next move. The presence of three large males in my personal space—not to mention the gay thing—has definitely thrown me off my game.

Steve prompts, "You want me to check out that flash drive, Melanie?"

I snap out of my trance and leap off the bed. "Oh, yeah, of course."

Billy points at my laptop sitting on the table. "Flash drive's already plugged in."

Steve settles in at the table. Paco and Billy hover over him. I squeeze in between them. Steve removes the flash drive from the USB port and examines it. He reaches in his jacket pocket, pulls out a compact disc. He looks up at us. "Do you mind backing off just a bit? What I'm doing may not be one hundred percent legal. *Si?*"

We back off. Paco drags me into the bathroom and whispers, "Who is this guy? He looks familiar."

I whisper back, "Long story. Tell you later."

Paco looks grumpy, but agrees.

"What's the story with Roxy?"

"Put her on the bus last night. Gave her money too."

We exchange a high five and I fill him in on what I learned last night. His eyes narrow ominously, but he waits until I'm done before he says, "I won't ask how you learned all that stuff and got the flash drive. Best I don't know."

"Any luck catching up with Myron?"

"No luck so far. Nick says he's in Portland, working his other job. He'll be back tomorrow. I'll check him out then."

"*Got it.*" Steve cries and we crowd around the table.

"Looks like a spread sheet," Billy says.

Column One: Names. *Column Two:* Date of purchase. *Column Three*: Amount of purchase in amounts ranging from $30,000 to $50,000.

I recognize the names at the bottom of the page. Michael and Pamela Kruger.

Chapter Thirty-Two

Steve looks up at me. "Is this list significant to you, Melanie?"

Billy and I exchange a glance. After breaking into their hotel room, Billy recognizes the Krugers' name, too. I don't have to be a mind reader to know what he's thinking and—it's exactly what I'm thinking. We're looking at a list of people who purchased babies from Rockwell, Breen and friends.

Paco peers at the list. "Well, damn," he mutters. "Is that what I think it is?"

Steve's leaning back in the chair, arms folded across his chest. He's listening but taking care to act disinterested. He doesn't know the back-story and I'm not willing to share it with him. At least, for now.

So, I give a noncommittal shrug. "Looks like it. No contact information, though. That makes it tough."

Steve looks around the room. "Do you have a printer?"

"No."

His fingers move rapidly over the keys. "I just emailed the list to myself. I'll print off a copy and bring it to you. Do you need phone numbers as well?"

I brighten at his words. "Can you get them?"

"Yes."

He stands. "Is there anything else?"

I like the fact he's not pumping me for information.

He showed up. He did his job. Now he's leaving. Just the way I like it.

"No. Thanks. You've been a big help."

He's on his way to the door when Aida's immigration issues surface in my mind.

"Wait." I close the gap between us. "I do have a question for you."

He stops and turns to face me. "Yes?"

"I have a friend who's in trouble. She was brought to this country illegally and is trapped in a very bad situation. I want to help her, but I'm afraid it will make things worse. If I go to the authorities, will they send her back home?"

Steve says, "They will place her in a detention center until they figure out her situation. But, yes, they will probably send her home."

I shake my head sadly, "That's what I thought."

Steve takes a step closer to me and gazes into my eyes. "Is she a good person?"

I know he's asking about Aida's soul. "Yes, she's a very good person. And, she's also pregnant."

He touches my arm. "Then, you must help her, Melanie." He leans close and whispers, "If they can't find her, they can't lock her up."

Light bulb moment. "What a great idea," I murmur, grinning at him.

He nods. "I'll be back soon with your list."

Before lumbering out the door, Paco pats the top of my head. "I'm right next door if you need me. Just pound on the wall."

"Pound on the wall?" I repeat.

"Yeah," he says. "I rented Number Eleven. Indefinitely."

I feel my mouth drop open in surprise. I look over at Billy who winks and inclines his head toward the bed. I get the picture. Number Eleven is the mirror image of Number Ten, which means Paco's headboard and mine are just inches apart. Heat rises in my cheeks. I manage to mutter, "Okay, Unc, thanks."

"And, don't forget to fill me in on this Steve guy."

Just as the door closes behind Paco, my phone chirps. I pounce on it, hoping it's Aida. It's Kendra and she's pissed off. "Is Billy with you?"

"Yes. Why?"

"He blew off this morning's session. The Vet Center's been trying to call him but it goes straight to voice mail. That's why they called me."

I hand my phone to Billy without saying a word.

"Yeah," he growls into the phone.

I hear Kendra's voice, shrill with emotion, but can't make out her words.

"Yeah, yeah," Billy says. "No biggie. I'll take care of it."

Another outburst from Kendra follows.

"*I said*, I'll take care of it. Jesus, Kendra, give me a break."

He listens a moment longer, then turns his back to me and lowers his voice. I hear him say, "I'm sorry, too."

He clicks off, sets my phone on the table and strides by me. "Gotta go."

"Why did you lie to me?"

He flushes and bristles up. His eyes are bright with anger. "Don't *you* start. I already took a load of crap from Kendra."

"Hey," I yell as he dashes through the door. "I'm

not the problem here. You are."

He climbs on his bike, punches it and peels out without looking back.

Paco emerges from Number Eleven, helmet in his hand. "Remember what I told you, little girl. Heebie jeebies. He's still got 'em."

I go back into my room, fighting tears. My first real relationship is turning into a shit storm of gigantic proportions. I feel like I'm starring in a daytime drama. Will Billy come to his senses? Can Melanie overlook Billy's lies? Will Billy get over his heebie jeebies? Tune in tomorrow.

I hear the purr of Paco's Harley as I fire up my computer and Google PTSD, something I should have done ages ago. Symptoms of Post Traumatic Stress Disorder could just as easily been labeled: Personality Profile of Billy the Kid. Trouble sleeping—check. Angry outbursts—check. Aggressive behavior—check. Easily startled—check. Distancing himself from loved ones—oh, yeah. The article goes on to say it's important for the person suffering from PTSD to have support from people close to him. How can I support Billy if he pushes me away?

I shut down my computer and try to figure out what to do next. I need to talk to Kendra but decide to wait until she cools off. I need the list of names from Steve, but will have to wait for them, too. Since I'm in limbo, I opt for a mindless chore and scrub the bathroom until the chrome fixtures shine and the toilet is gurgling with happiness.

Fifteen minutes later, Aida calls. Her voice is hushed. I hear Destiny babbling in the background. "Mel?"

"I'm here, Aida. What's happening?"

"Missus tell me I need to see doctor man. Make sure baby is okay."

"Is this your first check-up?"

"Yes."

I remember Aida telling me she was due in August which would make her about seven months pregnant. And this is her first check-up? The cynic in me believes the concern is not for Aida but for the infant they can sell for big bucks. After Larissa's problem, the Rockwells are suddenly concerned about Aida's ability to deliver a healthy baby. I say none of this, of course.

"Is the doctor coming to the house, or are you going to the clinic?"

"I go to clinic. They use machine to tell me boy or girl."

No doubt the Rockwells need the information for marketing purposes.

"When is your appointment?"

"Missus say we go early Monday morning. Eight o'clock."

"What about Destiny? Will she be with you?"

"Yes, baby will be with us."

"Will the clinic be open at eight?"

"Maybe. I don't know."

"Okay," I tell her. "I'll be in the clinic if it's open. Otherwise, I'll be outside, watching for you."

"So," Aida says, "If I see you, will you look like Mel or blond lady?"

I think about it. "I'll look like Mel. Don't worry. Nina Rockwell knows we've met. There are a lot of reasons I could be at the clinic. I want to make sure I see you walk out of there."

Aida gasps. "What you mean?"

"It's not safe for you at the Rockwells. You need to get out of their house before your baby is due. I'll find a safe place for you."

"But I can't, Mel. What about baby Addison? Who would take care of her? The Missus is terrible mother. I can't leave baby."

This had all started with Dani and Destiny. Now, it included Aida and her unborn child, among others. If this thing goes down the way I hope it will, Destiny would no longer be with the Rockwells. Whatever it takes, I'll make sure Destiny is in a good place.

"Yes," I say. "You can. Missus will find a new nanny. If you want to save your own baby, think about what I said."

I hear the hitch in her breath and know she's crying. "But, it's my job, Mel. I must take care of baby."

Frustrated, I tell her I'll see her Monday and hit the off button. I search for Jared Breen's card and find it crumpled up in the pocket of my black pants. I listen to all the options and press two for an appointment. When I tell the scheduler what I want—I have no intention of letting Dr. Feel Good peer into my private parts—she's says, "Oh, certainly. If you're interested in donating eggs, all you have to do is drop by and fill out some paper work. If Doctor wants to see you, we'll call."

Before I call Kendra, she calls me. No small talk. She snaps, "What did Billy tell you this morning. About why he wasn't at the vet center?"

I overlook her attitude because I know she's worried sick. "He said his counselor wouldn't be in until later."

She blows an enormous sigh. "Damn it. I can't believe he's already skipping out on his sessions."

"And lying about it," I added.

A long silence follows. I sense Kendra's trying to calm down. Finally, she says, "I guess we should cut him some slack. His counselor says it's fairly normal for people with PTSD to do the avoidance thing at first because they're afraid to face the emotional pain. How did he seem to you?"

"Okay, until I asked why he lied to me. Then, he blew up. Bad scene."

I hear her sniff and wonder if she's crying. "Look, it doesn't matter how much *we* want him to succeed, it's entirely up to him. He'll either get it together or he won't. We both need to back off and stop getting pissed at him. He's acting obnoxious because he's scared to death."

Kendra manages a chuckle. "Sounds like one of my kids."

"So, let's try to chill out and let him do it his way."

She sighs again. "Okay, I'll try."

I tell her about my father breaking into the flash drive and what we found. "He should be here soon with the list and phone numbers. I'll figure out a cover story and start calling."

"Keep me posted."

Excitement bubbles up inside me. "This could be a breakthrough, Kendra, the proof we need to take to the FBI or Homeland Security. They'll know what to do. But first, we need to get Aida out of that house and stashed someplace the Rockwells or the feds can't find her. If I go to the authorities, Aida will be put into a detention center and probably sent back to Kazakhstan.

She says she can't go back home. It would bring shame to her family. Is your extra room still available?"

"Yes, but what about Destiny?"

"Aida will have to leave her, but hopefully the Rockwells will be busted and then we can figure out what's best for Destiny."

Kendra sounds dubious. "I hope you're right."

"Me too."

Chapter Thirty-Three

An hour later, with the list clutched in my hand, I begin calling the phone numbers Steve provided. The first three calls go directly to voice mail.

Undeterred, I punch in the fourth. Gregory and Marcia Haywood of Lake Oswego, Oregon. A woman answers on the second ring. My mouth goes dry. *Don't blow this, Mel.*

"Is this Marcia Haywood?"

"Yes," comes the hesitant reply.

"My name is Desiree Wishkoski and I'm calling from the 3 Peaks, Oregon Fertility Clinic. Dr. Breen asked me to check up on you and your new baby. Little…"

I shuffle papers together as if I'm searching for the baby's name.

"Brady," she offers. "He's not exactly new anymore. Six months old yesterday."

"How is Brady doing? Any problems?"

"No, except for the sleep thing, but that's to be expected. He's doing better lately."

"Anything you'd like me to report to Dr. Breen?"

She says, "Yes. Tell him we might want another baby in a couple of years. Brady needs a little brother or sister."

"I'll certainly let him know."

"We'll have to save up first. Forty thousand dollars

is a lot of money. We didn't realize it was so expensive to adopt. Don't get me wrong, though. He's totally worth it."

My finger is poised over the *off* button. "Thank you, Mrs. Hayworth. Hugs to little Brady."

Before I can click off, she says, "Hold on. Are you calling everybody who adopted from Dr. Breen? Or just us?"

I scramble for a logical answer. "Oh, I should have told you earlier. We like to check when the baby is six months old to, you know, make sure everything is okay."

"Oh? Seems like a long time to wait." She sounds dubious.

Sweat pops out on my brow. "Doctor feels you would have let him know if there were issues early on."

"But, we signed the form."

Oops, now what? I shuffle papers some more. "Forgive me, but we have so many forms. Which one are you referring to?"

"The one about Dr. Breen not being responsible for after care. Before we took the baby, we had to provide the name of our pediatrician."

"Oh, *that* one," I babble. "Yes, it's true. Doctor is not a pediatrician. But recently, he decided it would be a good idea to do some follow-up on the babies. It's a brand new program. So, to answer your question, you're not the only one receiving this call. Thank you *so much,* Mrs. Haywood. And, continued good luck with Brady. Bye, now."

My hands are shaking when I set my cell phone on the table. I'd bungled the call. No doubt about it. At this very moment, Marcia Haywood is probably calling the clinic to ask about the legitimacy of Desiree with the weird last name.

Because of my blunder, I decide not to make any more phony calls. I'm in over my head and I know it. It's time to turn the list over to someone with the ability and manpower to investigate and hopefully shut down the Rockwells and Company. But then, there's Aida. I have to get her in a safe place before I go to the authorities. Feeling helpless, I pace back and forth across my tiny home. Eight steps from the door to the wall. About face. Eight steps back.

The frustration boiling inside me is tempered with sadness for the adoptive couples, the unknowing victims of such a heartless scheme, all in the name of greed. What will happen to their babies? Once again, I wonder if I'm doing the right thing. But I can't turn back now. Not with Aida due to give birth soon and Destiny in the cold clutches of Nina Rockwell.

I hear the rumble of Paco's bike and fling the door open and wave him inside. Before I can fill him in, he says, "Yesterday, I got Myron's address from Nick. Told him we were going to hang out. So, I've been checking his place. He got home this morning. He offloaded his stuff and got back in his car. I followed him. He pulled into a strip mall out on the highway where there's a Laundromat facing the street and a self-service car wash out back. No attendant in either one. Both open twenty-four hours. Just put money in and do your thing. Myron used a key to unlock the meters and took the cash out of both places. Then, I followed him to three different banks."

I have a sudden visual of my enormous uncle clomping around, spying on Myron. "You sure he didn't see you?"

Paco glares. "You think I don't know how to tail somebody?"

"Sorry, sorry. Just asking."

"So," he continues, "looks like Myron's got a couple of businesses that deal in cash and don't require employees. What does that tell you?"

I shrug and lift my hands.

"It's not just clothes and cars getting washed in those establishments."

I still don't get it. "Like what?"

"Money laundering," he says. "If he's the one who trashed your room—and I think he is—he's connected to the baby-selling people. If they are pimping the girls out after they give birth, there's cash money coming in, too. You have to be careful to spread the money out and filter it through a legit business. If you deposit ten thousand or more into your bank account, a report goes to the feds."

I don't ask how he knows this.

My head is swimming with information overload, so I tell him about my screwed up call to Marcia Haywood. He frowns, but says, "It's probably not as bad as you think. She'll get involved with her kid and forget all about it. Look at it this way, Mel. We now know for sure what's going down. The pieces are starting to come together. Probably wouldn't have happened without the flash drive."

I know he's trying to make me feel better, but I can't shake the feeling I've set something in motion that will come back to bite me in the butt.

Connie's cleaning cart rattles by and Paco perks up. "See you tonight," he says and charges through the door like a lion pursuing a three-legged wildebeest. I lock the door, flop face-down on the bed and try to turn my brain off. Apparently it works because I don't wake up until it's time to go to work.

Eddie's Russian friend, Mick shows up at seven thirty. He takes a small booth in my section. I offer him a menu. "Eating or drinking?"

He takes the menu and nails me with his intense gaze. "Both."

I look away, trying not to get sucked in. "Want your vodka now?"

"Yes. Grey Goose. But you already know that, Annabelle from Fargo."

My heart leaps in my chest and I stammer, "Wha-what did you call me?"

"You heard me. By the way, blond hair doesn't suit you."

"I have no idea what you're talking about." I whirl away and head for the bar to place his order. *Don't panic, Mel.*

Nick looks me over. "You okay? You're looking a little pale."

I remember what Nick told me about my reluctance in asking for help. Maybe now is the time. "Don't look now, but there's a guy sitting by himself in a booth. Blond hair. He's a little scary. Just keep an eye out. Okay?"

Nick pours the vodka over ice. "Want me to ask him to leave?"

I wave a hand. "No, no, just be aware."

"Did he threaten you?"

I definitely feel threatened, but the back-story is convoluted. Nick knows I worked a private party at the

Rockwells. He does not know I was in disguise. "Not really," I say. "He was at the Rockwell party. He's probably just hitting on me and doesn't realize he's coming on too strong."

Nick nods. "Too bad Billy's not around."

I grab the drink and deliver it to Mick. Without meeting his gaze, I pull out my order pad and pencil. "What would you like to eat?"

"Look at me, Mel."

Reluctantly, I look into his eyes. His soul is still unblemished. This confuses me. How can he hang out with Eddie and not have the telltale signs of evil stamped on his soul? I make a mental note to look for an answer in the notebook given to me by my father.

I snap, "Are you ready to order or not? I have other customers to wait on."

He smiles and a dimple appears in his left cheek. "Sassy," he says. "I'll have the meatloaf special with mashed potatoes."

I write down his order and turn to leave. His hand closes around my wrist. "Take care, Mel. Sometimes it's wise not to be too curious about things you can do nothing about."

I jerk free. "Being wise is not my strong suit."

"What is your strong suit?"

I lean close and stare into his eyes. "Helping people who can't help themselves."

Nick appears in my peripheral vision. "Everything all right here?"

I step away from the table. "Yes, I was just clarifying this gentleman's order."

As I walk away, I hear Nick say, "You're welcome to stay, but please, keep your hands off my waitress."

Truth-O-Meter time. I walk into the kitchen to deliver Mick's order. Myron looks up as I enter.

"Hey, Myron," I say. "You know that guy?" I point through the serving window toward Mick's booth.

Myron steps to the window. "Which guy?"

"He's sitting by himself. Blond hair."

Myron glances at Mick. His hooded gaze swings over to me. "Nah. I don't know him. Why?"

I stare into Myron' grimy soul and know he's lying. I shrug. "Just wondering."

Another dot connected.

Ten minutes later, Paco bangs through the door. He stops by the bar. I see Nick's head tilt toward Mick who is devouring his meatloaf, one arm wrapped around his plate as if protecting it from hungry hordes. I deliver a loaded tray to the Corral and see Paco standing over Mick, one giant hand gripping his shoulder. He points at me and leans close. I see Paco's lips moving and Mick nodding. He finishes his meat loaf, leaves me a $10 tip and exits the restaurant without looking back. With any luck, I won't be seeing Mick again.

Chapter Thirty-Four

It's seven-thirty a.m. Monday. Paco and I are sitting in a coffee shop across from Breen's clinic. Paco glances at his watch. "You said eight o'clock. Right?"

"Right."

"Here's what I'm thinking. This is a fertility clinic, not an obstetrician's office. A knocked up woman sitting in the waiting area would stick out like a hippo in a chicken coop. Know what I mean?"

He doesn't wait for an answer. "That's why I drove down the alley behind the clinic, to see if there's a back door. There is, so I'll bet that's the entrance they'll use."

"But we can't see it from here."

He rises. "You stay here 'til it's time for your appointment. I'll keep an eye on the back door. Got your cell phone?"

I nod.

"I'll call you if and when I see them. You do the same."

He chugs the rest of his coffee, pats the top of my head and leaves.

I finish my coffee and try to wake up. The last few days have been a blur. I'm sleep-deprived (thank you, Billy) and probably not at my best. I fight the urge to seek out a comfy chair and curl up for a nap.

At seven fifty, Paco calls. "A blond with a bun in

245

the oven and skinny black-haired woman just entered the clinic through the back door. The blond is lugging a kid. I'm guessing this is your girl."

"I'm guessing you're right." I stand and stretch. "Heading for the clinic now."

"I'll be around. If you need me, call."

When I arrive at the front door of the clinic, it's unlocked. I head for the receptionist and tell her my name.

She hands me a clipboard loaded with forms and lowers her voice although we're the only two in the room. "You're here about egg harvesting. Correct?"

The word *harvesting* startles me. A vivid image of Jared Breen pops up in my overactive brain like a bad movie. Clad in farmer overalls and ball cap, he's aboard a tractor and chasing me through a wheat field yelling, "Gimme your eggs."

"Um, yeah."

"No need to be embarrassed, dear. Lots of young ladies sell their eggs."

I nod my thanks and perch on a hardback chair; thumbing through the questionnaire I have no intention of actually filling out. My hand is poised over the first line (name) when I hear a baby howling in rage. It's faint at first, but growing louder. The clacking of high heels and the sound of a man's soothing voice follows. A door opens and Nina Rockwell appears with Destiny squirming in her arms. Jared Breen is a step behind her.

He points at a leather couch. "Have a seat, Nina. This won't take long."

Nina's face is tight with stress as she totters to the couch with Destiny. She makes a half-assed attempt to comfort the screaming baby, pounding on her back a little harder than necessary. Her hand is tipped with dagger-like scarlet nails. Still screeching, Destiny arches her back, churns her chubby legs and pushes away from Nina, all the while looking over her shoulder for Aida. Something akin to a feral expression flashes across Nina's face.

It scares me. I jump out of my chair. "Mrs. Rockwell? Can I help with the baby?"

She rakes me with a frosty glance. "Do I know you?"

"Yes. We met at Dani's funeral. I'm Aida's friend."

No pause to think it over. She shoves Destiny into my waiting arms. "Good luck. She's fussy today. "

"No problem." I hold Destiny next to my body and sway back and forth. When her sobs subside, I lift her up until we're eye to eye. "How are you, beautiful baby girl?"

Destiny studies my face and pops her thumb into her mouth. Her big blue eyes brim with tears. She looks so much like Dani I have to bite my lower lip to keep it from quivering.

I glance down at Nina who is using a tissue to dab at the baby slobber on her silk blouse. "Where's Aida today?"

"She'll be here shortly. Dr. Breen is giving her a prenatal check-up."

"Is Dr. Breen an obstetrician as well as a fertility doctor?"

She gives me a dismissive glance. "The check-up is a special favor to us. He's a friend of the family."

I'll bet he is. "Is she having a boy or girl?"

"They're doing an ultrasound right now."

Our conversation dies a natural death. I pace the floor with Destiny who's exhausted from her heavy-duty screaming fit. Her eyelids droop as she fights to stay awake. She finally gives in and drifts into a light slumber. Even though every fiber of my being resists, I sit on the couch next to Nina Rockwell who is skimming through a copy of Vogue.

She glances at me. "She asleep?"

I nod, waiting for her to say, "Thank you."

She doesn't. But she does say, "You trying to get pregnant?"

"No. I'm considering donating eggs. I need the money."

Her brows furrow like she's unable to grasp the concept of someone needing money, mouth opening and closing as she searches for an appropriate response.

Fifteen minutes later, a door opens and Dr. Breen steps through. "Nina? She's all done. I'll walk you out."

She springs from the couch and snatches up her Coach purse and designer diaper bag. Apparently she forgets she has a child, because she strides across the waiting room. I hurry along behind her, Destiny in my arms. Believe me, I *so* want to dash out the door and take the baby home with me. I want it so bad, I'm shaking.

When she gets to the door, Nina realizes she's missing something. She slams to a halt and turns to face me. "I'll take her now."

"It's okay," I say, ducking my chin in a timid manner. "Do you mind if I say hi to Aida?"

She looks at the baby sleeping in my arms. "I suppose."

For the first time, Jared Breen's gaze travels over

me. "And you are?"

The receptionist hears him, motions him to come closer and whispers the purpose of my visit.

Breen flashes a big toothy smile. "Excellent."

I follow Breen and Nina down a hall with six closed doors, presumably examination rooms. Is this where the Russian girls get impregnated while sedated? The door to one of the rooms opens and a woman walks out pushing an ultrasound machine. An antiseptic odor drifts from the room. Lysol and bleach overlaid with a room freshener smelling of rose petals. A chill crawls over my skin. No way do I ever want to be inside of one of those rooms.

We round a corner and find Aida waiting by the rear entrance door. When she sees me, her eyes widen in surprise. "Mel?"

"Hi, girlfriend," I chirp, handing over the baby. "I ran into Mrs. Rockwell in the waiting room and helped her with Addison."

Destiny stirs during the hand-off. Her eyes flutter open. She looks up at Aida, smiles and snuggles into her chest. I have to turn my face away so Breen and Rockwell don't see my tears.

I swipe at my eyes and put on a happy face. "Did you find out if your baby is a boy or girl?"

Aida drops a kiss on Destiny's head and places her right hand on her belly. "Doctor say I will have beautiful little girl." Her luminous eyes cloud with grief. "Her name will be Larissa."

Nina Rockwell is growing impatient. "Time to go, Aida. Thank you, Jason. We'll be in touch."

As they exit the clinic, I scamper back to the waiting room, not wanting to spend a single moment alone with Jared Breen. Now that Aida's safe, I tell the receptionist I will take the paper work with me and return it later…not.

She says, "Dr. Breen would like to see you before you leave."

All I can think about is the creepy examination rooms. "I'm kind of pressed for time."

"It won't take long. He's in his office." She points toward the hall. "First door on the left."

Curiosity trumps my desire to dash from the clinic. I rap on the closed door and hear, "Come in. Please."

I leave the door ajar when I enter. Dr. Breen pops up from behind his desk and waves me into a chair. "My receptionist tells me you're a possible egg donor." He pauses and flashes a brief, insincere smile. "I see you have our questionnaire.

"I'm thinking about it. I'll take the forms with me and look them over."

"I sense you're somewhat ambivalent. Perhaps, I can answer your questions."

I struggle to come up with a question, since, truly, *donating eggs* does not appear on my to do list. I blurt, "Does it hurt?"

Breen chuckles. "Normally, the first question is, 'How much will you pay me for my eggs?'"

I manage to smile back at him. "I guess I'm more concerned about pain. I'm not good with pain."

He rubs his hands together. "I respect that and I'll try to be as honest as possible. The procedure can be somewhat painful. In order to harvest the eggs, I have to insert a needle through the wall of the vagina into an ovary. However, I do everything possible to make the donor as comfortable as possible. And, the financial compensation is extremely generous."

I suppress a shudder. "Anything else I should know?"

"Yes," he says. "It's not a one-time shot or an instant procedure. It involves a four-week drug treatment program designed to stop your menstrual cycle. This keeps all your eggs in the ovaries. Also, you'll have to abstain from alcohol, recreational drugs and sexual intercourse."

He pauses to let his words sink in and waits for my response. When I don't have one, he adds, "Actually, I have some time right now. I could take a little peek and see if you're a good candidate."

No way is he going to take a peek, little or big. I spring from my chair. "Thanks, Doctor Breen, but let's wait until after I return the questionnaire."

"Sure, sure, no problem, my dear."

I'm at the door when he says, "If I'm not mistaken, you're Billy the Kid's girlfriend."

I turn to face him. "How do you know that?"

"You're a waitress at Nick's Place. Right?"

I nod. "I've never seen you at Nick's."

He winks at me. "Oh, word gets around. You know how it is."

I can't wait to get the hell out of this place, so I ignore the fact he answered my question with questions of his own. As I slip through the door, he says, "Hope to see you soon."

I fervently hope *not.*

When I get home, I know exactly what I have to do.

Chapter Thirty-Five

Kendra answers on the first ring. When she answers, I skip the small talk and go straight to the heart of the matter, "We have to kidnap Aida."

After a brief shocked silence, she says, "Are you crazy? Kidnapping is a federal offense. I have a husband and children. I know orange is the new black but I *cannot* end up in prison. You're on your own, girlie."

I need Kendra for this caper. Tact has never been one of my strong suits. Maybe I shouldn't have been so blunt. "Just listen. Okay?"

She says, "Mmm hmmm."

"Aida had an ultra sound today. Her baby is a little girl. She plans to name the baby Larissa after her dead sister. But, guess what? If we don't get Aida out of the Rockwell house, her baby will be taken away from her and named Emma or Sophia or Kaitlin. And the last name will likely by Johnson or Smith, not Doroshenko. And, Aida will be an unhappy hooker in Portland. Do you feel me?"

After a long silence, Kendra sighs. "Yeah, I feel you. What's the plan?"

"The problem is, Aida refuses to leave Destiny. Obviously, we can't kidnap Destiny, so we have to lure Aida out of the house and get her into your car. Preferably, in the middle of the night when everybody's sleeping. The next morning when she's safely stashed at your house, I go to the authorities, give them the flash drive and narc out the Rockwells. I'll tell them about Dani and Destiny and that Destiny may not be safe. Hopefully, they will act quickly."

"And if they don't act quickly? What about Destiny?"

"Trust me, Nina Rockwell will find a new nanny immediately. She likes the idea of having a child but wants nothing to do with the mothering part."

I think about Destiny's sweet face and innocent blue eyes and my tears start to flow again, robbing me of speech. *I'm so sorry, baby. I'm so sorry, Dani. Please trust me. Remember, we're Danimal! It will be okay.* I send my thoughts into the stratosphere, hoping they will be delivered.

"Are you crying?" Kendra says. Her tone is incredulous.

"Yes, Sherlock, I'm crying." I draw a hiccupping breath. "I hate the thought of leaving Destiny in that house. I held her in my arms today. I looked into her eyes and saw Dani. You have no idea how hard it was to give her back. I wanted to run out the door and bring her home with me. I wanted it so bad I could taste it."

My voice is choked with tears. I take a shaky breath and try to speak again. "We have to be smart, Kendra. We have to get Aida out and then we'll get Destiny away from the Rockwells. Believe me, I know she's not safe and it breaks my heart to leave her there. I saw something awful in Nina Rockwell's soul today and it scares the hell out of me. I don't know what else to do. If you can think of a better way, let me know."

By the time I finish, I'm in full-out meltdown

mode, barely able to string two words together.

I hear Kendra snuffle and know she's crying with me. When she speaks, her voice quivers. "It's okay, Mel. Count me in. We'll do it together."

She promises to pick me up in an hour and clicks off. I'm in the bathroom splashing cold water on my face when I hear a tentative rap on the door. I grab a towel and trot to the window where I part the drapes and peer out. Steve is standing in front of Number Ten.

Flustered, I open the door and babble, "Oh, hi. So you're still in 3 Peaks."

Obviously, Mel, since he's standing right in front of you.

"Do you mind if I come in? There's something I want to talk to you about."

I fling the door open and step back. "Sorry. Sure, come on in."

I wave him into a chair. "Is something wrong?"

He studies my face for a long moment. "Yes, I think something's wrong. I'm concerned about what's going on in your life. I sense you are involved in a troublesome situation. If you can get past your trust issues, I'm here to offer my assistance."

I perch on the end of the bed. "What makes you think I need help?"

"Let's just say the soul doesn't lie."

"What did my soul tell you?"

"Remember when I called you the girl with the rainbow in her soul?"

"Is the rainbow gone?"

"When last I looked, it is still present, but the colors are dimmer and now bleed into each other. This indicates you are under extreme stress. Also, I saw your reaction to the information on the flash drive. It's not hard to deduce you're dealing with an important, possibly dangerous, situation."

Decision time. His offer of help seems sincere. The least I can do is hear what he has to say. Still, I proceed with caution.

"What kind of help are you offering?"

"I'm concerned about your friend who has been brought to this country illegally. I assume her status is being used against her, to keep her from speaking out. Am I correct so far?"

"Yes."

"I have been in and out of the U.S. many times. I'm well acquainted with the immigration laws. I believe I can help your pregnant friend."

His offer is hard to refuse. "How, exactly, would you help her?"

"First, I need more information about her situation. How was she brought here? Who is the father of the baby? Is he still involved with her?"

There's no way I can tell him about Aida's situation without going into the baby-selling thing. Before I launch into the story, I pull out the Gideon Bible present in every motel room.

"Put your hand on the Bible and promise you won't reveal what I'm about to tell you—to anyone unless I tell you it's okay."

He suppresses a smile but complies. When I tuck the Bible back into the nightstand, Steve says, "You do realize if I was truly a bad guy, it would not bother me to lie."

I grin at him. "You think I didn't look into your soul to see if you were lying?"

He nods. "Excellent, Melanie. You're a quick study."

I fill him in on what I've learned so far. "The other day, you said if immigration can't find her, they wouldn't be able to detain her. It made me realize I need to get Aida to a safe place before I go to the authorities. I'm working on a plan right now."

I don't mention the plan involves a kidnapping.

He gives me a sharp glance. "Do you need help with your plan?"

I avert my eyes. "Not right now. But, thanks."

Steve stands. "I can see trust issues are still troubling you. Sometimes life requires a leap of faith, Melanie. I must go now. Please keep me informed of your progress and let me know how I can help."

He starts for the door. Somehow, I can't let him go.

"Wait. Do you want to know what I see in your soul?"

He smiles and again, I notice our marked resemblance. "Yes, I would appreciate it."

We sit across the table from each other. I stare into his eyes and see light reflecting off a sparkling body of water. But, hold on. The amorphous dark blob I'd seen before, flitting to and fro, is in a fixed position. Its darkness casts a long, narrow shadow over the water.

I drop my gaze, rub my eyes and take another look. It looks the same.

"What do you see?"

I describe the contents of his soul as clearly as possible.

"This dark shape you see," he begins. "Does it extend completely across the water?"

I take another look. "No. Not quite."

"Did you see it when we met at the coffee shop?"

"Yes, but it looked different. It was moving around."

"And now it's in a fixed position?"

"Yes."

He smiles. "Good, it means I am making the right decision."

"About what?"

"The direction of my life."

"So the black blobby thing is…"

"A problem I've been dealing with for years."

I finally connect the dots. *You're an idiot, Mel.* I struggle to find the right words. "You're talking about your, um…"

"Sexual preference," he finishes.

I avert my eyes. My cheeks grow hot. After all, he *is* my dad. "Yeah, that."

I struggle to find the right words. "Have you seen the dark shape in other people's souls?"

"Yes, in the souls of people who are struggling with a life-changing decision. Once the dark shape stays in a fixed position, it indicates the decision has been made."

"So, it's a good thing."

He rises and pats my cheek. Before he slips through the door, he says, "Yes, *mi hija,* it is a very good thing. I'll be in touch."

****

Kendra and I sit on a park bench while little Aaron plays in the sand box. He uses a plastic shovel to load sand in the back of his toy dump truck, pushes it a few feet, dumps it out and starts over again. This is accompanied by Aaron's special mantra: *beep beep*

beep screech ruuuump-pa-dump. The baby, parked in his stroller next to the sandbox, claps his chubby hands and squeals with delight each time Aaron dumps the load.

Kendra looks pale but determined. "Okay, what's the plan?"

"First, we have to get her out of the house. Aida doesn't want to leave Destiny, so we'll have to come up with something so compelling, so downright captivating, she won't be able to resist. And, it has to be in the middle of the night when the Rockwells are sleeping. That way, the baby won't be alone in the house."

"Sounds risky. They probably have an alarm system."

"I'm sure they do. I'll check and see if Aida knows the code."

"So, what's so compelling it will make Aida sneak out of Rockwell's house in the middle of the night?"

"I'm considering my options."

She rolls her eyes. "In other words, you don't have a clue."

"I'll come up with something."

Kendra stays quiet for a while. Finally, she asks, "Have you talked to Billy?"

"Not since he stormed out of my place in a snit."

"I don't think he should get involved in this. If something goes wrong, it might screw up his job opportunities."

"I agree. That's why we need Uncle Paco."

Kendra smiles. "Now things are getting interesting."

Chapter Thirty-Six

It's two forty in the a.m. and we're parked in the darkest place we can find adjacent to the Rockwell house. Kendra's behind the wheel of her minivan. I'm riding shotgun. Paco is directly behind us, his breath warm on our necks.

He says, "Remember, private security comes around every thirty minutes, on the top of the hour and thirty minutes later. Just like clockwork. I checked last night. If they see us parked here, they'll be on us like white on rice."

I glance at the clock again. "That gives us twenty minutes if Aida shows up on time."

Kendra shoots me a quick glance. "If."

"She'll be here. Maybe on time. Maybe not. If Destiny's fussy or the Rockwells are up for some reason, she'll have to wait. I told her to try and keep Destiny awake longer than usual so she's sleeping soundly when Aida leaves."

Kendra says, "Are you serious?"

She doesn't wait for an answer. "You don't know jack about babies, Mel. If they're tired, they sleep. Good luck trying to keep them awake."

I mutter, "It's worth a try."

Paco reaches over the seat back and massages my shoulders. "You're tight as a tick. Try to relax. We'll get her outta that house one way or another."

"Okay," Kendra says. "What *exactly* did you tell Aida that is so compelling, she'll come trotting out of Rockwell's house and jump into my car."

I'm getting a little ticked off. "Hey, I told you if you had a good idea, speak up."

Paco squeezes the back of my neck, hard enough to get my attention. When he speaks, it sounds like he's talking to a couple of two-year-olds. "Now, ladies. Let's not get hostile. Mel, I believe you should answer Kendra's question."

I take a big breath and begin. "I figured the only way to get Aida out of Rockwell's house was to tell her I had information about Larissa's baby."

I pause and glance over at Kendra. Her eyes are narrow with suspicion.

"So," I continue. "That's what I told her. I said I'd tell her where the baby is."

"Does she think you're taking her to the baby?"

"I may have given her that impression."

"Oh, she'll really like that. Especially when she finds out the kid is in San Francisco."

I say. "Once we get her into the car, hit the gas. She'll have no choice but to go with us."

Kendra shoots me a look. "That's your plan? Lie to the poor girl, get her into the car and then, speed away."

"Yep."

"What happens after that?"

"We take her to your house where you calm her down. Tell her you need her to help take care of the baby. Whatever. And, I'll explain about going to the authorities in the morning, so they can arrest the Rockwells and get Destiny."

"Oh, sweet Jesus," Kendra moans. "We're

doomed."

Paco comes to my rescue. "It could work. A lot of it depends on you, Kendra. Mel said this chick, Aida, is nuts about babies. So, she'll be going through baby withdrawal when she doesn't have Destiny. You've got a kid, right?"

I can tell Kendra is listening to Paco whereas; she was blowing me off. So I keep my lip zipped.

"Yes, I've got a couple of them."

"And one of them is a rug rat?"

"Six months old."

"Perfect," Paco declares. "Like Mel says, tell her you need help, big time. Without it, you might just have to go to the booby hatch and your hubby won't be able to cope without you."

Kendra thinks it over. "Yeah, I guess that might work."

While Paco is mesmerizing Kendra, I dash off a text to Aida. *R U coming?*

The answer comes quickly. *Baby fussy.*

I text back. *We'll wait.*

A few minutes before the hour, Paco says, "Better move the car."

I reach for the door handle. "I'm staying here in case she comes out and the car's gone." Before Paco can grab me, I slip out the door and scoot behind the trunk of a massive pine tree bordering the Rockwell property. I hear the car window zip down and Paco's hoarse whisper, "Damn it, Mel. Get your butt back in here."

"No way," I hiss. "I see headlights coming. Get going."

Kendra punches the accelerator before Paco can

come after me. My phone buzzes. Text from Aida. *Now I come.*

The security guy, driving a white pick-up, approaches the Rockwell's house. My hands are shaking as I fumble with my phone. *No, no. Wait 5 min. Security guy out front.* Geez, I had no idea kidnapping someone was so difficult.

The white truck stops a few yards away from my hiding place. The beam of a spotlight dances across the trees and shrubs. I pull the hood of my sweatshirt over my head and crouch at the base of the tree. I hold my breath, listen to my heart thudding in my chest and pray Aida sees my text. Finally, the truck pulls forward and I gasp for air. When I stand, my head swims and I see shooting stars behind my eyes. I brace my hands against my knees and take a couple of deep breaths until my vision clears.

I text Aida again. *He's gone, come now.*

I take a step away from the tree and see headlights again. Kendra or someone else? I duck back behind the tree until the minivan stops in the shadows.

I hurry over to the car. "She's coming. Get ready."

Kendra presses a button and the passenger door in the back slides open. I step away from the car and move to where I can see the front door, fully illuminated by a porch light. Suddenly, the light goes off and I think, *smart girl, Aida.* I peer through the darkness and see movement as Aida darts through sheltering trees, well away from the massive front lawn. She's almost to the car when I notice she's carrying something. Something wrapped in a blanket. Something making a mewling sound, I swear, my heart stops, just for a moment.

"Oh, shit." I cry. "She brought the baby. We can't

take the baby."

Yes, I panicked. Kidnapping an illegal immigrant is one thing, but the baby? Federal prison, here we come. I see shooting stars again and slump against the side of the car.

When Kendra speaks, her voice is calm and authoritative. "Don't panic. Get her in the car. We'll think of something."

I hear her but the words don't penetrate. "Aida," I whisper as she approaches. "Why did you bring the baby? We can't take her…we can't."

Aida narrows her eyes at me. "Baby fussy, so I bring."

"Oh, God, oh, God, oh, God," I moan.

Kendra appears by my side. "Hi Aida. I'm Mel's friend, Kendra. Why don't you get in the car and we'll get everything sorted out."

Kendra guides her into the back seat. Aida gives a little squeal of alarm when she sees Paco. He rumbles, "Hello, you sweet thing. I know I look like a big, mean Mexican, but actually, I'm really a nice guy. Just ask Mel. I'm her Uncle Paco."

Kendra grabs my arm. "Get a grip. We have to get Destiny back into Rockwell's house." She shoves me into the car, slams the door and trots around to the driver's side. Once inside, she turns to the back seat and coos, "I haven't seen Destiny forever. Can I hold her?"

Aida thinks it over for a moment and then hands her over. Kendra drops a kiss on the baby's forehead and bounces her until she stops fussing. Aida hands her the pacifier. "She likes her binky, too."

Kendra pops the binky into Destiny's mouth. "So, Aida, how did you get out of the house? Did you turn the alarm off?'

"Yes, I know code. I turn it off."

"So," Kendra says. "Is it still off? Can you get back in?"

"Yes, I turn it on when I go back inside. Door not locked."

Kendra thrusts Destiny into my arms and whispers, "Go. We'll drive around for a few minutes. If we're not here, wait behind the tree."

I tuck Destiny in the crook of my left arm and jump out of the van. As I shut the door, I hear Kendra engage the child locks and Aida wailing, "Noooo."

Kendra peels out. I'm filled with dread as I watch her taillights disappear around a corner. I glance down at the baby. She stops sucking on the pacifier and smiles up at me. I murmur, "I'm sorry, baby. I wish I didn't have to take you back." One of my tears plops down on her cheek and her eyes widen in surprise.

It takes every bit of will power I possess to re-trace Aida's path through the trees. First, I have to convince my feet to walk toward the house, not run in the opposite direction. I creep onto the darkened front porch and try the door. As promised, it is unlocked.

My next big hurdle is to actually enter the house. I make sure Destiny is still latched onto her pacifier before I step into the cavernous foyer. I shut the door behind me and wait a beat before heading for the stairs. My right foot is on the bottom step when I hear a toilet flush. I freeze. Frightening scenarios race through my mind. What if the Mister has the munchies and is heading downstairs for Cheese Doodles and a nightcap? What if the Missus needs a Perrier? Should I hide? Take the baby and run? What?

Apparently my panic translates to a tighter grip on Destiny. She squeaks in alarm. I loosen my grip and rock her back and forth. "Shhh, baby, it's okay."

The sound of receding footsteps emboldens me and I creep up the stairs, my heart pounding in my ears. I pause to listen when I reach the top and glance to the left where the Rockwell's bedroom is located. The door is ajar. Not good. Gripped by a sense of urgency, I turn right and creep down the hall to the nursery. A dim glow leaks from beneath the closed door. I open it carefully and slip through, closing it behind me. *Five steps to the crib, Mel, and you're outta here*. I'm so focused on the crib, I don't see the teddy bear lying on the floor. I step on it. The teddy bear emits a loud squeak. I stumble, almost fall and Destiny screams in fright. *Aw, shit.*

No time to panic. I plop Destiny into her crib and pat her back. She screams louder. I need to get out of here. Now. When I turn toward the door, I hear footsteps approaching the nursery. Out of options, I dash into Aida's darkened room, climb into her bed and pull the covers over my head.

The nursery door opens. I sense her presence before she speaks. When she does, her voice is sharp with anger. "Aida. For Christ's sake, get up and take care of Addison. Can't you hear her screaming her head off?"

I pray she won't flip on the overhead light. I peek out from beneath the blanket, making sure my hair is covered. In my best Aida imitation, I say, "So sorry, Missus. You go back to bed. I take care of baby. Coming right now." I fake a yawn, rustle the covers and plant one foot on the floor. She waits a beat, huffs her disgust, turns and stomps away.

Acutely aware of time passing, I do my best to comfort Destiny. I need to get out before Paco comes barreling into the house. When the baby's outraged screams subside to an occasional hiccup, I whisper my apology again. "Sorry to leave you, Destiny, but it won't be for long. I promise."

I make sure the pacifier is lodged firmly in her mouth before tiptoeing from the room. I have to force myself not to race down the stairs like a woman possessed. With my luck I'd probably miss a step, cartwheel to the bottom, break an ankle and get caught by the evil one. With this in mind, I make my stealthy exit from the Rockwell house without incident. Once outside, I pick up speed, praying the minivan will be parked in the shadows.

It's not. Of course it isn't. Could anything else go wrong with this royally fucked-up kidnapping? I duck behind my tree and wait.

Chapter Thirty-Seven

I soon find out why the troops are missing. Five minutes later—seems like an hour—the minivan cruises into the shadows and stops. I sprint to the car and jump into the front seat.

"Sorry, Mel," Kendra punches the accelerator. She leans close and whispers, "Aida was hysterical and screeching so loud I was afraid somebody would hear."

I turn and check out the back seat. Paco, crooning in Spanish, holds Aida against his chest, his free hand gently massaging her pregnant belly. She's whimpering and snuffling, but clings to Paco like he's the lone life raft in a tossing sea.

Kendra says, "What happened in there? Paco was about go in after you."

I fill her in on operation baby insertion. When I describe the teddy bear incident, she gasps.

Paco switches to English. "You were lucky, *chicka*. Never do that again. Promise Uncle Paco."

I nod vigorously.

Aida draws a hitching breath. "Addison is okay?"

"Yes. She was sleeping when I left. When she wakes up, the Missus will have to act like a mother for a change."

Oh, how I'd love to be a fly on the wall when she finds out Aida is gone.

"You take me to Larissa's baby now?"

Through gritted teeth, I whisper to Kendra. "You didn't tell her?"

Kendra flashes me a cheesy smile. "We decided to let you do the honors."

"Thanks a bunch."

I turn in my seat and reach for Aida's hand. She looks up at Paco. He nods and keeps patting her tummy.

I grip her hand and tell her Larissa's baby has now been sold to the Krugers and is living in California. I see shock register on her face. She makes a sound so mournful, so full of misery; I feel hot tears spring to my eyes.

"I'm so sorry, Aida. I didn't want to lie to you, but we had to get you away from the Rockwells or the same thing will happen to your baby. She will be taken from you and sold for a lot of money. And, what's worse, you'll end up in Portland, forced into prostitution."

She stops moaning. "What does this word mean? Prostitution?"

Paco defines the word, using graphic terms.

Aida gasps. "Oh, I cannot do that. It is for bad girls. I am a good girl."

"Exactly why we had to kidnap you tonight," I say.

"Kidnap?" she asks.

Paco explains.

"Now, what we do?"

Kendra says, "Now, you stay with me and help with my children. Would you do that for me?"

Aida thinks it over. She pats Paco's cheek. "Will big Mexican man be there?"

"As long as you need me, Sweet Cheeks."

"What are these cheeks you speak of?"

Paco tells her. She giggles.

I'm thinking, *thank God for Uncle Paco.*

It's an hour before dawn when we pull into Kendra's driveway. The house is lit up like a Christmas tree. Billy's Harley is parked next to the garage.

"Boyfriend alert. Get ready," Kendra says.

We pile out of the van, Aida still clinging to Paco.

Craig and Billy are in the kitchen, drinking coffee. Both look grim.

Craig strides to Kendra and pulls her into a hug. "What took you so long? I was getting worried."

She wraps her arms around his neck nuzzles his cheek. "Complications. Everything is okay." With a quick glance at Billy, she grabs Craig's hand. "Let's get Aida settled."

She drags him from the room, leaving me alone with Billy. His soul burns bright with fury and frustration.

He stands, arms folded across his chest, staring down at me. "What the hell, Minnie? Why didn't you tell me? We could have figured out a better way. Damn, girl, you just orchestrated a kidnapping. What if the Rockwells go to the cops?"

"They won't. They'll think Aida ran away. What are they going to do? Tell the world their illegal, pregnant nanny is missing? Trust me, they don't want to draw attention to themselves. Not with what's at stake."

I take a step toward him. Lift my hands in supplication. "Kendra and I thought it best not to involve you in case, you know, if…"

"Exactly." Billy says. "In case it went belly up and you got arrested. And that could have happened. Quite easily."

"We didn't want to jeopardize your future."

Billy grips my shoulders. His anger still burns but it's flagging. "What about your future?"

"I had to get Aida out of there. There was no other way."

His grip tightens. "You scare me, Minnie. You dive head first into things without thinking about the consequences."

I jerk away from him. "I don't need a daddy lecture. Yes, I thought about the consequences. Guess what? None of them is good. The Rockwells steal Aida's baby and sell her for big bucks and Aida is shipped off to Portland, locked up and forced to perform sexual acts for money. I don't care what you think, I won't let that happen."

Billy's jaw tightens. "And you didn't trust me enough to tell me?"

At that moment it occurs to me Billy is bummed because he didn't get to be part of the action. I send up a prayer for patience. "We covered that ground, Billy. Kendra and I talked it over. We want you fully present in your counseling and…"

"I'm not a child who needs to be protected."

"Well, you're acting like one now."

We're both breathing hard, glaring at each other, unwilling to give an inch. Finally, Billy sighs and holds out his arms. "Let's start over."

I should play hard to get, but I'm too damn tired to work up the energy. I step into his embrace, wrap my arms around his waist and snuggle into his chest. It feels like coming home after a long, hard day.

His lips graze my temple. "What god awful plan is next on your agenda?"

I stifle my urge to retaliate. "I'll give the flash drive to Home Land Security and ask them to get Destiny out of the Rockwell's house."

Billy tucks a finger under my chin and tilts my head back until I meet his gaze. "Do you realize that agency is in Portland?'

"Yes. I'll call this morning and hope I can convince an agent to come to 3 Peaks. If I have to, I'll go to Portland with the flash drive."

Billy releases me, takes a step back and bows from the waist. "Miss Melanie Sullivan, aka, Minnie Mouse, would you allow your humble servant, William Henry McCarty, to assist you. Pretty please."

My lips curve into an involuntary smile. "Maybe. What's *your* god awful plan?"

He grabs my hand and leads me to the kitchen table where we settle into chairs. "We go to the local authorities. I have friends there. They have a direct line to federal agencies whereas you, well, they might think you're a nut job."

I think about Rusty, the big policeman who scares Aida so. "We can't go there. Remember that guy I told you about? The one they call Rusty. He's involved in this mess, clear up to his mean little eyeballs."

"I have people I trust."

Before I can stop the words, I blurt, "Your ex girlfriend Candy?"

He blinks in surprise and drags a hand through his brush cut. "Oh, yeah, you met Candy. I forgot."

"I sure did and she still has the hots for your studly bod."

"Aw, come on, Minnie. That's ridiculous. Candy and I are a done deal."

"I don't think she feels that way."

He narrows his eyes at me. "You really want to talk about this now?"

"No."

"Good."

I take a big breath. Let it out. Hit the delete button. Expunge Candy Talbot from my memory banks. "Okay, it has to be tomorrow. I mean, today. What's your schedule?"

"I can get away at noon. I'll call Candy and make the arrangements."

I bite my lip to keep from saying something bitchy. "Okay."

Kendra bustles into the kitchen. "Aida is all settled. I've got the hide-a-bed in the family room made up for you, Mel. Stay with us tonight. Okay? "

Before I can answer, Billy says, "I'll take her home."

"Oh, no you won't. She's tired and it's practically morning. You're welcome to stay here too, but no hanky-panky. My kids get up early." She blows us kisses and heads for bed.

"How do you feel about spooning?" Billy says.

"Love it."

Before we crawl into the hide-a-bed, I check on Aida. Clad in one of Kendra's nightgowns, she's curled up on the queen-sized bed, sleeping soundly. Paco is sitting on a chair next to the bed, holding her hand.

I whisper, "Thanks, Unc, for everything. Looks like Aida bonded with you."

"Poor kid," he rumbles. "Damn shitheads want her baby. They'll have to get past me first."

I plop down on his lap and kiss his cheek. "You're

a pretty good guy, for a Mexican gang banger."

He wraps his free arm around me and squeezes. "Get some sleep, little girl. You did a damn good job tonight. I'm proud of you."

I press my cheek against his chest and listen to the strong beat of his heart. I must have dozed off because the next thing I remember is Billy lifting me in his arms and carrying me to the hide-a-bed.

Spooning is good.

Chapter Thirty-Eight

It's twelve twenty-two p.m. and Billy and I are in an interview room with his cop buddy, the comely Candace Talbot. When we arrived, I checked out her tiny cubicle of an office, one of many partitioned off by tri-fold room dividers and shook my head. No way was I going to spill my guts in the midst of a bunch of people I didn't know or trust. Hence, our re-location to the interview room.

Candy is looking sleek in tapered black trousers and a silky pale blue blouse clinging to her bodacious boobs like a second skin. Not that I'm jealous. Not much.

Billy does most of the talking since I'm too busy not being jealous. We agreed ahead of time, not to mention last night's little misadventure regarding Aida. The word *kidnapping* will remain unspoken in this building.

Candy tears her fascinated gaze from Billy and flicks a glance my way. "So, did you bring the flash drive?"

"Yes."

I'm *so* not going to give it to her.

"Can I see it?"

"I'm going to hang onto it for now."

Candy makes an exasperated sound. "If I'm going to contact Homeland Security, I'll need that flash drive."

I shake my head. "Like Billy said, it's a list of the people the babies were sold to, and the amount they paid for them. I know that for a fact because I made some phone calls."

Candy turns to Billy and lifts her hands in a helpless gesture. "Not sure what I can do if she won't give me the flash drive. I need proof."

Billy places a hand on her arm and flashes his thousand-watt smile. "Just do what you can. Please. Make the call. Try to convince an agent this is for real. We'll hang on to the flash drive for now. Would you do that for us, Candy?"

The famed Billy the Kid charm is working today. She reluctantly agrees. "I'll be in touch."

I stand and push back my chair. "Thanks, Candy. I hope you can make it happen soon. I'm extremely worried about Destiny. She isn't safe in the Rockwell house."

"How do you know that?" Her voice is sharp.

Now what, Mel? Do you tell her you've looked into Nina Rockwell's soul? "I, um, well…"

Billy stands and places a hand on my shoulder. "You need to trust her, Candy. She has good instincts about people."

Candy looks skeptical, but nods.

We turn to leave. The door to the interview room opens. The big cop, Rusty, steps through. My heart leaps into my throat as his hooded gaze lingers on me a little too long. Billy shoots me a warning glance.

"Hi, boss," Candy says. "Remember Billy the Kid?"

"Sure do." He shakes hands with Billy. "I hear

you'll be joining us soon."

Billy nods. "Hope so."

His gaze swings over to me. "Who's this pretty lady?"

Billy makes the introductions. I find I'm in the presence of Captain Rick (Rusty) McGowan.

He clasps my hand in both of his. "Nice to meet you, Miss Sullivan. Is there anything I can help you with?"

I pull my hand away, but not before I look into his soul. His eyes are gray. So is his soul, but with a few reddish purple streaks. I've been studying Steve's notes, so I know a soul that particular shade of gray indicates a withdrawal from societal norms as well as secretiveness. Many sociopaths have flat gray souls. The reddish purple streaks make it truly scary. That combination of colors tells me he has a nasty temper and is prone to aggression and violence.

I force a smile. "No, Candy took care of us. Nice to meet you too."

I can't wait to get out of this man's presence, but he's blocking the door.

Candy says, "I'll fill you in later, Captain."

Oh, hell no!

I turn toward Candy and extend my hand to her. My back is now turned to McGowan. Candy looks puzzled, but takes my hand. I shake it vigorously and say, "Thanks for your help." She tries to pull her hand away but I cling to it like a barnacle on the side of a tugboat. I see Billy watching me as I mouth the words, "No, don't tell him. He's in on it."

Her eyes widen a bit. She squeezes my hand and smiles. "You're welcome, Mel. I'll be in touch about the incident in your room."

Whew. Message received.

McGowan steps aside, allowing us to leave the room. I wonder if he's picked up on my body language and is about to grill Candy Talbot for information. For the first time, I feel empathy for her. We've just dumped a boatload of trouble on her doorstep.

Billy takes my hand and we exit the building. Neither of us speaks until we approach the Harley. Before we climb on, Billy loops an arm around my shoulders and gives me a squeeze. "Quick thinking in there. Good job."

My legs are still shaking. "Damn, that was scary. Do you trust her? Maybe Candy's part of the problem."

Billy cups my face in his hands and drops a kiss on my forehead. "There's no way she'd be involved."

I pull away. "Maybe it's hard for you to be objective since you two have a history."

He heaves a sigh. "Look, I know Candy can be a bitch, but she's a good cop."

"Kendra doesn't like her. She says Candy won't rest until she gets you back."

Billy shakes his head in disgust. "I thought we were talking about Candy's integrity, not our past relationship. Here's a thought. Maybe Kendra's being a bitch too. Can we please put this to rest? Trust me, Minnie. It's over."

I want to believe him. I do, but I can't help it. I take a little peek into his soul to see if he's telling the truth. He is. I feel a flush rise in my cheeks. When did I turn into the classic needy girlfriend? I'm acutely ashamed.

I place a hand on his arm. "Sorry. I guess I'm

acting like a bitch too."

Billy's grin lights up my world. "No worries. Obviously, I'm attracted to bitches."

Back at Number Ten, I dig the flash drive out of my pocket and hand it to him. "If word gets out I have the flash drive, it will be safer with you."

He nods and tucks it inside his jacket. After a warm, lingering kiss that leaves me weak in the knees and breathing hard, Billy says, "We finish early tonight. I'll be back."

"Promise?"

He nuzzles my neck. "I'd be crazy not to."

My cell phone buzzes as he pulls away. Paco.

He says, "Sorry I was sleeping when you left. How did the thing go with the cops?"

I fill him in, including my introduction to Captain McGowan.

"Hmm."

He stays quiet for a while, thinking things over. "I'll be there soon. You be careful, ya hear?"

I assure him I'm fine. "How's Aida doing?"

"Still worried about the kid."

"Maybe you should stay with her a while."

He chuckles. "That Kendra chick is something else. She's yakking a mile a minute and has Aida shoveling goopy stuff into the baby's mouth. I'll stick around for a bit. See how it goes."

I flop down on the bed, exhausted, but too tense to sleep. Whatever happens next is now up to Candy Talbot. Billy trusts her. I want to trust her too. Should I have given her the flash drive? My weary mind flits from one dilemma to another. What about Destiny? I'm swamped with guilt about leaving her in the Rockwell house. I try to put her out of my mind. Unsuccessfully.

I spring off the bed and change into my running clothes. Maybe working up a sweat will relieve my anxiety. After a long run and quick shower, I feel almost human when I report for work. Paco comes in around dinnertime.

I seat him in my section. "How's Aida?"

"Still confused and worried about the kid she left behind. She cried when I left."

I slip into the booth across from him. "Listen, Paco, Billy's coming by later. I'll be perfectly safe. After you eat, head back to Kendra's house. Obviously, Aida needs you."

His eyes brighten. "You sure?"

"Absolutely."

I deliver his food. He wolfs it down, leaves me a twenty-dollar tip and splits.

Billy calls at eleven-fifteen. I hear male voices in the background. "Can't make it tonight, Minnie. I'm involved in a bit of a crisis."

Alarmed, I say, "What kind of a crisis?"

"Not me. It's a guy in our group. He was freaking out, so a bunch of us are at his place, trying to talk him down."

I remember Paco's words. "Does he have the heebie jeebies?"

"Yeah, he does."

I'm disappointed of course. But I played the whiny girlfriend card earlier today. What kind of an asshole would ask her boyfriend to desert a buddy in crisis in order to make her happy? Not me.

"No problem. Maybe tomorrow."

"I hope so."

It's quitting time. After helping Helen and Nick clean up, I scurry across the parking lot to Number Ten. I step through the door, cursing myself for not leaving a light on. But, I did. Didn't I? I close the door and reach for the light switch. Before I can flick it on, a rough hand covers my mouth and I'm locked in a steely embrace. I feel a prick on the back of my neck and darkness swallows me up.

Chapter Thirty-Nine

I awaken slowly in the dark. My stomach is queasy and churning. My head hurts. Something—it feels like a hard metal object—is directly beneath it. I moan and try to shift my position. I squirm and wriggle, unable to move my arms and legs. Why? Oh, God, my wrists are bound and my ankles tied together. I'm trussed up like a turkey ready for the oven. Sick with fear, I try to summon my sluggish wits. Where the hell am I?

One by one, my senses return. I attempt to cry out, but a rag smelling of rancid motor oil is tied across my mouth. I roll my head from side to side and see nothing but blackness. The floor beneath me vibrates with the sound of an engine shifting gears. I lift my head and hear men's voices, but can't make out the words because of the music. Country music. Sounds like Johnny Cash; *A Boy Named Sue.*

Well, crap. I'm in the trunk of a car. A big car. Like Myron's Impala.

Do not panic, Mel. Try to remember what you're supposed to do when locked in a trunk. Surely Sandra covered that subject in one of her cautionary tales. Kick out the taillights? Find something sharp to rub against the ties binding my ankles and wrists? Make noise to attract attention when the car stops at a red light? Yes, all of the above.

I maneuver my body around and lash out with my

feet, hoping I'm in the general vicinity of the taillights. I'm rewarded with a loud thumping sound, which is good, because the gag muffles my screams. I keep it up while squirming around and feeling for something to grasp with my hands. My stomach gurgles ominously. Bitter bile rises in my throat. My fingers close around the metal object that had been beneath my head. A tire iron? It feels good in my hands even though there's no way I can use it with my wrists tied together. Nevertheless, I cling to it.

The car stops. A red light? I double my kicking efforts and cry out against the stinky rag binding my mouth. The engine dies with a *clunk*. The music stops. I hear doors slam and the sound of footsteps. The trunk flies open. Myron and Mick stare down at me like I'm a caged animal. Actually, I guess I am.

Myron drawls, "Well, looky here. Our little birdie is wide-awake. Let's get her inside." He snatches the tire iron from my hand. "Nice try, sweetheart."

Mick grabs me around the waist and flings me over his shoulder.

I'm borne across an asphalt parking lot. It looks familiar. I twist my head around and peek under Mick's arm to see where we're heading. Dr. Breen's fertility clinic. My worst nightmare. Momentary panic makes me struggle against Mick's steely grip. He whacks me across the butt. "Settle down."

We get to the back door and Myron presses a buzzer. My belly, pressed against Mick's shoulder, makes a formidable rumbling sound. I squirm and grunt, trying not to heave up my dinner. Mick pulls me off his shoulder and slams me against the side of the building. I go, "Mmmph, mummph." I roll my eyes like a panicked horse and tilt my chin toward my tummy.

In a thick Russian accent, Mick says, "She's trying to say something."

Myron chuckles again. "Yeah, like 'Ooo, let me go please, please.'"

He's wrong. I wouldn't utter the word *please* to him. Ever.

I make retching sounds. Mick removes the gag and takes a step back, like he knows what's about to happen. Maybe he does. I turn toward Myron and vomit spews out of my mouth like a volcanic eruption. It's a direct hit.

Splattered with the contents of my stomach, he jumps back, a few seconds too late. "Jesus Christ," he mutters, swiping at the mess.

I smile at him, determined to enjoy the moment. "Looks good on you, Myron, you asshole. I just have one question. Why did you run over my bike?"

He shakes his head in disbelief. "You're helpless, about to die and you want to know about your bike?"

"Yeah, I do. I think it was a simple act of meanness. Am I right?"

Before he can answer, the door opens and Jared Breen peeks out. "Take her to number four. I've got a baby on the way."

He pauses, sniffs and checks out Myron. "You're not coming in here smelling like puke."

Myron turns and shuffles away. "Got a change of clothes in the car."

Mick swipes my face with the gag and, once again, jams his shoulder into my midsection. I grunt as the air whooshes out of my lungs. Breen holds the door open. After Mick steps through, Breen tells him to wait for

Myron. Breen hurries away.

Since my projectile vomiting episode, I'm feeling much better. Spunky, even.

How can that be? I should be cowering in fear. Myron just told me of my impending death. Still, I'm thinking clearly, able to put everything into perspective. What's the worst thing that can happen if I die? Aida is safe. Her baby will be safe. Kendra and Paco will make sure of that. Billy has the flash drive and I know he won't rest until these evil people are behind bars. That is, unless Paco gets to them first. Strangely, I'm not afraid to die. I just hope it's quick. Not that I want to die. No way. I have things to do. Places to go.

Maybe it's because the blood is rushing to my head that I throw caution to the wind. "Hey, Mick," I say.

He grunts.

"You know what? I can read your soul. It's not like Myron's and Eddie's. Why are you involved with these nasty people? For money? Women from your homeland are being used and abused, turned into brood mares and sex slaves. You should be ashamed of yourself!"

"Stop talking." He whacks me on the butt again.

"Ow."

The buzzer sounds. Myron is now clad in jeans and a white tee, topped with a camouflage hunting vest. He keeps his distance from me. I can't help but taunt him. "What's the matter, big boy? Scared I'll hurl on you again?"

He snarls, "Shut the fuck up."

I hear laughter rumble in Mick's chest. "She got you good, bro."

Myron ignores the jibe and walks ahead of us down the hall. He pauses in front of an examination room, opens the door and turns on the light. "Put her on the table."

Mick plops me on the examination table, none too gently. I hear a woman crying out in pain. The sound is coming through the wall from the examination room next to ours. I picture Dr. Breen hovering between the pregnant girl's legs, poised and ready to deliver the baby and hand it over to a childless couple with a big bank account. It makes me sick. If I had anything left in my stomach, I'd throw up on Myron again.

I wait until for the pause between her screams and yell at the top of my lungs. "Don't let him take your baby. You'll never see it again and…"

I see the back of Myron's hand coming toward my face. I duck but it's too late.

Whack!

His heavy blow knocks me off the table. With my arms bound together, I can't break the fall. I crash to the floor. The right side of my body hits first. My head bounces off the tile. Blood drips from the gash on my cheek, compliments of Myron's heavy ring. Pain shoots through my right arm. Dizzy and hurting, I curl up in a little ball of misery.

Myron nudges me with a foot. He's breathing hard. "I told you to shut the fuck up. Do you believe me now?"

I squeeze my eyes shut to hold back the tears and nod.

The screams on the other side of the wall start up again, closer together now. Myron, arms folded across his chest, leans against the door. He tells Mick. "Put her back on the table."

Mick scoops me up. My arm throbs with pain. I

wonder if it's broken. When he sets me on the table, he places a finger across my mouth. "Didn't I tell you to stop talking?"

His words piss me off. I open my mouth and chomp down on his finger, hard enough to draw blood.

With a yip of pain, he yanks his finger away and snarls something in Russian that sounds like, "*okhu el.*"

I smile at him sweetly. "*Okhu el* to you too."

Apparently it's a really bad curse because he flushes. His hand curls into a fist. *Kiss your front teeth goodbye, Mel.*

My head is throbbing but my vision clears. Mick's pale blue eyes are cold as ice. He mutters something else in Russian. His hand relaxes and he steps away.

Myron chuckles. "Told ya she was a piece of work."

I turn my head toward Myron. "You gonna kill me now or what?"

Myron flashes his mirthless smile. "Now, it's pay back time. We put your feet in the stirrups. Mick and I have a little fun. Then, you die. How does that sound?"

Struggling to control the shockwaves of fear and pain coursing through my body, I force myself to meet his eyes. "You sure you want to get that close to me? After what happened earlier? Plus, I'm having a herpes flare-up right now. Hope you have a rubber."

Myron's right eye begins to twitch. An angry flush reddens his cheeks. "Knew you were a skank. Did you give it to Billy?"

"How do you know he didn't give it to me?"

We lock gazes. I refuse to blink. Our stare-down is interrupted by the sound of a baby crying. Myron pumps a fist in the air. "*Yes*. You know what that is?

It's the sound of money."

Several retorts spring to mind. All of them are inflammatory. Since I know he won't hesitate to light me up again, I keep my opinion to myself.

A few minutes later, the baby's cries stop suddenly. I hear a woman's voice, rising and falling, tinged with panic. A door opens and closes followed by the sound of footsteps. The door to our room opens. Breen steps through. "Mick. I need you to calm our new mother down. She needs someone who speaks her language."

Words burst from my mouth before I can stop them. "You want Mick to calm her down so you can sell her baby for big bucks. Right, doc?"

Breen's gaze swings over to me. "Do you think the young woman in the other room has any idea how to care for a baby? Trust me, she does not. She'd be on the streets or on welfare in a New York minute. Really, I'm doing her a tremendous favor. I'm giving her child the chance to grow up in a loving family."

I squirm up to a sitting position. "You're doing her a *favor?*" My voice is shrill with outrage. "Is that how you justify impregnating women without their knowledge and selling their babies? You know what you are? You're a giant carbuncle on the ass of society."

Myron takes a step toward me, one hand raised. I zip my lip.

Breen stares at me, blinking rapidly, rendered speechless by my comments. I'm certain no one has ever spoken to him like I did. In this clinic, he is the Supreme Being, worshipped by an adoring female staff and needy women desperate to conceive. And, I just called him a huge pus-filled blister. I bite back a smile of satisfaction. If I'm going to die, I may as well get my licks in.

Jared Breen leaves without saying a word. Mick pushes away from the wall and follows him.

The pain in my head throbs, echoing the beat of my heart. Dread and panic arrive in equal measure.

I am now alone with Myron who's already explained in graphic terms, what he intends to do to me.

Hang in there, Mel.

Chapter Forty

He strolls to the table, one hand in the pocket of his camo vest and pulls out a large hunting knife. He removes the scabbard and slides a finger down its length. The overhead light bounces off its razor sharp surface. I stop breathing, my gaze fixed on the blade.

He waves the knife in front of my face. I shrink back. "Here's the deal," he says. "You make me happy and your death will be quick. If you don't make me happy, well, let's just say your loving family will have a hard time collecting enough of you to bury."

I will myself to breathe. My brain needs oxygen. In my present trussed-up condition, my brain is the only part of me not under Myron's control. Think, Mel, think. Don't let fear paralyze you.

I heard Mick's voice coming through the wall. He's speaking in a low, measured tone. The woman responds, sounding calmer. I want to reach through the wall and claw his eyes out.

Myron leans close and licks his lips. "I've been watching that cute little ass of yours swishing around the restaurant for too long. 'Bout time I got a piece of it."

My wits are my only weapon. Since my wrists are bound, my upper body is useless. If he unties my legs so he can rape me, I might be able to strike him with a strong double-leg kick. Then what? Unless he's completely incapacitated—highly unlikely—he'll go to work with the hunting knife and pieces of my body will be scattered around 3 Peaks. It will be a grisly Honor Melanie Sullivan scavenger hunt.

Myron grabs the neck of my Nick's Place T-shirt with one meaty hand, pulls it away from my body and slices it from top to bottom. If falls away. He slips a finger under the center panel of my bra and uses the blade to cut it. It springs open, exposing both my breasts. He cups my left breast in his hand and squeezes. It hurts like hell. I grit my teeth to keep from crying out. He's humming under his breath, obviously a man who enjoys his work. His movements are slow and deliberate, designed to make me realize I'm totally under his control. Willing to do anything. Willing to beg for my life.

As if.

His face is close to mine. He's breathing hard and the bulge in his jeans tells me he's turned on by my helplessness.

I take a deep breath and lower my voice. "Look at me, Myron."

He glances into my eyes and snarls, "I give the orders. Not you."

To prove how manly he is, he grabs my hips and pulls me to the side of the table next to him. He rubs his erection against me. His breathing accelerates.

I force a bark of laughter. "I'm guessing the only way you can get it up is when a woman is tied up and helpless. I dare you to look into my eyes and tell me that's not true."

He keeps rubbing his disgusting organ against me and mumbles, "You're full of shit."

"Am I? You're scared to look into my eyes. No problem. I already looked in your nasty little soul. Yes, I can do that. Want to know what I saw there, beside the fact you served time in prison?"

Myron freezes. He lifts his flat gray gaze away from my lower body until he's looking directly into my eyes. It's what I hoped he would do. He's not the brightest star in the firmament, so I'm praying he's leery of things he doesn't understand.

Past. Present. Future. Words from Steve's soul-reading manual. In this case, I have to work backward. *Present* to *Past*. Make some educated guesses. Fingers crossed, I soldier on.

He stares, unblinking, into my eyes. "How did you know I was in prison?"

"When we first met, I looked into your soul and saw prison bars. Among other things."

"You're making this up."

"Am I?"

It's time for the truth-o-meter. "Myron's not even your real name."

"Hell, yes, it's my real name. Why wouldn't it be?"

I see the lie flash across his soul before he looks away.

"You changed your identity so you didn't have to put 'ex con' on job applications. Does Nick know?"

He doesn't answer.

"That's what I thought."

I'm far from safe so I pull out the big guns. "When I looked into your eyes just now, I saw something else. Something that's going to give you major Weenie Wilt." I emphasize the last two words like they are capitalized, the official Latin name for a troublesome medical condition.

I stare pointedly at the organ in question. It's already considerably smaller. "Are you ready?"

He steps away from me. "What are you? Some kind of Satan worshipper? A witch?"

I smile. "Maybe. Wanna know what I saw?"

His jaw tightens. Clearly, he doesn't.

Too bad.

"The prison bars in your soul are bigger than before, and darker. That means you're going back inside. Soon. Know what else I saw?"

There's uncertainty in his eyes when his gaze meets mine.

"Terrible images." I force a shudder. "Awful. They don't scare me, though, because I know what they mean. Everything you plan to do to me tonight will be done to you when you're locked up again. In triplicate. By men. Big, nasty, muscular men. The prison shower is a real danger zone."

This is such an outrageous lie; I almost choke on the words. I'm cheered by the fact Myron's face has gone pale.

He recovers quickly and blusters, "You're making this up."

"You sure about that?"

His eyes narrow into little slits of fury. Moving fast as a striking cobra, he grabs my ankles. One slash of the knife and my ankles are unbound. Clutching the waistband of my jeans, he yanks me to the end of the table, steps between my legs and grinds his crotch against me.

"Surefire cure for weenie wilt," he says with a sneer.

The pain shooting through my arm stalls me for a moment. It takes every ounce of strength I possess not to scream.

Okay, Mel, this is your last chance. Make it good.

"Guess you don't believe me," I pant. "Need more proof. I know what you served time for."

He keeps rubbing against me. "Go for it."

"Rape and aggravated assault."

He stops grinding and unzips his fly. "Lucky guess."

"The future doesn't look so lucky for you."

He gropes for the button on my jeans. "My future looks a whole lot better than yours. In case you've forgotten, you'll be dead soon."

He makes the mistake of looking into my eyes when he utters these words. I hold his gaze, and narrow my eyes. "In case *you've* forgotten, every single thing you do to me tonight will be done to you. Three times over."

He grimaces and wraps a hand around my throat. "*Shut up.*"

I squeeze out the words, "Three. Times. Over."

"*Shut the fuck up,*" he screams, but his grip loosens.

The door opens and Mick steps through. He takes in the scene with a single glance, but gives nothing away in his expression. "Talked to Rusty. He wants me to take care of her now. Not wait until morning."

Myron looks frustrated and pouty. "Gimme five minutes."

I *so* want to say, "Five minutes? Don't make me laugh." But, I don't.

Mick says, "No time, dude. Got to do it now. It'll

be light soon and I need to dump her in the dark."

My blood turns to ice. Despite his soul, Mick looks like a stone cold killer, totally impervious to emotion. A get-the-job-done-and-move-on kind of guy.

You're so screwed, Mel.

Still glowering at me, Myron takes a reluctant step back. "I'll drive you."

"Breen wants you to stay here in case he needs help with the woman and kid."

Myron hands over the keys. Mick pockets them, steps around Myron and reaches for me.

Their calm discussion around my impending demise makes me livid with rage. "Hey, assholes." I yell. "I'm half naked here. The least you can do is cover me up."

I double up my legs and land a good hard kick in the middle of Mick's chest. A brief grimace of pain flashes across his stoic face, but he's as unmovable as a stone statue. He pulls a roll of duct tape from his back pocket and lashes my ankles together. That done, he removes the flannel shirt he's wearing over a form-fitting black tee, drapes it around my upper body and buttons it.

"Happy now?"

"Ecstatic," I say. Since my hands are bound, I flip him the bird with my eyes.

Once again, I'm hoisted in the air and draped across Mick's left shoulder. The pain momentarily steals my breath away.

"Bye-bye, sweetheart," Myron mocks. "Sorry I didn't get to know you better."

"Roast in hell, Myron. You'll fit right in there."

"Witch." he snarls.

"Satan's minion." I respond, grunting to get out the words as I jounce up and down on Mick's shoulder.

"Bitch."

"Bastard." It's my parting shot as I'm borne out of the clinic.

No more options. No more tricks up my sleeves. I'm in the hands of a killer and I won't even have a chance to tell my mother goodbye.

Are you ready to die, Mel?

Chapter Forty-One

Mick opens the trunk of the Impala and places me inside. He starts to close the lid but reconsiders and pulls the gag from his pocket. He leans close. His eyes are cold and focused. "I have a decision to make and I know you won't keep your mouth shut while I'm thinking."

"What kind of decision? Like, how to kill me? Where to kill me?" My voice is quivering and semi-hysterical. "So, what do you want me to do? Be quiet while you decide where to dump my body?"

I'm trying hard not to cry, but after a stifled sob, I say, "I think Myron broke my arm. It hurts like hell."

"Keep your voice down or the gag goes on." He leans into the trunk and unbuttons the flannel shirt he'd draped around me. I feel his fingers probing my right arm. Just below the elbow, he wraps his hand around my arm. Squeezes. I inhale sharply, trying not to cry out in pain.

"Hmm," he says, buttoning the shirt and tying the filthy rag around my mouth. He slams the lid shut. *What did you expect, Mel? Sympathy?* I curl up on my non-injured side. Mick cranks the motor and the car pulls out of the clinic parking lot.

My tears begin to flow in earnest. Since my mother is foremost in my mind, I search my memory for advice she may have given me about how to deal with serial killers. Zilch. With pain throbbing in my arm, it's really hard to focus. But I do remember watching a true crime show on TV about serial killers and mass murderers. Are serial killers/mass murderers and hired killers different? Probably, since the latter gets paid for doing the deed, whereas the others do it for fun. I vaguely recall something about trying to establish rapport with the potential killer, something like, "Aw, come on, killing me would be like killing your little sister and I'm sure you don't want to do that."

Or, is that technique intended for kidnappers/murderers? My mind is definitely not functioning well. I'm learning something about pain. It absorbs all your energy, chasing all rational thoughts from your mind. *Focus, Mel. Try to save yourself. Nobody else will.*

Okay. When Mick opens the trunk and, if he doesn't kill me that instant, I'll try the rapport thing. Nothing to lose.

A few minutes later, I feel the Impala make a slow left hand turn and pull to a stop. I hear the car door open and close and the sound of receding footsteps. Is this the time to make noise? We were surely still in the heart of the city. I steel myself against the pain and squirm around until I can lash out with my bound feet. After a series of feeble thumps, the lid of the trunk flies open and Mick peers in. He's holding a plastic grocery sack.

"I'm going to remove the gag, but you need to be quiet. Nod if you understand."

I nod so vigorously, I probably look like a bobble head doll.

As soon as the gag comes off, I remember my vow

to make rapport. I whisper, "Hey, Mick? Do you have family back in Russia? Maybe a sister?"

He shoots me puzzled glance. "Why do you ask?"

Strangely, his accent has disappeared. I weigh and measure my response. What's the worst he can do? Torture me before he kills me? I don't think that's going to happen. There seems to be a big rush to get the job done before daylight and it will soon be dawn. Consequently, I choose to keep jabbering. "How does a guy like you become a paid killer anyway?"

He grunts a non-answer.

"Remember when I said I can read your soul?"

He ignores me and gropes around in a grocery sack.

"Well, anyway," I continue. "Here's the thing. I've looked into Myron's soul as well as Eddie's, Jared Breen's, the Rockwell's and your cop friend, Rusty. All of them have the signs of evil stamped on their souls. Their souls all but scream, 'I'm a bad, *bad* person.' Every single one of them. Except for yours. Souls don't lie. So, what's the story, Mick? And, by the way, what happened to your accent? I'm thinking you may not be who you say you are."

"Hush." He upends the grocery bag and reaches into his pocket.

I squint through the darkness. Is that a pocketknife in his hand? Oh, shit. I take a huge breath, ready to scream my lungs out.

His finger appears in front of my face. He lays it across my lips. "I'm not going to kill you. Do. Not. Bite. This. Finger."

Weak with relief, the air gushes out of my lungs. He removes his finger. I feel the blade of a knife saw through the duct tape binding my wrists and ankles. Then, something cold snugs up against my bad arm. "Frozen lima beans," he says. "It's the best I can do right now. I'm going to make a sling for your arm."

He helps me to a sitting position and uses what looks like a dishtowel to construct a makeshift sling for my throbbing arm. He then lifts me from the trunk and sets me on my feet. The sudden upright position makes my head spin. The ground beneath me seems to shift. My wobbly legs give way. With a cry of alarm, I fall to my knees. If not for Mick's grip on my uninjured arm, I'd be kissing the asphalt. He picks me up, this time cradling me in his arms. "Did you hit your head when Myron knocked you off the table?"

Too tired to answer, I nod.

Once I'm placed on the passenger seat (way better than the trunk) I have a bajillion questions I want to ask Mick. Strangely, the realization I'm no longer a potential murder victim has rendered me speechless. I can't put my thoughts into words. All I want to do is curl up in a ball and go to sleep.

Mick guides the big car out of the supermarket parking lot. My eyelids are heavy with fatigue and fall shut.

Mick's voice startles me. I awake with a jerk. "I'm taking you to my place. You'll have to stay there until the mission's completed."

Suddenly, I'm so irritated I want to slap him. He won't let me sleep and furthermore, he assumes I know exactly who he is and what's going on. My power of speech returns in a rush. "Who the hell are you? And, what's your mission? It damn well better include saving that poor girl who just gave birth. And, what about the

Rockwells and the baby they supposedly adopted? Guess what? Her asshole father who, by the way, probably killed his wife, who, incidentally, was my best friend, sold Destiny to the Rockwells. And…"

Mick holds up a hand. "Hold it. As long as we're getting personal, do you know how much trouble your nosiness caused us?"

"Who is *us*?"

"Homeland Security. In case you haven't figured it out, I was working the case undercover."

"How would I know that?"

"I didn't kill you, did I? That should have given you a clue."

I'm really ticked now. "What was I supposed to do? Forget about my friend? Forget about her baby? What about the Russian girls getting impregnated without their consent? Not to mention they're forced to turn tricks after their babies are taken away from them and sold for big bucks. If you think for one minute…"

"Where's Aida?"

I gulp. "Who?"

"You know damn well who I'm talking about. I saw you last night."

"No way."

"Oh, yeah. Threw you off your game when she came out with the baby, didn't it?"

Busted. "Where were you? Hiding in the bushes with camo paint on your face?"

"Let's just say I've been keeping an eye on the Rockwells. So, where's the girl?"

"In a safe place. I didn't want her arrested when I went to the authorities. I had it all planned out."

He stays quiet for a minute. I'm still steaming.

Finally, he says, "If not for our little interlude with *you*, the whole crew would be locked up right now. The go signal was set for two a.m. I had to abort when Rusty insisted we pick you up."

He glances at his watch. "It's three-fifteen now, but hopefully, we can still surprise them at five a.m."

"If you're waiting for me to apologize, forget it. Just go get them, okay?"

"That's exactly what's going to happen as soon as I stash you in a safe place."

"I want to go with you."

His eyes widen and he shakes his head. "Are you serious? No. You can't."

"Well, that's a mistake. I could be a big help to your operation."

The brakes squeal as he takes a quick left into the parking lot of an apartment complex whose name, according to the sign at the entrance, is High Desert Pines. He pulls up next to one of the units and helps me out of the car.

I'm still woozy, walking like a drunken sailor. He slips an arm around my waist and guides me into a dark, recessed entryway. He props me up against an outer wall, bracing me with his body while he unlocks the door to number 110. Once inside, he flicks on a light and guides me to a couch. "Sit. Stay."

Before I can voice my objections to the canine commands, he pivots and disappears into another room, presumably, the bedroom. A scant moment later, he returns with a glass of water, a prescription bottle and a mini mag light. He tilts my chin back and shines the flashlight directly into my eyes. The sudden brightness makes me squint. "Look at me," he commands. I force my eyes open.

"Pupils not dilated. Probably no concussion." He turns the light off and probes the knot on my head. "I'm going to give you a vicodin for the pain in your arm. When this is over, I'll take you to the hospital."

He thrusts the water glass into my hand and orders, "Open your mouth."

His bossiness is annoying, but I sense he's trying to help. I scorch him with my best dirty look but, dutifully, open my mouth. He places a pill on my tongue and I slurp up the water like I'm stranded in the Sahara Desert.

He vanishes again and returns with a blanket and a wife-beater undershirt. He rips the undershirt in half. "Here's the deal. The vicodin will probably make you drowsy. Take a little nap. Okay?'

"Or, you could take me home so I can sleep in my own bed."

"Not gonna happen."

"Why not?"

"I can't risk you running around like the Lone Ranger while we're busting our asses making arrests. When it's over, I'll be back."

"I insist you take me home."

He grins at me. "You insist? You're not exactly in a bargaining position."

"You're overstepping your bounds. I'll speak to your supervisor. Maybe even get you fired."

His grin gets bigger. "Did you forget I'm Homeland Security? Undercover? I have no boundaries."

"That sucks!" I screech, trying to get to my feet.

He pushes me down, whips a piece of the

undershirt around my ankles and ties them together with a complicated knot. He then pulls my uninjured arm flat against my body and ties my wrist to my left thigh.

"What are you doing? Did you decide to kill me after all? Since you have no boundaries?"

He stands and stares down at me. "No, but I can't risk you screwing up this operation."

Helpless, I glare up at him. "I really, really hate you."

He chuckles. "But, you really, really love my soul. At least, that's what you told me."

I close my eyes, regretting I've commented on the contents of his soul.

A moment ticks by. He says, "Do you plan to scream? If so, I'll have to duct tape your mouth shut."

I have great difficulty prying my eyes open. Apparently, the vicodin is working its magic. "Screw that. Go catch the bad guys."

Chapter Forty-Two

The pain in my arm begins to ease and I struggle to stay awake after he leaves. Maybe I'm not thinking clearly, but I have a point to prove. Why should I lie here and *take a little nap.* Who does he think he is? My nanny?

He should have taken me with him. Does he know all the players? I do. Plus, I know what will happen when they bust the Rockwells. Destiny will be put into the foster care system and it will be hellishly hard to get her out. True, I've been sidetracked with Aida and the others, but this whole thing started with Destiny. I promised Dani I'd fix it. I can't give up now.

I want out of here and I have two choices. I can scream my head off and wait for someone to call 911. Or, I can take the bull by the horns, get to the phone on the kitchen counter and make it happen. Since a 911 call will bring the police and I don't know the whereabouts of the evil Rusty, I choose the second option.

True, my good arm is taped to my leg, which puts it out of commission. The injured arm is in a sling but I can still use my fingers if I can get to the phone. Yes, it's a big *if.* But, what else do I have to do? Sit around and wait until someone hears my cries for help? Or, hang around until Mr. Homeland Security gets back? No way.

When (not if) I get to the phone, I'll call Uncle Paco. I know Billy will be pissed, but when it comes to shadowy, covert activities, Paco is my go-to guy.

I struggle to a sitting position, place my bound feet on the floor. Taking a deep breath, I slide off the couch until my butt hits the carpet and begin inching my way across a living room that seems as vast as a football field. Reach out with the feet. Dig the heels in and pull. Scoot on the butt. Try not to fall backward. Slow and steady wins the race. Eye on the prize. Beads of sweat form on my forehead, drip down my face and sting the gash on my cheek.

I'm breathing hard and have no idea how much time has passed when I reach the kitchen counter upon which the phone rests. Now for my next challenge: getting to my feet so I can reach the phone. There's only one way I can accomplish this feat. I squirm around until I can press my back against the cupboard beneath the counter top. I'll have to get my feet under me and push to a stand. I don't realize how weak I am until I try to do just that. The muscles in my thighs are quivering with fatigue. I'm woozy from the vicodin and long to curl up and take the little nap suggested by Mick. Grunting with effort, I press and push. Once upright, bright stars flash across my vision and I sag back against the counter. My empty stomach seizes up in a vicious cramp. Deep breathing helps. My vision clears.

Now, for the next step. Turn body toward the counter top without falling on my face. Use useless arm to reach for the phone. Hope and pray Paco has his cell phone turned on. I count to three, take another deep breath and pivot my body toward the counter. I brace my legs against the cupboard and flop my injured arm, sling and all, atop the counter. I'm howling with pain, but grit my teeth and somehow stay upright.

The clock on the kitchen stove tells me it's a few minutes before four a.m. If all goes according to plan, Mick's team will be busting down doors in an hour. I want—no—I *need* to be at the Rockwells when that happens. Do I have a plan beyond that? Sort of.

Whimpering in pain, I slide my injured arm across the counter, hook my fingers around the base and pull it toward me. The handset falls from the base, numbers down. I'm shaking so hard I can barely flip it over. I duck my head and wipe the sweat from my eyes on the dishtowel sling.

Praying the phone works, I hit the green button. The sound of a dial tone makes me weep with joy. I punch in Paco's number thinking, *please, please, have your phone on."*

It goes to voice mail and I yell, "Damn it, Paco. I need you. I'm at the High Desert Pines apartment complex. Number 110. You might have to bust down the door. Bring Aida. Please, help me."

Though I know it's futile. I call three more times, leaving increasingly hysterical messages. I have second thoughts about leaving Billy out of the loop and call him too. He doesn't answer. Finally, out of options, I sink to the floor, curl up in a ball and weep. Nothing to do now but wait. I try desperately to stay awake, but fall into a fitful sleep.

Bam. Bam. Crash.

Startled awake, I peer across the living room and see a large hand reach through a brand new hole in the front door, groping for the deadbolt lock. So much for shadowy, covert action. Paco has arrived.

A moment later, he bulls through the door, followed by Aida. He crosses the room and kneels next to me, tears streaming from his eyes "Oh, *chicka*, what has happened? It's my fault. I should have been with you."

"No worries, Unc. You're here now. That's what counts."

Aida leans close, touches the gash on my cheek and points at my injured arm. "Who has done these awful things to you? What is this place?"

"I'll explain later. Right now, we need to get to the Rockwells. I don't have a good feeling about Destiny."

Aida gasps. "What you mean? Is baby in danger?"

I can't explain the urgency I'm feeling, so I shrug and change the subject. "What time is it?"

"Four forty-five," Paco says, scooping me up in his arms. I bite back a yip of pain and mutter, "Actually, I can walk."

"Faster this way." He kicks the door open and charges toward the parking lot. He huffs out the story as he trots. "Had to wake up Kendra...needed the van...can't put three people on the bike...of course, she wanted to come along...luckily, Craig wouldn't let her."

We pile into the van. Paco cranks the motor and we speed through the mostly empty streets toward Broken Top. I relate an edited story of my capture, the certainty that I wouldn't live to see morning and the surprising turn of events when Mick revealed his true identity.

"I knew Myron was an asshole," Paco mutters. "Is he the one who hurt you?"

"Yeah. Mick tried to patch me up."

"What we do when we get to the Mister's house?" Aida says.

Good question. "Not sure. I just don't want them calling in social services for Destiny. Since you're her nanny, maybe they'll let us take Destiny."

Paco frowns. "Don't want to burst your bubble, kiddo, but that might not work. You know how the feds work. Everything by the book."

"I'm not sure that's true for Homeland Security. I'm hoping Mick will be there. He might listen to me."

It's a little past five when we cruise into the Rockwell's ritzy neighborhood. Dawn is breaking, but the sun has yet to appear over the mountains to the east. The expansive homes appear ghostly in the dim, gray light.

"How do you think the bust will go down?" I ask Paco.

"They'll have people covering all the exits and break down the door if they have to."

As we approach the Rockwell house, I see a black Suburban and a tan crew-cab pick-up parked in the shadows next to my favorite tree. No sign of the Impala. Not good. If Mick's not here, our chances of getting Destiny are zero to none.

Paco parks the minivan well away from the other vehicles and we walk back toward the Rockwell property just in time to see the lights come on inside the house. Standing beneath a massive pine tree, we watch as the front door flies open. Two men dressed in black march a handcuffed Ethan Rockwell onto the front lawn. He's struggling and yelling things that make me smile. "Do you know who I am? I'll have your badge."

"Oh," Aida breathes, "Police have the mister. What

about missus and baby?"

Shortly after, two more guys burst through the door and join the others. One of them is lugging a fat briefcase and the laptop computer from Rockwell's study. The other man is talking a mile a minute, gesticulating wildly and pointing back toward the house. I can't make out what he's saying, but the tension in his voice and body tells me something has gone wrong. No sign of Nina Rockwell or Destiny.

"You and Aida stay here," I whisper to Paco. "I need to get closer so I can hear what's going on."

Paco says, "I'll come too."

"No, they'll see you. I'll stay behind the bushes like I did before." I stand on my tiptoes and whisper in his ear. "Aida's scared. You need to stay with her."

He grudgingly agrees. I lower my body to a crouch and slink behind the living wall of tall arborvitaes. As I close the gap between the men and myself, I start to pick up snatches of their conversation. "…in the diaper bag…detonator…baby's in the crib…she wants…"

His voice drops before I can hear what she— probably Nina Rockwell—wants. One of the men gripping Rockwell's arm explodes in anger and I hear every word clearly. "Why the hell did you let her go into the kid's room?"

The other guy mumbles something I don't catch.

"*Jesus Christ*. Now we need a hostage negotiator. Did she say what she wants?"

"She wants a written statement, a guarantee, she'll be granted immunity if she narcs out the husband. She says he's the one running the show."

"That's a goddamn lie." Ethan Rockwell shouts. "It's her. It's always been her. There's never been enough of anything to suit her. Money. Things. Even the baby. She's the one who saw Eddie's kid and had to have her. I didn't want the baby. She did. And, believe me, she paid a bunch of money for her. And, she's the one bringing the girls over from Kazakhstan. It's her, not me."

"So, wise guy, tell me this. If she wanted a baby so bad, why does she have C-4 packed in the diaper bag and a detonator in her hand? She says she'll set it off and blow herself and the kid to kingdom come if we don't give her what she wants."

Shock waves rocket through my body. I clap a hand over my mouth to keep from crying out.

Rockwell says, "Honest to God, I didn't know she had that stuff in the house."

The guy in charge says, "What a goddamn, fucking mess." He points at the guy who screwed up. "Get Mick over here. I'll work on setting up communication with the Rockwell woman."

The guy steps away from the group, speaks into a slim hand-held device, then turns and gives his boss the thumbs up sign. Since we're in a holding pattern until Mick arrives, I scurry back to where Paco and Aida are standing behind a tree. If they think they're hidden, they are sadly mistaken. Both of their bellies are clearly visible.

Paco says, "What's going on?"

"I need your cell phone."

He hands it over. I punch in a number. After five rings, I hear a sleepy, "'Alo."

"Steve, it's Mel. I need your help."

"Where are you?"

I give him the address. He promises to be there

soon.

Now, all I have to do is convince Mick that my father and I can confront Nina Rockwell, figure out if she's lying and rescue Destiny without getting all four of us blown to smithereens.

Yes, I have a plan.

Chapter Forty-Three

The sun arrives along with a bevy of law enforcement vehicles and a handful of early-rising, nosy neighbors. A man wearing a jacket with the initials D.H.S. jumps out of his rig, strides to the pine tree and barks, "You three, out."

He herds us to the small band of rubbernecking spectators. We watch while yellow crime scene tape is strung across the perimeter. Ethan Rockwell, arms handcuffed behind his back, is marched to the black Suburban and locked inside.

Someone asks, "What's D.H.S.?"

Paco grunts, "Department of Homeland Security."

His words are followed by gasps of alarm and multitude of questions.

"Why is Homeland Security at the Rockwells?"

"Are we in danger?"

"Why were you hiding behind the tree?"

"I played golf with Ethan yesterday. Why are they arresting him?"

We claim ignorance and move away so we can speak freely. By now, Aida is sobbing and clinging to Paco's hairy, muscular arm with both hands. But, her remarks are addressed to me. "Mel, baby is in danger. You must get her out of house. Missus doesn't care about her."

I nod and watch as Myron's Impala screeches to a

stop next to the perimeter. The mere sight of the Impala evokes memories of my terror while locked inside its vile, stinky, trunk. My pulse kicks up a notch and I hold my breath. Somehow, my unreasoning lizard brain expects to see Myron pop out of the car, cursing and waving his hunting knife.

When Mick appears, I resume breathing. He's totally focused on the Rockwell house and pays no attention to the gathered crowd. He slams the car door and ducks under the yellow tape.

I rush toward him, calling, "Mick."

"Not now," he snarls and then does the classic double take. The first glance is quick and dismissive. The second one is longer and stops him dead in his tracks. He ducks back under the tape, staring down at me like he's seeing a ghost.

I smile up at him. "Surprise."

"No way," he growls.

"Yep, it's me. We need to talk. I can help. With the hostage thing, I mean."

He flaps a dismissive hand and turns away. "Forget about it. You're a civilian."

"Wait."

He pauses, but won't look at me.

I choose my next words carefully, knowing if I fail, I'll lose my only ally. My only hope. My voice is shaky with emotion when I speak. "Why do you think I busted my butt to get out of your apartment? It's not because I was in danger. It's because I know something that will save that innocent baby girl inside the Rockwell house. I don't give a shit about Nina Rockwell, but I made a promise to the baby's mother and I intend to keep it. Just try to stop me."

My last statement leaps from my mouth, surprising me as much as it does Mick.

Hands on hips, he turns to face me again. I see the ghost of a smile tug at his lips. "Oh, I think I can stop you."

I step closer, jut out my chin and mimic his pose by placing the hand of my uninjured arm on my hip. "Stop being an ass and listen."

He sighs and lifts his hands, palms up, in defeat. "You have sixty seconds to tell me what the hell you're talking about."

"Remember when I said I can read your soul?"

He rolls his eyes.

"Tell me this. Can your hostage negotiator tell if Nina Rockwell is lying about having C-4 in the diaper bag? Can he or she tell for sure?"

His gaze flicks away from mine and back. "They look for little tics that give the lie away. They're pretty good at what they do."

"But, can they be one-hundred percent certain?"

He makes a disgusted sound. "Nobody can."

"I can. My father too, and he's on his way."

He shakes his head and glances toward the action on the Rockwell's front lawn. "Do you know how crazy this sounds?"

Desperate, I pluck at his sleeve. "I *know* it sounds crazy, but my father and I are soul readers. He taught me how to tell if someone's lying. Here's what you need to do. Tell Nina Rockwell my dad is the hostage negotiator you're sending in, along with someone to help with the baby. That would be me. Tell us what questions to ask."

Unconvinced, he remains silent.

"I've looked into Nina's soul. I know she's too damn self-centered to kill herself. I know she's faking. I bet she's got a big old chunk of Silly Putty in that diaper bag. But, we need to make sure. And, I guarantee you, we'll know for sure. One hundred percent sure. All you have to do is try to suspend reality as you know it."

He stares deeply into my eyes. Once again, I'm amazed at the beauty of his soul. Finally, he says, "Wait here," and ducks under the tape.

He trots to the cluster of agents who gather around him, awaiting instructions. He begins talking and I can only imagine the expressions of disbelief registering on their faces. Mick points toward me. Should I smile and wave? Maybe not.

One of the agents throws up his hands and turns away, his body language indicating he thinks Mick has lost his mind. Several of them shift their weight, obviously uncomfortable.

Paco and Aida join me. Paco says, "What's happening?'

Have I mentioned Paco knows nothing about my soul-reading ability? Neither does he know Steve is my father.

I place a hand on his arm. "Uncle Paco. There are things you don't know about me. There's something I have to do here. Please trust me. I promise I'll tell you the truth, the whole truth and nothing but the truth after this is over."

Paco gives me a smirk and rotates his index finger next to his temple, the universal sign for *cuckoo*. "You think I don't know about that thing you can do? The mind-reading *woo-woo* thing?"

My mouth drops open. All I can do is stare at him.

"Oh, yeah," he says. "Your mother told me years ago."

When I find my voice, I say, "Um, well, that's good. But, there's something else. It's about Steve. He's…"

"Your father. I get it. Hey, I'm no rocket scientist, but it's totally obvious you two were picked from the same tree."

I shake my head in disbelief. "And yet, you didn't beat the crap out of him."

He shrugs. "Not my place."

Mick is still talking. His stance is now aggressive, one foot forward, his index finger stabbing the air as he makes his case.

Steve arrives and joins us. Paco nods a greeting, takes Aida's hand and backs away to give us privacy.

Steve looks me over and frowns. "I knew you were in danger and now, you are injured. What can I do to help?"

I fill him in quickly, ending with, "I kind of volunteered you for the job. If you don't want to, it's okay."

"Of course I will help you, Melanie. If the officers will allow me to do so."

Mick peels away from the group and trots back to the taped-off perimeter. He checks Steve out. "You the father?"

Steve nods.

Mick lifts the tape. "Come with me."

Steve ducks under. I follow.

Mick glances over his shoulder. "Not you."

"We're a team," I protest. "It's both of us or neither of us. Right, Steve?" I nod vigorously to encourage him.

Steve's face is a mask of indecision. He leans close and whispers, "You are injured, *mi hija*. Maybe I should do this on my own."

"No. I have to do this."

He turns to face Mick. "She is correct. We're a team."

I cross my fingers, hoping we haven't screwed ourselves over. Mick is not happy. He glares down at me. A muscle twitches in his jaw.

"One condition," he says through gritted teeth. "Steve will be acting as the official hostage negotiator. *He* will enter the nursery where Nina Rockwell is holed up. *He* will do all the talking."

He pauses and lowers his face until it's a scant few inches from mine. "*You* will be in the hall out of sight, until your father indicates it is safe for you to enter and retrieve the child. Do you understand?"

"Yes." I make sure my face is expressionless, but inside, I'm gloating.

He leads us to the group assembled on the lawn. A female agent hands an official Department of Homeland Security jacket to Steve along with a badge.

Mick points at the guy who flushed us from behind the tree, "Dave will brief you. I'll let Ms. Rockwell know you're coming in."

Dave rakes both of us with a flat, appraising gaze. "So you two are the genius mind-readers here to save the day, huh?"

I bristle up and draw a deep, preparatory breath. Steve puts a steadying hand on my arm and speaks calmly. "You may call us whatever you like, sir. My daughter and I are here to help. I trust your job is to help us do just that."

"Yeah, whatever," Dave mutters.

Mick, his ear pressed to a cell phone, pivots and gives Dave his death stare, resulting in an instant attitude adjustment.

"Okay, folks," Dave says, clapping a hand on Steve's shoulder. "Let's get you prepped."

Five minutes later, Steve and I walk through the Rockwell's front door. Instantly, a chill raises goose bumps on my flesh and I shiver. To me, the Rockwell house is steeped in the worst kind of evil. I can't wait to get Destiny out.

I point at the staircase and whisper, "The nursery is upstairs."

As we climb the stairs, Steve follows the directions given to us at the briefing. He calls, "Mrs. Rockwell? My name is Steve. I'm here to work out the details for your safe release. May I come into the nursery so we can talk face to face?"

We pause at the landing and wait for a response. I can hear Destiny whimpering and, oh my God, how I long to run to her. I take a step toward the nursery. Steve shakes his head and puts a finger to his lips.

A minute ticks by before she answers. "Yeah, okay. Just so you know, the detonator is in my hand. If you charge in here with weapons, I'm pressing the button."

Her voice is cold, matter of fact. As if killing herself and her child is of no consequence—probably because she has no intention of harming herself. Destiny is just an insurance policy.

Steve says, "I promise you I am unarmed. May I enter?"

In the same monotone, she replies, "Yes."

We creep down the hall. I press back against the wall as Steve steps into the nursery. His voice is soft. Soothing. "Hello, Nina. My supervisor is conferring with a judge. In a matter of minutes, he will have notarized documents granting you immunity in exchange for your help in identifying the perpetrators."

Damn, I think. *He's really good at this.*

During the silence that follows Steve's statement, I hear a soft footfall on the stairs. Still pressed against the wall, I turn my head slowly and see Mick on the landing. He places a finger against his lips. I roll my eyes as he approaches. Why am I surprised? I should have known it's physically impossible for him to stay away from the action.

We listen as Nina says, "Full immunity. Right? No charges against me. I'll give you names, bank accounts, whatever you need if you let me walk."

"Fine, fine," Steve murmurs. "Just a few questions. Naturally, we need information about the explosive in the diaper bag. I believe you mentioned C-4. Is that right?"

I *so* want to peek into the room as Steve gazes into Nina's evil soul. In fact, I push away from the wall. Mick grabs the back of my shirt and pulls me back.

"Yes," Nina replies. "It's C-4. Enough to blow the house up, not to mention, you, me and the baby."

"So," Steve continues. "You're not afraid to die."

"No."

"What about your daughter?"

There's a slight hesitation before she says, "We haven't really bonded yet. It will be fast. She won't suffer."

Steve continues probing, using the questions suggested in the briefing. I edge closer to the door, Mick close on my heels.

Finally, after a long pause, Steve says, "Do you mind if I pick up the child? She seems unhappy."

This is the identifying phrase Steve and I agreed upon when we entered the house. The phrase that says, *I know she's lying.* I whirl away from Mick and charge into the nursery. Steve stands next to the crib. Nina Rockwell is seated in the nursery rocking chair, the fake detonator in her hand. When she sees me, her eyes spark with fury.

"You. You're supposed to be dead."

"Yet, here I am, you lying bitch."

Her thumb hovers over the detonator.

I have to make sure. "Tell us again how you're going to blow us up."

Howling in rage, she wings the detonator at my head and springs from the chair. Granted, I'm not in tiptop shape, but my BJJ training kicks in. She charges at me, arms outstretched. Despite the pain in my arm, I sidestep quickly and use a strong leg sweep to knock her to the floor.

She's growling like a feral cat when Mick plants a booted foot in the middle of her back. He grins at me. "Good job."

I nod my thanks and use my good arm to lift Destiny from her crib. I cradle her next to my body and rock her back and forth until her pitiful cries cease. Steve wraps his arms around the both of us and pats my back like I'm the infant, not Destiny. At some level, I'm aware Nina Rockwell is taken into custody and led away.

I feel the sobs building in my chest, but hold it together until we leave the house. I *will not* have a meltdown in front of Mick and his steely-eyed agents. I tell Steve I need a moment alone and head for a wrought-iron bench next to a dogwood tree in full bloom. I sit; hold the baby close to my body and allow my tears to flow unchecked, a seemingly endless stream.

Destiny seems to understand, but doesn't join in. Instead, she grips my shirt with both chubby fists and lifts her blue-eyed gaze to mine. I feel Dani's gentle presence as the blossoms of the dogwood tree stir and flutter in the early morning breeze. A pale pink petal drifts down and kisses the top of Destiny's blond head.

It's then I remember a poem about the dogwood tree, recited by my stepfather, Abel, in the Godmobile. *Slender and twisted it will always be. With cross-shaped blossoms for all to see. The petals shall have bloodstains marked with brown. And, in the center, a thorny crown.*

I take a hitching breath and turn my tear-stained face to the brightening sky. "We did it, Dani. Destiny is safe. Thank God, she's safe. Rest in peace, my friend."

I dry my tears, stand and walk toward to the front of the Rockwell property. Paco, Aida, Steve—and Billy. Waiting for me.

Chapter Forty-Four

It's party time at Nick's. Two days have passed since headlines in the local paper screamed, *Human Trafficking/Baby Selling Scheme in 3 Peaks.* The Rockwells are behind bars. Ditto Jason Breen, Myron, and the judge. Fortunately, Rusty saved local taxpayers a butt load of money. When Mick and crew stormed into his house, he pulled out his department issued Glock and splattered his brains all over the wall.

A trip to the local emergency room revealed I have a broken olecranon—that's the official name for the pointy end of the elbow. My right arm is now immobilized in a hospital-provided splint and sling. The sling is remarkably similar to the one Mick fashioned from a dishtowel purchased at the super market.

Since it's a private party, Nick's is closed to the public. Still, the place is crowded with family, friends and well wishers. A huge banner hangs over the bar. It says: MESS WITH MEL AND SHE'LL KICK YOUR ASS!

I'm seated in a booth with Sandra and Abel. Sandra in 3 Peaks? Of course she is. Where else would she be when her daughter has a broken olecranon? Not to mention said daughter was assaulted by a miscreant who does not deserve to draw another breath. Fortunately for Myron, he is safely behind bars.

Sandra is wide-eyed as she gazes around the room.

"You've made this many friends since you arrived in 3 Peaks? Who are all these people?"

I'm equally surprised to see the size of the crowd. Mick and his Homeland Security pals are whooping it up in the Corral alongside some of Paco's crew who recently returned to the area. An uneasy alliance has developed between the two factions.

Helen is busting her buns delivering drinks and food. Thanks to Nick, everything is on the house. Since I'm officially the guest of honor and one-armed, I'm not allowed to help. Connie, Queen of the Motel Maids, has been pressed into service. After her lustful glances at Paco are deflected, she zeros in on Steve who is seated at the bar, chatting with Billy. Should I tell her not to waste her time? Maybe not. Who am I to dash her hopes?

The predatory Candace Talbot is also at the bar where Nick is serving up free drinks. Candy looks hot in tight faded jeans, hand-tooled cowboy boots and a black V-neck, cleavage-revealing tee that says: *Saddle up. Shut up. Hold on Tight*. Judging from her outfit, I assume her horse is patiently waiting in the parking lot. Trust me, I'm keeping an eye on Candy.

Kendra, Craig and family are also present, enjoying chicken nuggets and raw baby carrots dipped in ranch dressing. I'm a big supporter of Kendra's theory: Greasy foods plus raw vegetables equal zero harm.

Paco and Aida have a booth of their own, large enough to accommodate their expanding bellies. Destiny is in her car seat on top of the table. She has a tight grip on Paco's pointer finger and is chomping down on it like it's filet mignon. Aida tells me she's teething again. Paco is gazing at Aida like a lovesick calf.

Mick pulled some strings to allow Kendra temporary custody of Destiny until all the details can be worked out. She says she won't rest until Destiny is legally a member of her family. Aida is still under the radar. Mick obviously knows she's here, but he's taking the high road and pretending she's invisible. If a threat to her legal status arises, I'm sure Paco will be on bended knee, proposing marriage.

Mick grudgingly filled me in on some of the details. While the Rockwells and friends were taken into custody in 3 Peaks, another team hit the prostitution ring in Portland. Paco was correct. The money flowing in from prostitution was laundered through the self-service car wash and coin-operated Laundromat. After checking Rockwell's records, the bean counters determined he was in the process of setting up an offshore account to hide some of the ill-gotten gains.

When I asked Mick about the fate of the women forced into prostitution, he became close-lipped and replied, "Yet to be determined." Nagging proved fruitless.

However, he did tell me Larissa's death was an accident, due to placental abruption. She died shortly after the baby was born. Eddie and Myron were the cleanup guys. They rented a room at the Rest Inn, used a fake credit card and dumped poor Larissa there. After I yelled at Mick for ten long minutes, he agreed to cut loose some of Rockwell's impounded money to arrange a decent burial for her.

Still, I'm not fully satisfied with the results of Homeland Security's investigation. They're crowing about their victory, obsessed with the big picture. But, what about Dani? She died to protect her daughter. I'm certain Eddie had a hand (or fist) in her death. Mick promises me they will question him, but with nothing remaining but Dani's ashes, Eddie's complicity in her death will be impossible to prove unless he confesses. I know that won't happen. Mentally, I mark it down as *Unfinished Business.*

Billy wanders over and slides in next to me, carefully placing an arm around my shoulders. I lift my face to his. After a quick glance at Sandra, he gives me a chaste peck on the lips.

My mother snickers. "Bet you do better than that when I'm not around."

Billy grins. "Don't want to get her all riled up until she's back in fighting shape."

I fake a punch at his chin. "I'm tougher than you think."

Billy narrows his eyes and pats my injured arm. "You're made of flesh, blood and bone like the rest of us. You scared the hell out of me the other night. When I got to the apartment and saw the busted door, I was sure that was the end of you."

When he couldn't find me, he figured the action was either at the clinic or the Rockwells. He arrived in time to see me leave the Rockwell's house holding Destiny, and was, of course, pissed off he'd missed all the action.

"What is it with your daughter?" he asks Sandra. "Does she have to do everything on her own? Damn, but she hates to ask for help."

"That's the way I raised her."

Sandra glances over her shoulder at Steve sitting at

the bar. "It was just the three of us. Hope, Honor and me. We had to be tough. Then, we lost Hope. Hope the child, and hope in the literal sense. That's when Melanie decided she didn't deserve the name Honor. It was a rough time for us."

She pauses and swipes at her eyes. "When you lose one child and see the other one in terrible emotional pain, there is only one option. Do whatever it takes to fix her. If that means she turns out bull-headed and unwilling to ask for help, so be it."

Billy drops his gaze and murmurs, "Yes, ma'am."

Abel reaches across the table and takes my hand. "If anyone deserves the name Honor, it's you, and that's what I intend to call you from now on."

I've never liked being the center of attention. Time to change the subject. "Hey, Sandra, how did it go with Steve? Did you two duke it out?"

The last two days have been a blur of doctor appointments, debriefing by law enforcement officials, long hours of restorative sleep and no alone time with my mother.

She says, "After you told me about his little problem…"

Little problem? "You mean the fact that he's gay?"

She nods. "That and the whole family expectation thing. I guess I've become more forgiving as I've grown older." She takes Abel's hand. "Plus, I have a wonderful husband. Who could ask for a better man?"

Billy smooches the top of my head and rises. "I think I'll have a word with that guy in Paco's—um, group. You know the one who had the same problem as me."

I squeeze his hand. "Okay."

"One more week and I'll be a free man," he says and heads for the Corral.

I'm not sure what happened, but Billy's attitude toward PTSD counseling has undergone a profound adjustment. His boiling anger and resentment have subsided into a gentle simmer of acceptance, seasoned with an occasional dash of the heebie-jeebies. The fire in his soul still burns, but the smoke has cleared and the flames are tinged with a clean blue-violet glow. His future looks bright.

Will Honor Melanie Sullivan be part of that future? My heart wishes it were so. Though I try to suppress them, random thoughts bombard my mind. Can people like me have normal relationships? If Billy lies to me—and I'm discovering everybody lies—will it destroy my ability to trust him? Isn't trust the basic foundation for a healthy relationship? I could stop reading souls, but why should I? Until recently, I've spent most of my life looking down. Now, it's time to look up—and forward.

The troublesome thoughts circle through my brain on an endless loop. Since I have no answers, I push them away.

After Billy leaves, Mick stops at our table. He greets Sandra and Abel, plants both hands on the table and turns his probing gaze to me. "I need to speak to you. Alone."

Sandra's eyes brighten with curiosity. "We were just leaving."

She blows me a kiss. "We'll talk later."

Translation: *I want to know all the details.*

After their departure, Mick slides in next to me. I scoot over to give him room. He takes the additional space like he owns it. I feel heat radiating from his body, but refuse to give him another inch. He's either hitting on me or he's had too much *wodka.*

I'm squirming with discomfort. I point across the table. "You might want to sit over there."

He looks at me and winks. "Too close for comfort?"

"For your information, I have a boyfriend."

"You sure about that?"

Now, he's pissing me off. "What's that supposed to mean?"

"If you were my girlfriend, I wouldn't leave you sitting here all alone. Just saying."

I stiffen in outrage. "I think that qualifies as none of your damn business. Furthermore, I wasn't sitting here all alone. I was with my parents."

I jab him in the ribs with my uninjured elbow. Hard. "Move."

He chuckles and takes a seat on the opposite bench. "We need to talk."

"About what?"

"Your dad did a hell of a job the other night."

Like an afterthought, he points at me. "You too, of course."

"Gee, thanks," I mutter. *You chauvinistic pig.*

"Here's the deal," he continues. "I'm not the only one whose cover was blown the other night."

"What does that have to do with me?"

Mick lowers his voice. "It's the soul-reading thing. I'm talking about the blabathon when you thought you were about to die?"

"Blabathon?" I huff. "I was trying to save my life. I believe I presented a well-drafted argument designed to…"

Mick raises a hand to stop me. "Whatever. My point is, during your *blabathon,* you told me only a few people know about your ability to read souls. After the Rockwell bust, a whole lot of people know."

"Yeah, Homeland Security people. I assumed they could keep secrets."

Mick rises and steps out of the booth. "You and your father are unique. Your ability to figure out if someone is lying is a marketable skill. The two of you should open a consulting business. Hell, D.H.S. would hire you. Think of the possibilities in law enforcement alone. Not to mention other fields like employment agencies and jury selection."

I'm trying to absorb what he's saying, but old habits don't die easy. My instinct for secrecy and self-preservation leap to the surface and I blurt, "That would mean everyone would know."

Mick stares at me for a long moment. "Maybe I'm wrong, but I had you pegged as a girl who doesn't give a shit about what other people think."

I open my mouth to answer, but no words come out. Mick slides out of the booth. "Talk to your dad. Think about what I said."

After Mick heads back to his buddies, Billy returns. He slides in next to me. "I saw that D.H.S. guy here. You okay?"

I nod. "Just surprised, that's all. He thinks Steve and I should start a consulting business."

"Oh, really." His voice gives nothing away.

"Do you think it's a good idea?"

He shrugs. "Do you?"

"The idea scares me a little."

He smiles. "I totally get that. You don't have to

decide right now. Whatever you decide, I'll support you."

Tears spring into my eyes. This is Billy being nice. I like it.

I swipe at my eyes. "I never got a chance to tell you I'm sorry."

"For what?"

"For not including you in the grand finale—the whole saving baby Destiny thing. I know you would have been a big help."

He shrugs. "Let's not forget who set it in motion. If you hadn't been so damn nosy and stubborn, there might have been a different ending." He glances at his watch. "Gotta go. Counseling session." He rises. "Later?"

Before he leaves, I reach out and take his hand. "For sure, later. Maybe at your place?"

He reaches down and pulls me in for one last hug. "Yeah. I'd say it's about time."

A word about the author…

Marilee Brothers is a former teacher, coach, counselor, and the author of nine books so far. Marilee and her husband are the parents of three grown sons and live in central Washington State. After writing six young adult books, Marilee is once again writing romantic suspense for the adult market. She loves hearing from people who have read her books. You will find those available elsewhere listed on her website.

Marilee's *Book Blather* blog is where she features aspiring and published authors as well as some tidbits of her own.

Feel free to contact her at any of the following:

http://www.marileebrothers.com

www.facebook.com/marilee.author

Twitter @MarileeB.

http://bookblatherblog.blogspot.com

www.ingramcontent.com/pod-product-compliance
Lightning Source LLC
Chambersburg PA
CBHW071524260626
47170CB00002B/496